A Proper Proposal

"Will you marry me?"

Priscilla stared at him in amazement and vexation. Never in her dreams had she anticipated an offer from an earl.

He moved to take Priscilla's hand, drawing her to her feet. "This is sudden, you may say."

"True, it is, my lord."

"Your father seemed to think you might welcome my advance."

"That is also true. I cannot think of any young woman who would not be pleased to have the attentions from so handsome and polished a gentleman." Her voice was soft and low, intimately husky.

"Priscilla, I care not for what other young women might like. I want to know what you want." At the confusion he saw in her eyes, he instinctively drew her close and placed a kiss he intended to be chaste and brief on her lips. Only the kiss did not go as planned. Her innocent response aroused his senses. He deepened the kiss, his ardor unconsciously released.

Marrying to make his family respectable suddenly became enormously appealing.

Get swept away with these Emily Hendrickson romances

Lord Nick's Folly
The Ivory Dragon
Lord Huntingdon's Legacy
The Rake's Revenge
A Perilous Engagement
The Dangerous Baron Leigh
Miss Haycroft's Suitors

Pursuing Priscilla

Emily Hendrickson

A SIGNET BOOK

SIGNET
Published by New American Library, a division of
Penguin Putnam Inc., 375 Hudson Street,
New York, New York 10014, U.S.A.
Penguin Books Ltd, 80 Strand,
London WC2R 0RL, England
Penguin Books Australia Ltd, 250 Camberwell Road,
Camberwell, Victoria 3124, Australia
Penguin Books Canada Ltd, 10 Alcorn Avenue,
Toronto, Ontario, Canada M4V 3B2
Penguin Books (N.Z.) Ltd, Cnr Rosedale and Airborne Roads,
Albany, Auckland 1310, New Zealand

Penguin Books Ltd, Registered Offices:
Harmondsworth, Middlesex, England

First published by Signet, an imprint of New American Library,
a division of Penguin Putnam Inc.

First Printing, February 2003
10 9 8 7 6 5 4 3 2 1

"Let other pens dwell on guilt and misery. I quit such odious subjects as soon as I can."

—Jane Austen
Mansfield Park, 1814

"Manners are what vex or soothe, corrupt or purify, exalt or debase, barbarize or refine us, by a constant, steady, uniform, insensible operation like that of the air we breathe in. They give their whole form and color to our lives. According to their quality, they aid morals, they supply them, or they totally destroy them.

—Edmund Burke, 1796

Prologue

A decided hush hung over the table when Mrs. Herbert concluded reading the astounding letter to her family—at least those who were still there. Two daughters had previously left the bosom of the family for other parts; three remained for the moment. And it seemed highly likely that another daughter would be gone in a matter of days!

Cautiously, Priscilla, the one affected by the letter, voiced her thoughts. "I am to go? To London? But why?"

"Your father's sister, your aunt Mercy Herbert, does not precisely say, love. I suspect she wishes to entertain her goddaughter since she has no children of her own." If Charlotte Herbert thought it would help were Mercy to find a splendid husband for Priscilla, she didn't say so. After all, her husband's income was modest, and with so many children any help at all was appreciated.

"London," the other girls at the table breathed with proper reverence.

"Indeed," Mrs. Herbert seconded. She rose from the table to be followed by her daughters. Left at the table, the Reverend Mr. Herbert, Esq., and his only son, Adam, shared a look of understanding before turning their attention to other matters.

In the small front parlor where most concerns of any importance were handled, Priscilla wandered to the window, staring out at the main road that cut through their small village as though she might conjure up her aunt at once.

"I can scarce believe that letter to be real, Mama. Out of the blue like this, and so soon after Nympha went north to be with Great-Aunt Coxmoor. You will be almost alone with three of us gone." Priscilla smiled at her mother. Claudia had fortunately married well, a prosperous gentleman who lived not too far away. With Nympha up north, life had altered its pattern. And now this change!

"I imagine I will cope. Drusilla is practicing household management very nicely, and Tabitha is always a help to both me and her father. She has done a commendable job with his study. He can actually find his books now that she finished organizing them." She nodded to her younger daughters, then turned back to Priscilla. "But you, dear child, must have the opportunity offered. You will go with your aunt Mercy and do as she instructs. She may be a single woman, but she knows simply everyone, it seems. And she is wealthy—she has carefully managed the money bequeathed from your father's mother to her, as well as the dowry she received when she reached twenty-five and was still unwed. You should learn household management from her, I would imagine. I fancy that money and excellent family connections can overcome a great deal." The Herberts might be gentry, but without money a name meant little.

"We must consider our good fortune at being the grandnieces of none other than the Earl of Stanwell, with his son, Viscount Rawlinson, an active member of London Society." Priscilla didn't sound as sardonic as she felt. The connections were excellent, true. But little good it had done them to this point in time. Her father was no better paid, although he earned more than many rectors of country churches. But, oh, to have him a bishop! Why had not the Earl of Stanwell seen to that, pray tell!

"We had best get busy organizing Priscilla's clothes." Drusilla rose from the chair by the fireplace to study her older sister. "Not that what you have is the least presentable in London, love. However, we shall wash and mend what you want to take with you. Even if Aunt Mercy buys you a new wardrobe, it may be comforting to have old, familiar garments for quiet times." She paused a moment before adding, "Just think of all you will see!"

The three girls hurried from the room, mindful of the letter that indicated Aunt Mercy could arrive at any time. Their excited chatter drifted back to the parlor.

Mrs. Herbert settled back in her chair, wondering what had prompted this invitation, but thankful it had come when it did. There was little prospect of finding a husband in their village. The only presentable man was Baron Rothson, and she doubted he was around long enough to know a pretty girl of proper lineage existed here. She smiled at the memory of the letter she had written to her husband's sister some time ago. Perhaps it had some influence on the invitation? Charlotte Herbert was not one to sit quietly back and let nature take its course.

Chapter One

*I*t was two days later that Miss Herbert arrived in a post chaise with her personal maid, Rose. Her modest assortment of baggage promised a brief stay, but the warmth of her greetings to her family was all one could wish. A delicate scent of honeysuckle clung to her, and her clothes might seem unassuming until you realized the high quality and subtle blending of color that bespoke a superior knowledge of style. And stylish she was. Enthusiastic, too.

"My dear Charlotte," she cried, "how well you all look, and such charming daughters." She immediately picked out the oldest of the trio. "This must be Priscilla—the blonde with enchanting blue eyes. Hmm, she has a neat figure, pleasing face, and promising hair. I shall have a most interesting time with her in London. I have such plans . . ."

Priscilla absorbed the understated elegance of her father's sister, and quaked at the very thought of going to London in her country garments. However, practical to her core, she knew that her aunt understood the restrictions of the rectory family. Living in a very rural society was not conducive to high style! And why should her hair be promising?

If Priscilla had experienced any qualms about her aunt's company, they vanished at her kindness, especially about the paucity of Priscilla's wardrobe.

"Dear girl, I expected nothing less. I know full well how it must be for you. We shall get you a fine wardrobe as soon as may be once in Town." She waved her hand over the humble collection of garments awaiting placement in a small trunk. "Take what you please and do not worry about a thing. As your godmother and aunt, I feel compelled to do my most for you."

That said, she ordered the maid the girls shared to pack the dresses and all else set out on the bed.

Her words filtered through Priscilla's mind, leaving her to wonder what the "most" involved.

It took three days to organize Priscilla's things to suit Aunt Mercy and to indulge in a pleasant bit of visiting. She was generous, encouraging Priscilla to bring along little treasured items, favorite books, and an old stuffed toy—a cat with a dubious heritage. The time she spent with Charlotte Herbert was private, but appeared highly satisfactory to both.

When the post chaise returned as she had ordered, it took a little time for the luggage to be stowed—some behind, some on top, and the trunk fitted neatly above the front wheels. Rose perched on the seat up behind the body of the chaise while Aunt Mercy and Priscilla settled inside.

Before she knew it, Priscilla had waved her last to her family. The neatly dressed postboys were astride their horses, urging them to a fast and steady pace, leaving her village far behind.

Priscilla was breathless. It seemed so sudden, this miraculous change in her life. Yet she was eager to sample all that London offered a young lady—a young *unmarried* lady. Hope rose within that perhaps she might find her heart's desire, a gentleman of worth who could care for her. She and her sisters had often discussed the topic of marriage, all agreeing that love for a husband was to be ardently desired by both parties.

If her aunt intended her to wed some worthy cleric, Priscilla would thwart that notion. Not that she felt above such a match. But she had lived in the rectory all her life, and couldn't imagine spending the rest of her days in a like situation. She was not cut out to be a vicar's mate. Just whom she might marry, she didn't know. But not a cleric.

The trip seemed endless, cooped up as they were inside the swaying, bouncing chaise. Fortunately, the weather proved excellent, and Rose seemed to enjoy being in the fresh air. When she remarked on this to her aunt, Mercy Herbert chuckled.

"Rose would not thank you to be brought inside the carriage. She becomes dreadfully ill if confined within."

Once the city loomed on the horizon, Priscilla peered from the window, trying to see everything at once. Aunt Mercy tolerated her curiosity until they entered the Town itself.

"Contain yourself, dear child. It is not seemly to be too curious. You will become familiar with London before you realize it. Come, relax, for we are almost there."

Relax? How impossible! But Priscilla leaned back against the cushions, curbing her impatience as her aunt wished. It would not do to be taken for a country miss, even if that was precisely what she was.

But her curiosity overcame prudence, for when they reached the better part of Town, she once again gazed from the window to better see the imposing houses. And they were *most* impressive, rising several floors in great splendor.

She was about to draw her head inside when she spotted a fine gentleman leaving his house. She was no stranger to men's fashion, having seen such before, but this man was perfection personified. Every item of his apparel was so right, she knew he must be of the supreme *ton* to be in such style. Those superbly fitting dove-gray breeches topped by a dark blue coat over what appeared to be a subtly striped waistcoat of some richness could never have come from a provincial tailor. Her brother had once remarked he would like to have a hat from the superior shop of Lock's. She would wager that is where this unknown gentleman's hat was made. He appeared true quality from his polished boots to that smashing beaver hat. She exhaled a wistful sigh.

The coach moved so quickly she had little chance to retreat. His eyes met hers for a moment. Priscilla blushed at her forward behavior. She deserved his casual dismissal of faint scorn. But, oh, how she would like to meet this sample of male incomparability.

The chaise stopped only a few doors along the street. Was this, then, where she was to live for the next few months? In one of these grand stone houses with their fine windows and lovely ironwork?

"Here we are. Come, let us get inside, for there is a chilly wind." Aunt Mercy left the chaise, motioning the forward postboy to follow her while the other kept an eye on the horses and chaise.

Once paid they were impatient to be off. Aunt Mercy's footman swiftly unloaded the chaise, and the carriage swept away with a flourish of the postboy's whip.

Priscilla paused at the door, looking to the neat park in the center of the street, a rectangle of green. At least she would have a tiny bit of country nearby.

"Come, come. We will have a spot of tea, perhaps a light supper before we head for bed. I'll wager you are near exhausted with this traveling. I am." Her aunt bustled along the passage to a tasteful dining room furnished simply in great style.

Priscilla agreed as she felt expected, thinking she would have a hard time falling to sleep. London! She was here! There was so much that could be seen and done. Her excitement bubbled through her. What would tomorrow bring?

Aunt Mercy's notion of a light supper was substantial. Once Priscilla had eaten the delicious food on her plate, drunk several cups of the finest Bohea tea, she felt more than ready to find a bed.

Her room was a delight, although it would seem strange to have a bedroom all to herself. Decorated in willow-green and rose, and rich walnut furniture inlaid with satinwood trim, it was far and away the loveliest bedroom she had ever beheld. The four-poster bed with artistically draped rose hangings proved as welcoming as the house. She was soundly asleep a few moments after her head touched the plump feather pillow.

Morning brought the discovery that Aunt Mercy put a whirlwind to shame. She had the day organized to the last minute.

"First, we go to Madame Clotilde's. She will be in alt to have an ash-blonde possessing melting blue eyes as well as excellent posture. And such skin—delicate rosy pink such as you seldom see. You have a good figure, child. Use it to best advantage. Oh, I do not mean you flaunt it. Indeed, not! Rather be guided by Madame in finding the look that suits you best, shows off that delectable shape in the nicest possible manner." Aunt Mercy shooed her niece up the stairs to her room with the admonition to be ready in a trice.

Silenced by her aunt's surprising compliments, Priscilla donned the prettiest of her gowns and her best bonnet before joining her aunt in the entryway.

"Well, you are so pretty that no one seeing you will notice your gown. Come." She beckoned Priscilla to follow her from the house into a carriage that while it looked plain was of the highest quality. Even though Priscilla knew little about such things, she could appreciate the excellent leather seats and other fine appointments.

Priscilla soon learned that "come" seemed to be one of her aunt's favorite words. In the ensuing hours she heard it often. Only when sequestered with Madame Clotilde did her aunt retire to one side, allowing Madame full sway in the selection of materials and styles.

With the promise of an awesome number of gowns to be delivered as soon as possible, they left the elegant salon for the happy prospect of choosing slippers, reticules, and bonnets.

Then she saw him again, the man she had observed when they arrived. Although dressed differently, she could not forget that poise, that air of assurance such as she had never seen before. Again, his garments were impeccable, his taste the most refined she could imagine. He truly was a handsome creature, well-built, with obvious polish.

They were on Bond Street, intent upon reaching the tempting environs of Grafton House, a shop where Aunt assured her the finest ribbons, gloves, and other feminine fripperies could be found, not to mention muslin of the highest quality.

He was on the other side of the street and had paused to chat with a gentleman, a man Priscilla at once dismissed as a dandy. His wine coat had excessive padding, and those knit pantaloons looked as though he'd never be able to sit down in them. Her brother had informed her that while a good fit was desirable, it was helpful to be able to sit down to dinner!

Fortunately, Aunt Mercy had paused to study a display in a shop window so Priscilla could stand at her side, innocently looking around her. She watched him, wondering who he was, if he was married, if she would ever meet him. She had never before desired an introduction to a man, but she did now.

"What has your attention, girl? It is clear I don't." When Aunt noted the direction of Priscilla's gaze before she could transfer it elsewhere, Aunt Mercy cleared her throat. "I believe that is Lord Latimer with your cousin, Viscount Rawlinson—the gentleman in the wine coat and gray pantaloons. Perhaps when you are properly gowned, your hair suitably trimmed, and so forth, you might encounter him at a party to make his acquaintance. I am well-known in London, having lived here for so many years—so we shall receive many invitations. Your cousin is the highest *ton*, and I daresay will be of help one way or another. Anyone I do not know, he does. I know little about Lord Latimer, as our paths have not crossed. I know who he is when I see him— that is all. Come."

Priscilla obediently trotted along at her aunt's side, wishing she dare glance back at the handsome Lord Latimer. She knew better, of course. That didn't make her stop desiring otherwise.

The lure of the treasures found in Grafton House swept Lord Latimer and her cousin from her mind. What young lady did not find lace-edged handkerchiefs, gloves in every subtle color and length imaginable, lace ruffs to flatter a face, and beautiful ribbons of every hue and design intriguing?

At last, after handing countless parcels over to the groom, Aunt decreed a pause at Gunter's. "You will find this a most acceptable little shop. Every hostess seeks his wares to complete parties and dinners, and I do so enjoy a dish of his pineapple ice. Come."

Priscilla smiled and went.

It was over an orange ice that her thoughts returned to the distinguished gentleman who was acquainted with her cousin, that is her unknown Lord Rawlinson.

"What is Lord Rawlinson's Christian name?" she inquired. "Is it likely that we will encounter him?"

"Aylwin. I shall send a note around to where he lives so you might meet him. He has rooms at the Albany—that is a residence for single gentlemen," she informed Priscilla. "He will come, as I have money and he has hopes to be named in my will. Come, I wish to arrange for your hair to be cut and styled."

Priscilla marveled that her aunt could be so matter-of-fact regarding her will, and the wishes of someone to inherit from the same. But if one had a great deal of money, she supposed it was not surprising that there would be relatives wanting to benefit from it.

When the hairdresser came later in the day, Priscilla was glad to find her tresses needed no more than a bit of trimming to look *au courant*.

The following day was another surprise. Rather than shop, her aunt suggested she put on that same simple gown to join her in visiting a charity school she helped finance. It proved to be an eye-opening experience.

Located in a modest brick structure, the school was clean, simply furnished, with scrubbed wooden floors and a small stove in the corner of each schoolroom.

"Fireplaces waste heat," Aunt Mercy lectured. "I found these in Germany. They have proven effective. I'll tolerate no half-frozen students in these rooms. Who could learn when chilled to the bone?"

Priscilla nodded, while looking everywhere about her. The children were simply dressed in plain, but clean, garments, faces scrubbed, hair neatly combed. "They learn their letters and numbers?"

"Indeed, and a few Bible verses as well. They will be able to get a better job if they have a smattering of education—even the girls."

Priscilla eyed her aunt with growing respect. She had heard the same from her father, so she wasn't too surprised to hear her aunt was of the same opinion. It boded well for an agreeable visit that they would concur on matters like this. It was comforting to know that her aunt was not solely given to entertainment, but worthy causes as well. She was using her money wisely, in Priscilla's estimation.

The trip back to the house on Hanover Street was accomplished in silence. Once there, the following day had to be planned. It seemed that shopping was not the only item on the coming agenda; there would be interesting sites to see as well. Priscilla could not contain her pleasure at the thought of actually seeing the Tower of London and all the other sights of curiosity.

Having sent off a note to her nephew, Miss Herbert regaled her niece with tales of Society over the ample tea she considered proper. Priscilla had not expected her to be quite so fashionable. That is, to be interested in worthy causes as well as balls and dinners, and attending the most desirable parties. Her time at Hanover Square promised to be both entertaining and enlightening.

Not too many streets away, Lord Latimer, known to his closest friends as Felix, left a fashionable address in a state of frozen politeness. His family! He, the heir to the Marquess of Silverstone, rejected because of his family! The girl whose hand he had thought to seek in marriage was pretty, an empty-headed bit of fluff that would have been pleasant to escort about and entertain his friends, but he assuredly had not been more than faintly fond of her. She possessed a decent pedigree, passing good looks, and from all he had heard, an excellent dowry. He'd been rejected.

His family! He could scarce take it in. His family was deemed too improper for an alliance with Miss Anne Bolsolver. And who was she? The daughter of a viscount who ought to be thrilled to marry an earl who had the prospect of inheriting a marquessate. Not only did he have a title, but his careful management of his estates ensured him a tidy income, unlike his many relatives who seemed to be in perpetual need of funds. Except his Aunt Beatrice. She never approached him for money, thank goodness. Not that he saw her all that often, for she was still in disgrace after all these years.

Disgraceful relatives seemed to surround him, parading their scandalous behavior for one and all to enjoy. Felix winced at the recollection of the scathing words from Lord Bolsolver. No daughter of his would align herself with the house of Sutton. He uttered the words as though the very name of Sutton was beyond the pale.

Felix burned with the thought of all the various Sutton

family members scampering about London in gaming, chasing women, turning up their collective noses at Society.

"What ho, Latimer?" a familiar voice inquired.

"Renshaw! Just the chap I wanted to see. I can do with a bit of cheer." Felix matched his stride with that of his friend, heading toward White's and a bottle of comfort.

"Never say he rejected your offer," Chauncy Renshaw inquired in horror after Felix revealed the source of his annoyance. "But Bolsolver is only a viscount. Surely he'd not pass up an earl destined to be a marquess? And you with a handsome income to boot!"

"It seems he finds my family highly objectionable." Felix was careful not to allow his distress to show. Even Chauncy was not to know the full depth of Felix's embarrassment over the Sutton family foibles. Just when he thought the peak of nonsense had been achieved, one of them reached a new height in scandal. But, by heaven, he wasn't like that! He lived a reasonably proper life by London standards.

They reached White's in due time. Before entering, Felix paused to caution his good friend. "Not a hint of this to anyone, mind you. I'd not have my dirty linen aired in public, if you know what I mean."

Renshaw nodded. "I know only too well. A juicy bit like this gets around, and you might as well head for the country."

"Not I," Felix countered. "I have yet to find a person I can't stare out of countenance, but it would be easier if I didn't have to bother."

They settled down over a listless game of cards and a bottle of fine claret. Chauncy tossed a card down on the table, studying his friend. "So what do you intend to do?"

"I'm not sure," Felix admitted. "It is time and more that I wed. My father reminds me every now and again that I am not getting any younger."

"He should know," Chauncy said with care.

"I have a mind to find me the most proper girl in London and marry her regardless. That would show all these prattle-boxes that the Sutton family can lay claim to fine manners. I shall restore the family name!"

"And where would *you* find a truly proper young

woman, one who would marry you if word of this rejection gets around? I suspect it is far too juicy a tidbit for Bolsolver to keep to himself."

Felix acknowledged the truth of that remark, then called for a second bottle of claret.

"Well, look who is here," Chauncy murmured. "If it isn't Rawlinson. Thought he was planning to rusticate."

"He is usually under the hatches," Felix replied, turning to study the elegant dandy who had just entered the room. "We are to be favored with his conversation, it seems."

"Latimer, Renshaw, how does it?" Lord Rawlinson eased himself into a chair, taking care not to crease his coat of the wildest shade of peacock green to be found. That he had to lounge back to consider the tight fit of his pantaloons didn't surprise anyone.

"Tolerable," Felix replied quickly. "And you? I thought you planned to leave Town."

"M'aunt returned. Summoned me to her house to meet a cousin of mine. Girl stands to inherit a bundle from what I gather. Gentry—parson's daughter. Probably as plain as a pikestaff, but with a lot of lovely money, who's to care?"

"Not you, I gather." Felix knew a moment of pity for the parson's daughter, whoever she might be.

"Hadn't thought of tossing the handkerchief, but if enough blunt is on the line, why not? I can always leave her in the country." Lord Rawlinson gave his audience a pleased smile as though he was the first man to think of such a scheme.

"True." Felix wondered how such a blockhead as Rawlinson managed to get through life without being strangled.

"She might prove to be a fetching wench." Chauncy gave Rawlinson a grin that allowed the gleam in his eyes to shine without suspicion.

"Hadn't thought of that," Rawlinson admitted. "See her tomorrow. Promised to call on them. Girl has to get her hair properly cut and be outfitted in the latest fashion, of course. Bound to be provincial."

"Naturally." Felix concealed a yawn behind a raised hand.

Chauncy rose from the table, glancing at the clock on the far wall. "Best to take our leave now, Latimer. Remember you wanted to inspect that horse at Tatt's?"

"How could I forget!" Felix rose with the languid grace that other men—like Rawlinson—could admire but rarely emulate.

With Tatt's as an excuse, the pair hastily left the haven of White's to saunter along the pavement.

"That was good thinking. I pity the poor girl who is to be leg-shackled to Rawlinson." Felix deftly spun his cane, glancing at his friend, a pronounced twinkle in his eyes.

"Tatt's is always a good excuse if you want a reason to leave in a hurry." Chauncy thought a bit, then added, "So where do you intend to meet your paragon of virtue?"

Felix stopped to stare at his friend. "Are you serious?"

"I thought you were."

They resumed their stroll in the vague direction of Tattersall's, where horses could be viewed with the possible thought of purchase. "Maybe I am. Could I find a truly proper young lady of decent background and acceptable appearance, I would wed her and begin the restoration of the Sutton name!"

"I should like to see that." Chauncy gave Felix a considering look. "And do you know, I believe you might just do it."

"I will. See if I don't." Felix figured it would be a simple matter to find a truly proper young miss of presentable birth and background. Why, there must be any number of them perched on pews.

"Where will you find her?" Chauncy frowned.

"Where do you see a proper lady? In church, of course, or one of those worthy institutions catering to the unfortunate, the sort some women find so appealing to their better natures."

"You, in church?" Chauncy cleared his throat of a sudden obstruction. "I'll join you. I'd not miss this for the world."

Chapter Two

"*I* had no idea there are so many churches in London." Felix left the evensong service at St. Michael's with a decidedly brisk step.

"How many have we visited so far?" Chauncy inquired, fascinated at this new aspect of his friend.

"Too many."

"No likely candidate in view?" Chauncy shook his head. "I don't know, old fellow. I have seen one or two rather possible prospects. None to suit you?"

"If you see one you think likely, you marry her! So far I've not seen a young woman I could tolerate viewing across the breakfast table year in and year out."

"Hadn't thought of it precisely that way." Chauncy glanced at Felix, then fell silent for a few moments. "Good aspect to consider. Imagine gazing at a few of those we saw? Give me the shudders, it does."

"It isn't that I am overly fastidious. But I should like a wife who has a certain charm, an air of breeding, and above all a solid respectability." Felix entered his carriage, waited for Chauncy to join him, then gave a nod to his groom to hand over the reins and hop up behind. They set off at a pace suitable for one who was in a reflective mood.

"Sounds reasonable to me." Chauncy settled back against the seat, crossed his arms, and waited.

"I believe that somewhere in one of these churches is the right woman for me. There must be someone with a good reputation whose face doesn't frighten children."

"True." Chauncy nodded. "We have spotted more than a few of those kind, old chap."

"There is a display at a small museum I want to see tomorrow. Come with me?"

Chauncy shook his head. "Afraid not. Promised Whittaker I would go with him. Has to see his mother, and you can imagine that sets him quaking in his boots."

"You are the most noble of fellows, Chauncy. Think of all the men who depend on your support." Felix gave his good friend a grin. "Ah, well, I shall give you a full report. Chances are there won't be a respectable woman in sight anyway. After all, how many women give a rap for new inventions?"

"That certainly is true. What say we go for a good bit of beef and a bottle of claret?"

"My house, I believe. I pay that chef enough so that he ought to find us something along that line."

They headed for Hanover Square and the prospect of a good meal.

Priscilla found a moment of triumph when she convinced her aunt that it would be perfectly proper for her to attend the little museum where a display of the latest inventions could be seen. "After all, I doubt anyone fashionable will go there."

"Take your new maid with you. Daisy . . . Poppy . . . whatever her name is. And dress well. While it might be unlikely you may meet someone, you never know, my dear. I intend to go calling." Aunt Mercy exchanged a knowing look with her niece. The calls would be paid to those with connections—in particular the elderly Countess of Stanwell. It was a pity their first son died before he inherited the earldom, but his son, who would be a second cousin to Priscilla, filled his shoes admirably, assuming the viscountcy with aplomb.

"I have been taught my manners, and you may be certain that I will ignore anyone I do not know. Which means I will not talk to anyone, for I've not met a soul since we arrived." Priscilla gave her aunt a grin, hoping she would understand that meeting people was not at the top of Priscilla's list of things to do.

"You will soon enough. That is a pretty gown Madame Clotilde sent over. A simple round gown of that particular shade of celestial blue does something for you. Mind you, wear the new bonnet with the cluster of blue ribands on it." Aunt Mercy smiled and waved Priscilla off before returning to her perusal of the morning paper.

Excited at the prospect of leaving the house on her own, with no one other than her maid, Lily, along, Priscilla hurried up the stairs to fetch her bonnet. A glance at the large looking glass in her room told her that her bonnet was not only tied properly, but was vastly becoming as well. What a difference it made to have fashionable clothing! As to the round gown, it had to be the softest muslin ever, quite fetching if she did say so. She tugged on her gloves before gathering up her reticule. With Lily trailing behind, she left the house with a pleasant smile for the butler, the elderly Simpkins.

He had spoken to the coachman, for the man knew just where she wished to go. Priscilla settled back against the squabs, thinking life could not get much better than this. So far there had been no talk of finding a husband. Perhaps her aunt intended to take her time, which suited Priscilla.

She glanced off to one side, noting that the man who lived a few doors down was also leaving his home. Was there ever a time when he didn't look the pattern card of elegance? He was so polished and refined, he must outshine every buck and beau in London.

This time she took care that he should not see her peeking at him. Heaven only knew what he would think of such provincial manners! Assuming he might care.

Once the museum was reached, she paused by the coachman. "John you may as well take the carriage back rather than wait for me here. My aunt likely has need of you. I have change, so we can take a hackney back."

The coachman nodded at her wisdom. Priscilla watched the carriage disappear down the street, and felt a thrill of adventure sweep over her. She was on her own. In London.

The museum had a musty smell, but she quickly forgot it when she began her stroll past the displays. They led from one room to another, nicely arranged.

And then she spotted a magic lantern. It was more

detailed than any she had seen before, with three projection lenses and fancy brass trim on the oak case. It fascinated her. Why, with something like this, the picture show could be kept going without pause. The one she had seen had but one projection lens. And it had kept her, along with a roomful of usually antsy children, enthralled.

"I see you are beguiled by the stereopticon."

The male voice came from somewhere behind her. She was not so stupid as to twirl around to see who had the wildly seductive voice. She would remain calm, tell those silly butterflies that had abruptly taken residence in her stomach to go away. And do nothing. She did not speak to strange men. Period. No matter how enticing their voices might be, and this voice was utterly enchanting.

"It is the latest development, you know. Notice the fine detailing in the case, and the large size of the lenses. I would wager that it projects a very large picture on whatever is used as a screen for viewing."

She couldn't help herself. She simply had to turn her head. She did not need to turn a great deal, as the gentleman had stepped up and stood by her side. So she looked.

He smiled. At her!

Priscilla wondered if hearts actually ceased beating, then started again. She cleared her throat. She ought not speak to him. Yet didn't those good manners she had learned also say that she should be polite? It was the man she had seen after leaving the house. After all, this man was a neighbor of her aunt's. They might know one another. It was possible. Anything was possible.

"I find it quite, quite wonderful." She had to smile. He was just as perfect as when she had seen him earlier. In fact, he was even better close up. Oh, he was the culmination of all manly aspirations. And probably too good to be true. But those shoulders and that voice. Topped by his devastating smile, he would win any prize.

He was staring at her, making her wonder if she had a bit of smut on her nose or something. She hesitantly touched her nose, raising her brows in a silent query. "Is there something amiss?"

"Not in the least, miss." There was a fervency in his voice that assured her all was well with her nose. Face, too, likely. Although he did stare at her.

"I adore magic lantern shows. They truly *are* magical, you know. I have seen a room packed with fidgety children turn as still as stone when the lantern was lit and the images projected on a wall." She sighed with the happy memory of the last one that had ventured to her village.

"Perhaps I could arrange for you to see one?"

"That would not likely be correct, sir." He was going beyond what was proper, and she knew it. Tossing him a reproving look, and with Lily in tow, she hastily left the little museum with a regretful sigh. With an attraction like that man, all the other offerings paled in comparison. Besides, he might think she wanted to strike up an acquaintance with him. While it was true, she couldn't let him know that!

Felix stood by the stereopticon display like a flummoxed fish. That was the one! She was beautiful. She liked magic lanterns, just as he did. She had a genteel manner of speaking, and her voice was that of an angel. Those blue eyes had sparkled when she talked about the children viewing the lantern show. Did that mean she was a governess? No, that was not possible. No governess would have a maid in attendance. Besides, she was garbed in the latest fashion. The blue muslin blended with her luscious skin in tempting contrast to her eyes, the blue of which brought a summer sky to mind.

Coming to his wits, he hurried from the museum to see if he had lost her. A hackney was just setting forth. Perhaps she was inside? Felix raised his arm to summon another hackney, but by the time he was able to enter, the first had disappeared from view. He had indeed lost his paragon, the woman who was undoubtedly very respectable as well as desirable. Witness how she caught herself, quickly silencing her tongue and leaving at once when she realized the impropriety of speaking with him. She had not flirted with him, recalling what was proper before he could learn more about her.

But he couldn't help wish he knew who she was.

The carriage jounced over the cobbles until Felix signaled the jarvey to let him down.

"Chauncy! Just the one I wanted to see. I have found her!" he announced when he joined his friend.

"Where is she?" Chauncy looked around as though the woman was concealed behind Felix.

"I don't know," Felix admitted with a sigh. "I discovered this beautiful creature . . . and let her get away from me."

"I don't believe it. You? Let a woman escape? One you have been hunting for weeks?" Chauncy goggled at him.

"I didn't expect to find her at the museum, you see. But there she was, staring at the stereopticon display." Felix caught himself just in time from sighing again. If he weren't careful, he would sound like one of those lovesick lads who annoyed people.

"I see," Chauncy replied with caution. It was clear he didn't comprehend in the least, but was too polite to say so. "What do you do now?"

"Keep looking. At least I know there is a perfect creature out there, somewhere in Town." He clamped his mouth shut. Even Chauncy had his limits, and so did Felix. He would not soar into raptures over a miss he had yet to meet. There might be a flaw not readily visible. It was best to be cautious. But . . . somehow he doubted his bewitching female had any defects. She had looked very good to his somewhat jaded eyes.

"Did you hear the latest?" Chauncy inquired as they set off toward White's.

By a force of willpower, Felix listened to the latest gossip about a chap he truly disliked. But only with half an ear. The rest of his mind fastened on the matter of finding this original: a beautiful girl with manners to match.

They were relaxing at White's when Chauncy—seeing that his friend's mind was elsewhere—inquired, "Have you tried St. George's?"

"On Hanover Square? Not yet. The entire neighborhood attends there. I doubt there is anyone I don't know." The memory—quite forgotten—of a pretty face at a post chaise window returned. "That is not to say that there might not be a visitor. I shall attend this Sunday."

Chauncy scanned the room, then nudged Felix on his arm. "I say, isn't that your estimable cousin over there? Fancy seeing him here, of all places."

Felix promptly twisted around in his chair to see the most worthy Archdeacon Pallant, from his mother's side of the family, of course. Best of all, he had seen Felix and hadn't cut him.

"Cousin Pallant, good to see you." Felix rose to shake hands with his illustrious relative.

"Latimer, nice to see you well and about."

Felix wondered how he meant that. Then a curious notion occurred to him. "Please join us."

The archdeacon drew back a chair and lowered himself onto it with stately grace. He inquired about the family, but only in a vague manner such as one does when one does not really want to know.

"I wonder if you might be of help to me," Felix asked after exchanging some pleasant conversation. "I need some information." Felix got the instant impression that as long as he wasn't asking for money, the archdeacon would be only too happy to oblige.

"Could you list a number of charities that ladies of quality sponsor, especially involving children?"

"I trust this is an entirely proper inquiry?" There was a hint of frost underlying his words that brought Felix up sharp. Drat his family and their reputations!

"Indeed, it is. I, ah, thought to present a stereopticon showing for the less fortunate children. I am reliably informed that even the most restless of youngsters become as still as stone while viewing such a display."

"Hmm. I will have to consider that a bit. What do you say I send over the list first thing in the morning? Would that do?" Archdeacon Pallant actually smiled on Felix without a trace of censure.

"That would be fine. Just fine." Felix offered his cousin a glass of wine that was quickly accepted. The gentleman remained a little longer in general conversation before taking his leave, a ponderous action that was clearly a result of years of practice.

"Clever," muttered Chauncy. "You intend to visit every

charity in London with your stereopticon in tow?" His eyebrows raised to where his sandy hair flopped over his brow.

"I believe I will. Considering my aims, it would greatly help my ambition to restore the family name. If I manage to locate a certain delicious blonde at the same time, well and good." He grinned at Chauncy, who promptly grinned back.

"You will help me, of course," Felix asked, but was aware he sounded more like he was giving an order.

"You know . . . I believe I will. I fancy those magic lantern shows myself. And I'd not miss a chance to see that delicious blonde you mentioned. I suppose she has blue eyes as well?"

"She does."

"And pretty?" When Felix nodded by way of reply, Chauncy shook his head. "A delectable blue-eyed blonde, and you think to keep her from all the other lads in Town? I wish you well."

Felix softly groaned. "Oh, oh. I think we had better leave for more agreeable pastures, my friend. None other than Lord Bolsolver has come into the room. I'd prefer to avoid him if possible. Somehow, having him present a lecture to the members present on the inadvisability of allowing riffraff to enter these hallowed halls doesn't appeal."

"This way." Chauncy nudged Felix ahead of him, keeping an eye on where Bolsolver had paused to chat with someone. His back was to them, and with any luck at all, they should be able to be out and away without being caught.

When they reached the hall without being spotted by the vituperative Bolsolver, both breathed a sigh of relief. They silently ran down the stairs to the entry, gathered their hats, gloves and Felix's cane before escaping.

"That went rather well." Felix swung his cane back and forth a bit. "You know, ordinarily I might have stayed to give that old goat a set-down. It isn't part of my new image."

"Well, he is a prime pain and deserves a set-down for castigating your family in toto. I rather like your Uncle George."

"That is because he taught you how to win at whist."

"True, he did. But he is a good sort, for all his propensity to gamble. He doesn't ask you for money, does he?" Chauncy paused at the corner of Piccadilly and St. James' streets, eyeing the passing carriages with a knowledgeable eye before peering at Felix.

"Once in a while. He pays me back if he wins."

"There! You see? He certainly can't be all black."

"Bolsolver thinks so and states it in the loudest possible voice." Felix sounded as grim as he looked.

"Best thing to do is ignore the man."

"I wish his charming daughter good luck. Do you realize how few eligible men there are who do not have a skeleton in some closet?" Felix forced a smile to cover his annoyance at having to leave his club to avoid a disagreeable scene.

Chauncy snorted with derision. "Especially one who happens to be an earl and due to become a marquess in time."

"There is that. Come, let's wander along to see what is on offer at Hatchard's."

They entered the bookshop to head for the area where scientific literature might be found. Chauncy was well aware where his friend's true interests were and went along with his usual amiable nature.

Felix had buried his head in a treatise on some experiments that were being done with silver and the theory that one might produce images. Photography, this Frenchman called it, using a camera obscura and paper that had been sensitized with chloride of silver. It didn't sound too promising to Felix, but was curiously interesting all the same. Felix knew that Thomas Wedgwood had recorded images on paper sensitized with silver nitrate, but the silhouettes he created faded away in no time. It seemed to Felix that sunlight was simply too weak a source for . . .

"I say, there is a fetching blonde. Over there—just paying for some books." Chauncy poked Felix in the arm.

Felix tore himself from the treatise to see a familiar figure in a blue round gown and a bonnet trimmed with blue ribands. He dropped the booklet, taking a step toward the front of the store. Then he stopped. It was useless. He doubted he would gain her respect if he dashed out to chase after her like a lad just down from Oxford lacking town bronze.

"Was she the wrong one?" Chauncy was clearly disappointed.

"On the contrary. She is the right one. But wouldn't I look a figure of fun to go dashing after her out of Hatchard's, old boy? Very proper, I'd appear, too. If I want someone respectable, I had better act in like manner."

"You know, you'll turn into a dull dog if you keep this up."

"Don't you think it is time and enough that someone in my family does?"

Chauncy shook his head. "I think you make too much of this, Felix. You know what Bolsolver is, a nastier piece of goods isn't to be found. As a matter of fact, I think you are well shot of that daughter of his. She might grow to be just like her father—or worse yet, her mother!"

"That does happen. Let me pay for this booklet"—Felix stooped to pick up the item he had dropped when Chauncy poked him—"and we will find a more interesting pastime."

"Must say it is comforting to see your old twinkle return to your eyes. I was afraid you would turn into another archdeacon."

Felix paid for his booklet, then ushered Chauncy out the front door to the pavement. "Heaven forbid! I believe one to a family is the limit."

Priscilla hurried from the hackney, so absorbed in her thoughts that she paid little attention to Lily skipping along behind her. She had found a copy of the very latest novel by a writer she admired. And . . . she had glimpsed that gentleman again. There had been another man with him, but she had no doubt that the handsome neighbor was the one she spotted by the scientific publications.

It was nice to know he had worthwhile interests. From all she had heard, too many of the gentlemen in London were interested only in gambling and collecting pretty women.

"Priscilla! Home at last." Aunt Mercy greeted her niece with a welcoming smile. "Come. Enjoy some tea with me and tell me all about your trip to the museum. Did you enjoy it?"

Priscilla immediately launched into a rapturous description of the stereopticon she had seen. "And I saw one of your neighbors there. Of course I said nothing as to who I am, or where I had seen him before."

"And just which of my neighbors did you meet?" Aunt Mercy asked with idle curiosity.

"I believe you identified him as Lord Latimer. I saw him a few doors down the street the day we arrived. Then next I saw him chatting with Cousin Rawlinson."

"Hmm, I know who you mean. His name is Felix, one of the Sutton family. He is Earl Latimer, son of the Marquess of Silverstone. Quite a catch, so I am told. I confess I have not paid the slightest bit of attention to him. He does not often appear in the bits and scraps of gossip found in the newspapers—although his father does, as does his Uncle George Sutton, his aunt, Lady Beatrice, and a cousin I've been told is a trifle wild. Your cousin would know more about him, I imagine."

"Lord Latimer has a very nice smile." Priscilla stared into the fireplace at the glowing embers, thinking they gave the same sort of warmth as that smile. "A lovely voice as well. Do you think we will meet him?"

"He saw you, spoke to you—briefly of course—and about impersonal matters?"

Priscilla nodded gravely, her eyes widening at her aunt's smile.

"He is young, personable, and unmarried. I daresay we will see him sooner or later." She raised her handkerchief to her lips to cover a slight cough.

"Does he have a reputation?" Priscilla lowered her voice at this query, wanting to know, yet hoping that the reply would be favorable.

"I have no idea. Come, pour us some tea and do try one of the little biscuits Cook baked. I think you will like them."

Priscilla also thought that she would like to know Lord Latimer better. The biscuits were easier to get.

The first thing the following morning Felix opened a missive from Archdeacon Pallant containing a brief list of charities that were financed by the gentry and various peers.

Felix studied the list with care. It was no more than a stab in the dark, but if the blonde with blue was around children, and she was as proper as she seemed, it was likely that she might just be involved in some worthy cause. He had hunted through the various balls and parties being offered and not seen her. Of course it was early in the Season, and London was thin of company yet. But still, even if she was in the process of acquiring an up-to-date wardrobe, she might be visiting a charity school.

When Chauncy arrived, he found the stereopticon had been packed up along with a nice variety of painted slides. Fortunately, Felix had one depicting a familiar fairy tale, so it would appeal to youngsters. Chauncy had been around at holiday time, and enjoyed it as much as the children.

His cousin, the archdeacon, appeared just as the pair were ready to leave Felix's house.

"I thought I had best go with you. I am known to the various directors of these charity schools. They might be more receptive if I am there to introduce you. I must see for myself this venture by a Sutton into altruistic efforts." He beamed a benevolent smile on Felix.

Felix wondered if his cousin realized how stuffy he sounded. "You are welcome to join us. Chauncy and I can set up the stereopticon while you deal with the director or whoever must be dealt with at each of these places. We will cover what we can today. I do not expect you to go with us every day, that is asking too much of your time." Felix managed a grim smile.

"No trouble at all, my boy. Glad to partake in such a worthwhile effort." The archdeacon picked up the box holding the glass slides and followed Felix and Chauncy to the carriage waiting for them.

It was an exhausting day, producing absolutely nothing other than the reward of eager, happy faces as he showed his slides telling the fairy tale. They clapped little hands and said their thanks, prompted only slightly by the directress. The next day brought the same results.

The following day Felix almost didn't go. Only the arrival of Chauncy and his cousin, the Archdeacon Pallant, persuaded him to repeat the performances.

It was late in the afternoon when they set up in a schoolroom for a final performance. It was a neat, clean place. The children seemed better fed, certainly better clothed than the previous schools they had visited. He completed adjusting his stereopticon when a young woman dressed in pale aqua entered with a group of children. She paused when she saw him. And stared.

Felix smiled.

The dragon who entered the room behind her appeared vaguely familiar. His cousin followed them into the room, looking even more pompous then usual, if such a thing were possible.

"Felix, here is one of your neighbors! Miss Herbert, this is my cousin, Lord Latimer. He graciously offered to provide a showing of a few of his slides to the children."

The dragon smiled, revealing a not-quite-so-formidable lady. "And this is my niece, who is helping me today with the children, Miss Priscilla Herbert. Dear, come and meet my neighbor, Lord Latimer."

The smile that lit her eyes brought an answering smile to his lips. His goddess was here!

"It is a pleasure to meet a gentleman who is willing to devote an hour or two to a worthy cause. I am pleased to make your acquaintance, sir." She held out her hand to shake his. Felix wanted to clasp hers for longer than proper. It was a slender hand, and her skin as soft as an angel's wing would be. The faint scent of honeysuckle lingered about her, pleasing and fresh, just like her voice.

"And I am delighted to meet a young lady who not only enjoys stereopticon shows, but shares that pleasure with the children." Good grief, was that actually him, spouting off like his archdeacon cousin?

"As I said, they are captivating."

Felix thought she was far more captivating, but merely

bowed his head, then went about completing preparations for his fairy-tale show. "*Cinderella, or The Glass Slipper* seems to be a favorite with the children." He almost apologized for not having a Bible story, but stopped, fearing he would sound like his cousin again.

The children were silent, enraptured with the tale as it unfolded. At the conclusion when pretty Cinderella wed her prince, the children all clapped and began chattering among themselves.

"That was very nice. Think what hope it gives to these little girls. If that poor girl could marry a prince, they might perhaps marry the owner of a shop."

Felix studied the enchanting face belonging to Priscilla Herbert. "Do you hope to marry a prince of your own?" he asked before he considered what he was saying.

"Oh, I should like to very much, but from what I have heard, the princes in London are not such as would please me." She repressed a grin, but her eyes revealed her amusement.

"Wise girl." He glanced about to note the others were in conversation. "Could I call on you, Miss Herbert? Perhaps you would enjoy a stroll in the park?"

"Yes. I believe I would, Lord Latimer."

Felix smiled again and packed his gear away, his heart and mind set on the path he wanted to pursue. "I shall see you tomorrow."

"Tomorrow, indeed, sir."

Chapter Three

"*That* is splendid, dear. I think Lord Latimer is a nice young man, and I am pleased you will take a nice walk with him." Aunt Mercy nodded her head in affirmation of her words.

She poured herself another cup of Bohea tea, thereupon settled back in her chair, a superb example of Mr. Sheraton's finer work. Indeed, the mahogany carving was delicately detailed and suited to Aunt Mercy, who was still what her father called a fine figure of a woman. Garbed in a lilac morning gown with an impressive lace cap on her head, she was the epitome of London fashion. Even the paintings on the wall were restful scenes of English countryside, rather than the frowning ancestors found in so many dining rooms. Priscilla liked the room, as well as her aunt.

Perhaps there were no frowning ancestors, but Priscilla frowned. Somehow, she felt that the word "nice" was inadequate to describe Lord Latimer. Handsome, tempting, refined, cultured—they might do as a beginning. And she rated a walk with him far above an insipid "nice." Alluring? Perhaps enchanting? Certainly better than *nice*!

"There is a play on this evening that sounds interesting. I have obtained tickets for it. Madame Clotilde sent two gowns for you. Perhaps one of them will be suitable for an evening at the theater? I should like you to look nice." Her aunt peered up from her morning newspaper to regard her niece with a smile. "Oh, your cousin Aylwin will join us. He makes a nice escort."

"Oh, my. Thank you!" Priscilla left the luncheon table on eager feet. Why had no one told her that a parcel had arrived for her? Well, it was a marvelous surprise.

Once in her room, she soon found the gowns. At her request Lily held up a gown made of lilac silk, the neckline of which seemed daringly low to Priscilla. The beautiful gown was trimmed with darker lilac velvet ribands and gold embroidery at the hem and on the sleeves.

The second dress was spread out on the bed. The simple round gown had a dainty leaf print in delicate green on the fabric. Both gowns were simple in cut and design, neither had frills, something for which she was very thankful. She had never looked good in frilly garments. Or perhaps it was that she was more comfortable in modest things?

"I shall wear that lilac silk this evening. I know my aunt wishes me to look proper." She admired the silk gown again, noting how the fabric shimmered as Lily carried it. How gratifying it would be to look her best. One never knew who might be at the theater.

She returned below to again thank her aunt for the two gowns, and announced that she intended to wear the lilac silk.

"That will look very nice with your eyes and hair, my dear. I believe I have a pair of amethyst ear bobs that you can wear. They will be the finishing touch, I vow."

The talk turned to the weather and planning the coming days. Aunt Mercy had a considerable list of places she thought her niece ought to see.

Before long the time came to prepare for her walk in the park with Lord Latimer. Naturally Priscilla wished to look fetching for this auspicious event. Even if he had no serious intentions, it behooved her to look good. It was entirely possible he might introduce her to a gentleman who would do quite nicely as a husband! She doubted she would catch an earl as a husband—even if he smiled at her so.

Her thoughts were muddled as she went up the stairs to her room. She was sensible enough to know that gentlemen were often whimsical when it came to women. As to his taking her for a walk, he might simply like her company. It didn't mean he was serious. She was a new face in Town, and she had heard tales . . . Not that Lord Latimer wasn't proper—at least, so far. It was some of the other types Adam had mentioned she ought to avoid. No gamblers, no flirts, no poets reading odes to her eyes, and above all no man who would spirit her away with promises of a marriage in Scotland!

So, garbed in a pastel amaranth walking dress trimmed with rows of blonde lace and cream ribands with a pelisse of blue cloth that had cunning black cord frogs to close the front, she made her way to the drawing room to receive her aunt's opinion. "Will I do, ma'am?"

"Let me see." Aunt Mercy looked up from her embroidery. "Gloves? Parasol? Reticule? I do like that villager hat we found. And were we not clever to match the cream ribands to your dress! Simplicity is always smart. You are prompt, too. I suspect that gentlemen do not like to be kept waiting, although so many women I know make a practice of doing so. They seem to fancy that a man will be all the more delighted to see them once they finally make an appearance."

"I think it is rude to keep someone waiting." Particularly when it was someone she wanted to see.

Not much later Simpkins cleared his throat before entering the drawing room. "Lord Latimer, ma'am."

Again, that confusing sensation swept over Priscilla. He was more than good-looking. He could well be that prince of whom they had joked. He was anything but ordinary in his tobacco brown coat over biscuit pantaloons. Those highly polished boots added to his smart appearance. The final touch to his apparel was a biscuit-colored waistcoat with a woven design of gold stripes that contrasted nicely with a simply arranged cravat. He bowed to Aunt Mercy, then turned to face Priscilla. He appeared to like what he saw. A smile lit up his eyes, their gleam more than satisfying.

"Good afternoon, Lord Latimer." Aunt Mercy nodded as she spoke. "It is a pleasant day for a stroll in the park. Just do not be out too long, for we attend the theater this evening. Now go, and have a nice time."

It seemed to Priscilla that "nice" and "come" were two of her aunt's favorite words. However, she was such a dear person, it would be silly to cavil over it. Instead,

Priscilla kissed her aunt's cheek before joining Lord Latimer to leave the house.

His carriage awaited them in front. She regarded him with surprise. Lily climbed up to the seat behind at once.

"I did notice you have walking boots on, but I think we will drive to the park, then walk. That is agreeable?"

"Certainly." Priscilla didn't know what to say. She was accustomed to walking miles at home. But this wasn't home. She allowed him to assist her into the curricle.

She had never had to make conversation with a gentleman of his elevated position, and now she discovered she was tongue-tied! True, there had been a few titled people at home, but she'd had little enough to do with them.

Within moments, she was put at ease by his flow of agreeable comments on the weather and life in London.

"I find it all quite wonderful, you know," Priscilla responded to one of his remarks. "My aunt has a list of interesting places I may venture to explore. I can scarce wait!" Priscilla couldn't contain her pleasure at the thought of seeing so much of London.

Felix took note of those delightful, sparkling blue eyes, and wondered if there was an employee in the Herbert household known by a servant in his own. It would be very useful for him if he could learn in advance just where Miss Priscilla was headed every day. Not that he would pursue her to each and every one. That might overwhelm her, give her the feeling of being hounded. No, he would pop up when she least expected it. Then, too, perhaps her aunt would permit him to escort her niece. As long as the maid tailed along there ought to be not the slightest problem. He wanted utmost propriety. There would not be the faintest hint of scandal about the woman he chose to marry. It had pleased him when Cousin Pallant approved of this young lady. No less than an archdeacon ought to spot respectability!

"Perhaps I may be of service there. Elderly ladies tire and I would be happy to offer my escort to some of the places on your list. I like showing London to someone truly interested in what the city has to offer."

It seemed to him that no word of his scandalous family had touched her aunt's ears at any rate. If it had, he doubted he would have the happiness of this afternoon jaunt.

Once in the park, he pulled off the main road to hand the reins to his groom. The maid agilely made her way to the ground, and stood ready to fall in behind them. He approved of that seemliness even if he would have liked to be alone with his lovely creature.

"I am surprised you own a stereopticon, my lord. How did you come to be interested in such a thing? To my knowledge it is a clever invention used by those itinerants who travel from village to village, offering a bit of enjoyment to the folk there. And you are far from being an itinerant showman. I did relish your tale of *Cinderella, or The Glass Slipper.*"

"I am glad I could please you." He would have to find another tale that would entertain her. What a delight she was. So often a woman pretended to be in transports over some diversion he liked. It was not long before he learned it was feigned. Priscilla appeared to be natural in her responses, and that he could truly appreciate.

"Do you know I have wondered if that was really a glass slipper in that tale." She grinned at him. "My brother insists it must have been something else, as glass is far too unlikely. I suppose he is right. But tell me, how do you come to have this fascinating interest?"

"I have always liked unusual things—scientific inventions and what have you. That is why I inspect the latest offerings, with a view to owning them or perhaps improving on them. I suppose you might say I enjoy dabbling." He placed her hand on his arm, the better to guide her along the path, naturally.

"Well, if that is dabbling, I say it is impressive."

Felix preened slightly, for it was rather pleasing to be praised for what he did. Few people knew of his interests. He wondered if his cousin the archdeacon would keep his stereopticon in mind for future use. Felix thought it could be a helpful teaching tool. Not that he wanted to be at his Cousin Pallant's beck and call. But he owed him for helping to find the estimable Miss Priscilla Herbert.

The horse chestnuts were coming into blossom, the creamy blooms bursting forth with exuberance. And there were tiny daisies to dot the grass, like little stars, presenting a pleasant prospect for them as they meandered along the path. They chatted politely about London in general, the sights to be viewed and Miss Herbert's partialities.

He glanced off to the right and almost stopped in his tracks. There, along with several others he knew slightly, was none other than Miss Anne Bolsolver. They were headed straight for Felix and Miss Herbert. There was no side path where they might casually bypass the group. He took a fortifying breath and cleared his throat.

"Did you say something, sir?" He could almost feel Miss Herbert's speculative gaze on him. Her hand likely detected the tensing of his arm.

"No, merely a frog in my throat. I do believe that the daffodils are quite special this year. There is a drift of them over there—look completely natural. Would you like to inspect them more closely?" He edged toward that direction with the hope she would accept his lead.

She gave him a thoughtful look, checked the group approaching, and quickly replied, "I believe that would be delightful. I do admire daffodils."

Felix executed a sharp turn that should have earned him a questioning stare. Miss Herbert merely turned with him, and marched at his side to the very ordinary scattering of daffodils, the bright yellow a charming contrast to the rich green grass. The daisies punctuated the green here as well, offering a pretty counterpoint.

He felt a bit foolish, rushing her away from Miss Bolsolver and her friends. But he did not want his walk with Miss Herbert spoiled by any nasty gibes from the woman whose father had rejected his offer of marriage. From what Chauncy said, Miss Bolsolver had a temper. Seeing him with another woman would be tempting her. He feared her words would be anything but agreeable.

"I like that shade of yellow. I always have. It is such a merry color, full of promise for the summer to come." Miss Herbert bestowed a smile on him that was far more gracious than he deserved.

Bless the girl, what tact she had, something his family had always lacked. Felix murmured a few words of concurrence.

"It is drawing late. Perhaps we ought to take this other path back to the road where your carriage awaits us?" Miss Herbert gestured in the direction opposite to that taken by the Bolsolver party.

And still more tact! "I think that an excellent notion. After all, if you intend to go to the theater this evening, you will want to rest a bit before dinner and dressing. I have been told this is no hasty matter." He glanced over his shoulder to note the other group was now some distance away. Never in his life had he nattered on in such a mundane way. He felt like a fool. It was a distinct change for him to be so concerned with propriety—not that he had ever led a young lady astray. But he had enjoyed a bit of flirting, to be sure.

"Not having been to the theater before, I scarce know. I look forward to seeing the drama."

"And the farce that likely follows?" There was nearly always a farce or some sort of comedy, the theatergoers expecting full measure for their shillings.

"Oh, indeed, there is nothing like a good farce."

Her tone was dry and her expression far too shrewd. Why did he suspect she was thinking of more than the evening's entertainment?

Priscilla allowed herself to be entertained by his flow of words as they strolled back to where the carriage awaited them. He assisted her into the vehicle, took note that Lily had climbed to her place before accepting the reins from his groom.

He drove well. No fussy mannerisms or excessive flourishes spoiled his handling of the reins. Her brother, dear Adam, prided himself on his driving, and had commented more than once another chap's clumsy treatment of his horses. They navigated the streets at a slow pace, likely incurring the wrath of those in a hurry. She didn't know why Lord Latimer dawdled, but she could hope it was because he liked her company.

"Where do you wish to explore tomorrow?" His voice sounded friendly, and he seemed actually interested in how she planned to spend her day.

She darted a glance at him, a frown creasing her brow as she considered his query. She would have thought he would be flooded with more invitations than most mortals could possibly accept in a year. Was she overly suspicious as to his motive? Was he being polite, or did he intend to accompany her? "I'm not certain," she said at last.

The image of the modishly dressed young woman they had seen in the park returned. He obviously did not wish to meet her, or introduce her to Priscilla. Why? It would be interesting to know. Not that she intended to scorn his escort around Town. He proved to be a clever companion, with witty stories and information on a variety of topics at the ready. She had learned early on to accept the good that came her way without too much questioning. She had discovered *that* often brought trouble.

They reached her aunt's home just down from Hanover Square. She paused before the house after he had handed her from the carriage. "Would you care for a cup of tea—for that frog in your throat, you know." Her gaze met his with a directness that seemed to amuse him.

His answering smile held a tinge of humor. "I should like that very much." He turned to his groom. "I shall walk home from here."

Lily slipped inside behind them, while the groom took the carriage off to the mews.

Priscilla paused before going up to the drawing room, handing her bonnet and gloves to Lily while Simpkins accepted Lord Latimer's hat and gloves.

"Tea if you please, Simpkins. We have had an exceedingly invigorating walk."

He bowed before marching to the rear of the house.

Lord Latimer joined her on the stairs, walking with ease. Certainly nothing was perturbing him!

"I enjoyed our outing, sir. Seeing daffodils and daisies reminded me of home. Not that I am homesick, for I am not. There is too much to do and see in London for that. But it is agreeable to see nature."

"You are a sensible young woman."

"So my father has remarked." She flashed him a smile that made it plain she didn't expect a reply. She would have liked to know just who that woman was, and why he didn't wish to meet her, but that would have been a shocking bit of curiosity. "You asked what I plan tomorrow. I would like to see the British Museum, if such can be managed. My guidebook says that it is somewhat easier to access than in the past. Is that true? And why was it difficult before?" She was finding it all too pleasant to walk at his side, her arm brushing against his from time to time. The faint scent of bay rum teased her nose, and she rather liked it.

"Hmm. I shall see what I can do about that for you. I am not unknown to the governors. Do not be surprised if we must put it off for a day, possibly two. I have no idea why the powers-that-be limit the inspection of the collections, then guide people around as though herding a flock of sheep. It is about time that improved."

"Please realize that I do not expect you to conduct me to all the sights I want to view." They had reached the top of the stairs and were close to the entrance to the drawing room when she halted to face him. She frowned slightly, wanting him to know she was in earnest, not flirting. It would be dreadful if she was considered a pushing female! It wasn't that she didn't desire him— she did, and that was likely a problem, at least for her.

"As I said before, I enjoy showing London to someone who is truly interested. What about seeing Miss Linwood's Gallery of embroidery pictures, or perhaps Bullock's Egyptian Museum? Both promise diversion."

She stared up at him in an attempt to assess his sincerity. Well, if he offered, she would accept in like manner. "The Egyptian Museum, I believe. I think one of the panoramas might do as well. It is agreeable to have something indoors in the event the weather is nasty." She turned away from him to enter the drawing room, where her aunt awaited them.

Aunt Mercy wore an afternoon gown of plum kerseymere that had an interesting sleeve. The ruff of foaming lace at her neck flattered her, as did the lace cap she wore.

"Come, tell me how your walk in the park went. Are the daffodils in bloom yet?" Miss Herbert beckoned them to where she sat on a blue-and-cream-striped satin sofa.

Priscilla glided to her aunt's side to kiss her cheek in an affectionate greeting. "Indeed, dearest aunt. It is a fine day. The daffodils are at their peak of bloom, and the horse chestnuts were lovely. Lord Latimer made certain I saw them all." She turned her head just slightly to give him a conscious look. She could not forget that attractive young woman whom he did not want her to meet. The more that she considered it, the more curious she became. Curiosity is a besetting sin, her father lectured. Yet she would give a shilling to know why the confrontation was avoided, for confrontation she sensed it would have been.

"I should think there would be more gardens in the park." Aunt Mercy nodded decisively. "I always think of a park having flowers. The London parks have trees and some shrubbery, and *that* is nothing spectacular." She invited Lord Latimer to be seated near her. Priscilla perched on a comfortable chair close by.

"Perhaps you should write a letter about it to one of the papers? Or contact whoever it is that oversees the parks? Surely there is merit in your points." Lord Latimer quite won her aunt with his seemingly sincere attention.

"I like flowers. Most women do, you know. There should be a walk in the park where we might admire them," Aunt Mercy pointed out, then greeted Simpkins when he entered the room with a tray holding the pot of tea as well as necessary china, and a plate of dainty biscuits. "Do pour, Priscilla. It is so pleasant to have a nice young lady to do things for me. One thing I must say for my niece, she was reared to be proper. My sister-in-law is charming and quite aware of our family connections."

"Aunt Mercy," Priscilla cautioned. She detested having her relatives trot out the relationship to the Earl of Stanwell, not to mention Viscount Rawlinson.

"Tell me about them," Lord Latimer prompted.

He was entertained by a concise account of the illustrious relatives on her side of Priscilla's family. The earldom was discussed, with the wealth of details regarding the original granting of same. She also commented on Viscount Rawlinson. "Such a pity his father died so young. I must say, Aylwin is behaving with more aplomb than I would have expected. I had thought him to be a bit of a rattle-pate, you know. Young men so often are."

Lord Latimer took this bit of wisdom in stride before begging his leave. He placed his teacup down with a clink. "Perhaps I may see you this evening?" He seemed to depart with genuine reluctance. Priscilla wondered if that was real or feigned. And his "perhaps" left him a great deal of room in which to maneuver, although he had asked what play they intended to see.

Once they were alone, the two women plunged into the preparations for the coming evening. The amethyst ear bobs were found and declared a perfect compliment to the new gown. They also lent a hint of violet to her blue eyes that Priscilla considered intriguing. She had a narrow gold bracelet her aunt thought quite fine.

"I suggest you wear it. With all the other women decked out like a jeweler's shop window, you will stand out in your simplicity. Good taste is always an aim, and I mean to see that you are always arrayed in the nicest of taste."

Priscilla hugged her dearest aunt with genuine liking. How blest she was to have been granted this wondrous trip to London. Best of all, it appeared her aunt had no intention of settling Priscilla on an impecunious curate. She hadn't met a one yet!

They dined early, and Priscilla took care not to spill a crumb on her new gown. Aunt Mercy looked perfect in her rose silk trained gown. It had very pretty lace around the modestly cut neck and edges of the sleeves. In short, she was an excellent example of pleasing taste.

Cousin Aylwin arrived promptly to escort them. Lord Rawlinson moved with an innate grace that Priscilla envied. His understated garb could only draw attention from the fact it was so refined, so unremarkable, yet certainly of highest quality. And if Lord Latimer looked for propriety, she judged her relative ranked high on any list.

The theater, when they arrived, proved to be a sad crush of people. They crammed into the lobby with seeming disregard for others, totally intent upon reaching their seats.

"Hold fast to me, dear girl," Aunt Mercy begged. "If I ever lost you in this madhouse, I'd have trouble finding you again." Aylwin linked his arm with Priscilla, the same thought in mind, supposedly.

"Have no worry. I shall cling like a limpet until we find our seats. Is it always this crowded?" Priscilla gazed about her with wide eyes, taking note of distinguished gentlemen and beautifully garbed women. *This* was London, the London she had longed to see.

"I fancy it is. At least when I have come. One is tempted to arrive late to avoid the crush, but I hate to think of missing something."

"I should think it rude to enter during the play, thus possibly distracting an actor."

Her aunt chuckled. "You have yet to see real rudeness. London theatergoers have perfected the art of being rude."

At last, settled in the box her aunt had rented, Priscilla was able to study the theater interior as well as those who attended the production. She found herself distracted from the design and furnishings by the audience. Never in her life had she seen so many gorgeous gowns on so many plump women. Not that there were no slender females, it merely seemed to her that far too many revealed far too much!

Aylwin offered comments on the interior, then continued to point out the various personages. He seemed a trifle fawning to Priscilla, but perhaps that was merely his manner.

"What do you think?" Aunt Mercy queried.

"Opulent. Ravishing. Stunning. And who is that creature in the ivory satin with the magnificent tiara seated opposite us?" Priscilla discreetly wafted her fan in the direction of the young woman she had seen in the park—the woman Lord Latimer had not wanted her to meet.

"Miss Anne Bolsolver," Aylwin replied. "Her father inherited a fortune from his father—who, it is rumored, was in trade. She is a pretty thing, is she not? I heard something about her nearing an engagement. Nothing came of it, so she is still fishing in the pond of London nobility. Rumor also has it that her father will settle for nothing less than a peer."

Miss Bolsolver had assembled a decent-sized court about her, for her box was crowded with young men, the same ones that escorted her in the park if memory served. Priscilla had to admit that the woman was exquisitely garbed, her dark hair utter perfection, and she had elevated flirting to an art form from what Priscilla could see.

"Miss Herbert," a familiar voice said from behind Priscilla. "May I join you?" Lord Latimer entered to offer a courtly bow to Aunt Mercy, then turned to Priscilla.

She knew she blushed at his perusal. Perhaps this neckline was a bit too low. Oh, dear, and he appeared to set such store by propriety! Lord Latimer's face wore a shuttered expression, so she had no clue as to his thoughts when he viewed her cousin. But she was totally pleased with Aylwin. How lovely to have a male relative of whom she might be gratified. That Aylwin wore a resigned expression, she quite missed.

"You take my breath away, Miss Priscilla. Such fresh, natural beauty is seldom seen in London. Lilac becomes you well, I must say." He pulled forth a chair to seat himself between them, after which he proceeded to identify the various people Aunt Mercy didn't know and Aylwin had omitted to mention.

Priscilla was entranced.

The play began. Priscilla soon understood what her aunt meant about rudeness. People chatted loudly, came and went with abandon, and in general behaved more like unruly children than mature adults. She was relieved when the act ended. The chattering increased in volume, however.

At intermission they were joined by a young man introduced as Mr. Chauncy Renshaw. He was an agreeable person, certainly good-natured. Mr. Renshaw reminded her of a puppy they had at home.

Greetings were made; it seemed the gentlemen knew each other. Conversation became general, but Lord Latimer focused his attention on Priscilla. A glance now and again at the box where Miss Bolsolver sat caught her staring at them. Priscilla gave her a cool look in return.

Aylwin cleared his throat. "I can see the coming farce is going to be fascinating." That he studied Lord Latimer instead of the stage puzzled Priscilla greatly, but there was no time to inquire what he meant. And later she forgot.

Chapter Four

"*W*hat on earth do you suppose Aylwin meant when he said the farce was to be fascinating? He spoke in such a strange, meaningful manner. And how he stared at me. I was quite transfixed—at least for several moments. Then he scarce watched the thing!" Priscilla walked up the stairs with her aunt, wanting to prolong the evening that had proved so exciting, not to mention perplexing.

"I daresay he had some cryptic notion in his mind. That branch of the family is given to odd whims and starts. However, you must admit he did you credit, my dear. He was dressed to the nines and has such *ton*. If he seems a trifle eccentric, no matter." Aunt Mercy waved her fan in a dismissing manner. "And on your other side, Lord Latimer almost outdid Aylwin. The very cream of male elegance surrounded us, for even Mr. Renshaw looked quite fine in his charcoal coat with that interesting peacock-green waistcoat over cream breeches. I vow, it was enough to send a number of ladies I know into a green melancholy, to see a new-comer *so* surrounded."

Priscilla allowed that to pass for the moment. "Did you notice that Miss Bolsolver seemed to cast more than a few stares at our box?" Priscilla wondered if she had imagined it, and had not dared to ask Lord Latimer. If he wanted to avoid mentioning that beautiful young woman, it was fine with Priscilla.

"As a matter of fact, I did catch her watching us a time or two. I fancy it is because you are new in Town.

A young lady like Miss Bolsolver probably wants to keep note of competitors—and in that delicate lilac silk, you are a challenger to her position of reigning diamond."

"Never say so! I will be quite pleased to explore London and see all the interesting sights. I have no desire to queen it in Society!" Priscilla bestowed a horrified stare on her aunt even as she knew a secret thrill to be deemed well enough in looks to occupy such a position.

"I doubt any other young lady in Town has an earl dancing attendance on her—merely to show her around! Not only that, but a viscount cousin who shines like a star in the firmament of Society." Aunt Mercy's tone was exceedingly dry. "I observed that Lord Latimer was very careful not to introduce you to any other young men—other than Mr. Renshaw, who is more like a puppy than a threat to him in any way."

"Oh, you thought him a puppy, too? He reminded me of Rex, our spaniel—the same eyes, if you gather my meaning. However, I am not sorry that I did not meet any other young men. I was quite content with the gentlemen in your box. Although I suppose I should, if I am to find a worthy husband—meet other men, that is." Priscilla sighed slightly at the mere thought of such a deserving gentleman.

"Worthy? What a dreary word that is. I may be the sister of a rector, but I should hope I am good *ton* as the niece of the estimable Earl of Stanwell, and far above settling you on someone who is merely worthy."

Priscilla digested this in silence until they reached the top of the stairs. She glanced at her aunt, thinking she was a remarkably attractive woman for her age.

"I am surprised *you* never married. You are a lovely woman. You must have been quite beautiful when young." Priscilla paused at the door to the drawing room, turning to study her aunt once more.

"I had my share of beaux, true." Mercy Herbert's smile was wistful. "I did care for one gentleman very much, but he wed another. That is the way of life at times. One learns to go on, make the best of things. But I never found another to take his place in my heart."

"Dearest aunt, I am so sorry. I ought not have asked.

Forgive me for prying." Priscilla was appalled that she might have inadvertently hurt her aunt's feelings.

"Think no more about it, and it was not prying. It is rather comforting to have someone care, if truth be told. Now, let us enjoy a cup of tea before we head for our beds and a good sleep."

Simpkins approached with the tea tray, obviously well acquainted with his employer's habits.

Priscilla carefully poured their tea, again taking great care with her new lilac gown. Cook had sent up a selection of tarts and biscuits to enjoy with the tea. Priscilla had quickly learned that when her aunt said a "cup of tea," she meant far more than mere liquid refreshment!

Morning brought a gray day, but no rain. To her great delight Priscilla found that a posy of spring flowers had been delivered to her—from the earl, no less.

"Sent you flowers, has he?" The elder Miss Herbert studied the pretty bouquet with a contemplative eye. "Thoughtful of him. Not for him the ordinary bouquet of roses from some forcing house. He has selected a fine assortment of spring blossoms—tulips, windflowers, and bluebells from heaven knows where. Such delicate, fragile blooms are not to be despised." Aunt Mercy considered the glow on Priscilla's cheeks and smiled. "Where are you off to today, my dear?"

"Well, I asked to visit the British Museum, but it seems as though it is not like just *any* museum. One must apply in advance." Priscilla nibbled at her lower lip, giving her aunt a questioning look as she did. She hoped that his lordship was not making excuses to avoid going to that museum.

"True. That is the case with a number of privately owned painting collections as well. I shall see if there isn't some way I can obtain permission for you to view a few of these. Some of them are magnificent."

"This is wonderful. Before I came to London I did not dream of seeing so many lovely things. Lord Latimer suggested we visit the Egyptian Museum today, and he mentioned Miss Linwood's Gallery of embroidery on Leicester Square. I think that would be pleasing. Also, I should like to see one of the panoramas. One of our neighbors had been to see the one of Copenhagen and spoke highly of it."

A smile hovered on Aunt Mercy's lips. "Your days will be full. I shall not have to worry about seeing you are occupied while in London." She picked up her morning paper that had been properly ironed to set the ink, dismissing Priscilla with a nod.

Priscilla gave her aunt what she hoped was a demure smile, then clutched her posy to her while she returned to her room, sniffing the fresh scent of the flowers from time to time as she marched up the stairs. Bluebells had always been one of her favorite flowers; she loved the fragrance of them.

Lily had arranged the leaf-patterned dress on the bed, the pretty design blending nicely with the willow green and rose of her bed hangings and the coverlet. Handsome green Roman slippers awaited her, along with a matching green reticule and the palest of green gloves.

Priscilla stuck her posy into a glass of water atop the chest of drawers. She stood still while Lily undid the tapes of her morning gown, then set it aside. She eased the leaf-patterned dress over Priscilla's head. A check in the mirror revealed the dress was delightful, quite as fetching as she had hoped with the addition of a deep green spencer. By the time Lily had positioned the neat straw bonnet on Priscilla's blond curls, she was quite optimistic that Lord Latimer would find her more than acceptable. She was aware he found her sensible, but she wanted to appear attractive to him as well.

Not, she chided herself, that she was so foolish as to think he might seek to marry her. He was an earl, heir to a marquessate. He could look as high as he pleased for a wife. She was a diversion, nothing more, and she had better keep that in the back of her mind at all times. But perhaps if another gentleman saw her out and about with such a peerless gentleman, he might be intrigued, want to meet her. Thus she must look her best—regardless of her feelings for Lord Latimer. And she had to confess—if only to herself—that she found the gentleman far too entrancing for comfort.

"You look a treat, Miss Priscilla," Lily offered when she stood back to see the culmination of her efforts.

"Thank you. Isn't it amazing what a pretty gown can do?" She grinned at her maid and, before leaving to await her escort in the drawing room, requested the posy be put in a proper vase. She wanted to enjoy it as long as possible.

Aunt Mercy was seated near the window of the drawing room working at her piece of embroidery when Priscilla entered. She looked up at her niece. "How nice. I vow you will outshine everyone around in your new dress. How fortunate that spencer picks up the leaf color so well."

Priscilla curtsied politely. "I trust I shall do you credit, ma'am."

"I have no fear on that score. How fortuitous it is that you were with me when Lord Latimer deigned to show his lantern slides to the children that day. To my knowledge it is the first time he had ever done so for our tots, which makes your meeting all the more remarkable. All quite as though ordained from on high." She paused a moment in reflection. "I had no idea that he was related to Archdeacon Pallant. He, you must know, is a highly respectable gentleman. Indeed, I cannot but think he approved of you."

Priscilla felt her cheeks heat with a blush. "I cannot imagine why he should, but I am pleased if he did."

"Your father may merely be a rector of a small village church, but he has written some fine articles that have met critical acclaim among churchmen. You did not know this? He is too modest." Aunt Mercy set aside her embroidery, straightened her skirt, and shifted in her place to face the doorway. She, like Priscilla, had heard footsteps on the stairs.

Before Priscilla could reply to the last bit of wisdom, Simpkins ushered in Lord Latimer. She gazed her fill for a few moments until she realized that staring at the gentleman simply would not do. He correctly held his hat in his hand, advanced to stand before Aunt Mercy, and bowed. His dark hair gleamed, and his green eyes had a depth of sparkle in them that utterly enchanted her.

How fortunate she had worn her leaf-print dress with the dark green spencer over it. It went admirably with the corbeau coat he wore over biscuit pantaloons and a splendid cream waistcoat. How her brother Adam would admire this man's attire. She did, and she knew nothing of the finer points of male dress.

"You are in looks, Miss Priscilla. I trust you are ready to walk about the Egyptian Museum? It is an odd assortment of artifacts, but interesting. Shall we take our leave?" He turned to Aunt Mercy and inclined his head. "I promise to take very good care of your niece, ma'am." He glanced behind him to find Lily standing at attention by the door, waiting to follow as proper.

Felix wondered at his own sanity. He insisted that he wanted a proper, respectable bride. Here she was with her equally proper maid to serve as watchdog, and all he could think of was getting Priscilla Herbert alone! A more delectable bundle of femininity he couldn't imagine. He would have to bring this courting business to a swift conclusion before he lost what mind he had.

Priscilla had to be the most delicious, delightful creature he had met in a long time—and that included the ones thrust at him, not to mention the ones who contrived to "happen" in his way. He would have to be sharp to keep her from meeting any of the single men he knew. Once any of those chaps got to know her, listen to her astute remarks, hear her charming laugh, he would possibly have a contest on his hands. He had no illusion that she cared for his title. Sensible girl that she was, he felt she would only marry a man for whom she truly cared. Most likely she took after her spinsterish aunt.

He put aside the state of the unwed aunt to escort Priscilla to where his carriage awaited them. He assisted her into the curricle, took note the maid was settled up behind, then entered the vehicle from the other side, gathering the reins up from his groom as he did, and they set off. The groom joined Lily up behind, skilled at hopping up behind a moving carriage.

Priscilla looked about her as they went. The square was behind them. The four acres had been planted with shrubs and small trees, all of which were surrounded by a wooden fence. She thought it might be a pleasing place to walk when she was not otherwise occupied.

The fashionable church of St. George's, Hanover

Square, was behind them as well. The Earl of Harewood had a home on the north side of the square—not that she had glimpsed the man. Aunt Mercy told her of his amazing collection of old china for which vast sums had been offered. The earl had declined, which made Priscilla quite long to see his acquisitions. His house might not be large or grand, but Aunt assured her that all was of the finest quality. He was of the highest *ton*, Aunt insisted. He was also old and very plump, much like his good friend the Prince Regent.

The houses they passed on the way to Piccadilly Street were fine brick and stone edifices, with impressive doors and ornamentation. Aunt said they were about eighty years old, being of the style popular in the time of George I.

When they turned onto Piccadilly, Priscilla found the traffic much increased. She marveled at the ease with which the earl made his way through the utter chaos of drays, gigs, cabriolets, and sedan chairs—the men appearing dangerously daring to her country eyes.

People strolled along the side pavement, pausing to greet friends, look at shopwindow displays, and in general enjoy the mild day. She noticed not a few stares at their carriage, or perhaps those who were in it. She was not privy to the earl's choice of lady friends, but she suspected he probably didn't drive with just anyone, which made his selecting her all the more curious. Perhaps it was as he had said—he merely wished to kindly escort her on her seeing the sights of London.

Whatever the reason, she found it delightful to be in the carriage with such a handsome gentleman. If only her sisters might see her now!

Priscilla caught sight of a fine jeweler's shop, the window glittering with costly trinkets, valuable gems the likes of which she doubted she would ever own. Still it was lovely to see these things, imagine she might have such someday. She glanced at her escort, tooling along through the carriages and the pedestrians crossing Piccadilly. *He* could have anything he desired, yet she did not get the feeling he reveled in it. Perhaps he was like their neighbor, Baron Rothson, who appeared to take his wealth for granted, much as one might take the sunshine.

"Hatchard's is along here, you know," Lord Latimer said, suddenly interrupting her thoughts. "It is just two doors along from the museum. I suppose you have found time to visit that bookshop?"

"Indeed, I have. I found a couple of books I like very much." She did not mention seeing him.

He brought the curricle to a halt before a strange-looking building. He spoke quietly to his groom, who had jumped down to take the reins.

Priscilla accepted his lordship's hand, taking note that Lily had managed to leave her seat at the back of the curricle. It seemed strange to have a maid constantly at her heels. Such propriety was a must in the City but hardly necessary in the country, and she wasn't accustomed to such attention.

Pulling her small copy of the *Picture of London* from her reticule, Priscilla opened it to the page wherein Bullock's Museum was described. She noted that nothing was written about the curious exterior that featured a decidedly Egyptian look, with very tall figures—one male, one female—above the door. She supposed they represented Egyptians. She couldn't swear to it, not much acquainted with their history. They were decidedly *not* English.

"It says here that there are more than thirty thousand articles on display within." She valiantly ignored the sensations his touch on her arm sent through her. If his touch could do this through her spencer, what in the world would it be like if he actually touched her skin! Then he tucked her arm next to him. She hadn't been prepared for this. Yet it was a wondrous feeling, a protected, cared for sort of thing that she very much liked once she calmed her racing pulse.

"You do not need that thing. I shall guide you."

Priscilla thought that for a guide he was too attractive for her peace of mind. Surely no guide set a girl's heart to beating far too fast, or caused her to surreptitiously study his finely chiseled mouth, those unusual green eyes. She was definitely a country mouse!

"Here is a catalog for you." At the entry he offered her a handsomely printed booklet. Their hands met and once again she felt that shocking impulse rush through her. This must cease! She had to steel herself against his attraction. He would be vastly amused were he to realize how greatly he affected her. As they entered the museum proper, she trailed along at his side, half bemused, half alert.

She obediently listened as he commented on the South Sea curiosities brought, for the most part, by Captain Cook.

A hat of feathers caught her eye. "What a beautiful thing. I can think of many women who would relish that clutch of feathers. I suppose it was worn by a chief." She turned away to see a war club of hard black stone, menacing and lethal-looking. "I would not want *that* around, however."

He smiled. "I cannot think you would ever be in need of a war club, Miss Herbert. Somehow you seem a more delicate sort of woman, not one such as Boadicea."

"Heavens above, I should hope I do never seem warlike! I far prefer peaceful beings." Priscilla flashed him a look of amusement. He thought her a delicate sort? She would wager she was far more hardy than many of the beautiful women she had seen while in London— like Miss Bolsolver, who had caused Lord Latimer to abruptly turn from the path while in Hyde Park. Being the daughter of a village rector did not encourage delicacy of nerves or of body. There was too much to do, too much that needed tending. She did everything from feeding the chickens to picking autumn fruit. No, she was not delicate at all.

They strolled on to inspect the curiosities from North and South America. "That wampum belt looks practical, but there are more of those war clubs, as well as axes. Between the bows and arrows and those, the natives were equipped to battle one way or another." When they reached the African section, she sighed, meeting his gaze with rueful eyes. "More hatchets, daggers, and other queer items. The natives all seem to be very warlike."

"Particularly with those poisoned darts."

Priscilla fancifully wondered if one of those darts tipped with a potion had stabbed her heart, causing her to become enamored of Lord Latimer. She certainly wasn't her sensible self. She murmured what she hoped was a suitable reply, thankful when they passed the native displays to inspect the area with works of art.

"Now, this Chinese pagoda is worth noting. I wonder if the prince saw this and was inspired to create his place in Brighton." He chuckled, so Priscilla supposed it was intended to be an amusing observation. Since she hadn't been to Brighton or seen any drawings of the palace the Prince Regent built there, she had no response.

The giraffe in the natural history part of the museum was truly impressive. She could not help but clutch at his arm as they approached the stuffed animal that surely must have been seventeen feet high. "I am very glad we do not have these creatures here. I do not think I would like to meet a live one—not in the least." She looked from the giraffe to the elephant and could not help a small shudder. "Are all the animals from Africa so immense? Remind me never to travel there!"

"Ah, no. There is a tiny antelope—a dik-dik I think it is called. Just as small as those chaps are enormous—perhaps fourteen inches high. But, I'd not have thought you so timid, Miss Herbert."

"Not timid, my lord, just sensible!"

They didn't linger very long in the other sections with stuffed birds—which Priscilla deplored—turtles, fishes, and a wealth of insects of every variety, some quite beautiful.

The display of the Napoleonic relics completed the visit as far as Priscilla was concerned. "I had no idea he was such a practical creature—to have a bulletproof carriage is above all things prudent for a little general who wanted to conquer the world." She looked at the other items with great curiosity, ceasing when she felt the man at her side stiffen.

One peek was all it took to realize the cause. Miss Anne Bolsolver had wafted into the room, looking quite as ethereal as she had before. Her dark curls peeped out from under a fashionable bonnet of satin, and those ice-blue eyes flicked over Priscilla as though she was an object on display, and one not worth looking at.

"I have seen enough to satisfy my curiosity, should you wish to depart, my lord." Priscilla spoke in a soft tone that was not likely to carry far. She wasn't certain if he wished to acknowledge the young lady. She wasn't even sure if she wanted to make her acquaintance, for all that she was curious about the girl. There was some mystery here, but it was none of her business.

He totally ignored the others who had entered the Napoleonic display room, merely patting Priscilla on her hand, before turning away and heading to the exit.

"What a thoughtful woman you are, Miss Herbert. You guessed I had no desire to greet those people. Discretion is a trait I admire above all." He also spoke quietly, obviously intent upon leaving without conversation with the invaders.

They did not reach the door without incident, however.

"Lord Latimer! Fancy meeting you here. I cannot believe I see *you* escorting a country miss about Town." The musical titter was one Priscilla would wager had been practiced with great care.

He stopped, turned to face Miss Bolsolver, and placed his hand more firmly upon Priscilla's trembling one, covering it with a comforting clasp. "I would vouchsafe that she is no more a country miss than you are, Miss Bolsolver—since I know you hale from Suffolk. Furthermore, I believe she has a nicety of Town manners to be envied by any lady of breeding. Good day."

Priscilla observed the spark of anger that briefly lit Miss Bolsolver's eyes. This was tossing down a gauntlet, indeed. To be told one lacked breeding was a high insult. What had this woman done to Lord Latimer to give him such a dislike of her? The icy chill in his voice was such that Priscilla hoped never to have directed at her.

The young woman's escort murmured something to her. They turned aside to study the carriage.

"Come, let us find more agreeable surroundings." Lord Latimer didn't bother to lower his voice. Priscilla thought it would be impossible for the young woman and her escort not to have heard his words. What retort that might have brought was beyond her imagination.

She was not going to ask about Miss Bolsolver. That there was animosity was putting it mildly. What caused it was beyond her and likely to remain that way.

"Shall we proceed to Miss Linwood's exhibit? Or would you rather call it a day?"

"I would like to see more, but my feet tell me otherwise. There was an enormous amount to see, and we skimmed over much of it—not that I complain. It would take all day to examine everything, possibly two days. I thank you for showing me so much."

Felix wondered if he might simply propose now and save a lot of time. She possessed not only discretion, but also a fine sense of tact—and sympathy, unless he was mistaken. That was something no one else in his ramshackle family knew much about. Small wonder Bolsolver disdained an alliance with him. Still, he had to be thankful for that rejection. Miss Bolsolver would not make an agreeable wife!

"Why do we not drive over to Gunter's to enjoy one of his ices? It is too chilly to sit beneath the trees, but it is acceptable to go inside. You shall likely have a choice of raspberry or pineapple." He glanced at her face to see a gleam of anticipation light her eyes. "Perhaps both!"

"That sounds delicious."

Felix thought she looked delicious as well. Her blue eyes held a warmth he hoped augured well for his pursuit.

His groom, summoned by a convenient lad, brought the carriage to the entrance within minutes. Lily, her mind likely whirling with all the strange and unusual things she had seen, clambered up behind. Priscilla accepted Felix's assistance into the carriage, arranging her skirts properly, but not before he glimpsed a very neat ankle.

It was a pleasure to drive this young woman through the streets of London. She garnered more than her share of notice. He enjoyed the stares from various chaps he knew. That they would demand to learn where he had met this glorious creature amused him. If he told them his archdeacon cousin introduced them, he doubted they would believe him. Either that or they would insist upon having Pallant bring forth equally charming girls for their diversion.

No one had any inkling of his intentions at this moment. Miss Herbert seemed satisfied that he merely wished to escort her about Town, since she lacked a suitable male guide. No one in his right mind would expect Lord Rawlinson to appear in a place like the museum.

Felix did not propose to allow matters to dangle for long. Within as brief a time as possible, he intended to make his intentions clear. That she would welcome his address, he had no doubt. After all, he knew his worth.

Chapter Five

*W*hen they arrived at Gunter's Tea Shop, Felix noted that the door under the sign of the pineapple at No. 7–8 Berkeley Square was busy with patrons going in and out. He smiled, satisfied that many of the *beau monde* would be present and wonder about his association with a beautiful young lady as yet unknown to them. He'd wager a goodly sum that Miss Herbert would be inundated with invitations in the near future once word of her identity was spread about.

The niece of the admirable Miss Mercy Herbert who was herself the niece of the Earl of Stanwell was excellent *ton*. And then there was Viscount Rawlinson, that dashing gentleman about Town. He would likely see that his cousin entered the cream of Society now that he had observed she was a diamond of the first water.

He didn't underestimate his own contribution to Miss Priscilla Herbert's success. He merely wanted to capture this suitable young lady before some other chap caught sight of her and learned what a delight she was, not to mention how eminently respectable.

Once again he turned over the reins to his groom, signaled the maid to remain with him, and then offered his arm to his chosen lady. It was a bit chilly to enjoy their ices under the shade of the trees in Berkeley Square as customary so they would go inside. Gunter's was one place in London where it was perfectly respectable for a lady to be seen alone with a gentleman in the afternoon.

Miss Herbert gazed about her with apparent pleasure.

"My aunt took me here recently after shopping. Do they truly obtain their ice from Greenland? Aunt Mercy read that they had received a shipment of ice recently. Amazing what can be accomplished nowadays."

Felix liked the way Miss Herbert appeared to notice everything, yet was so modest in her demeanor. There were no bold looks, no excited cries that drew attention to her.

"Indeed, the ice comes a great distance. We must doubly enjoy our treats, don't you think?"

"I know I shall." Her simple, direct reply pleased him. He supposed there might be something about her that could irritate him. He hadn't found it as yet!

They were fortunate to find an unoccupied table.

"How thoughtful of you, my lord," Miss Herbert said with glowing enthusiasm. "This is a special treat I will remember with pleasure."

"I insist you shall try both the raspberry and pineapple ices. Then you can give me your verdict as to which is the best."

"That will not be an easy task, I should think."

He overheard an order for a wedding cake being placed and wondered if the elder Miss Herbert would order their cake from the most fashionable supplier of such in all of London. He hoped so. They had delicious cake.

"Most of the *ton*'s wedding cakes come from here. I have sampled a few and found them outstanding." Felix exchanged a warm look with Priscilla Herbert. Could he place a thought in her head regarding weddings? Or did every woman instinctively think of her own marriage when a wedding cake was mentioned?

Priscilla studied his expression as she tasted the first of her ices the waiter had set before her. Now, why would he offer that particular comment? To her knowledge most unmarried gentlemen avoided the topic of marriage like the plague. She thought she would ignore his comment about wedding cakes. She couldn't think of anything appropriate other than a polite murmur.

"The raspberry is marvelous, quite like fresh fruit, in fact." She ran her tongue over her lips, savoring the delicious flavor of crushed raspberries. How in the world did the proprietor obtain raspberries out of season? Or perhaps these were preserved? No matter, all she had to do was enjoy the ice.

"Go on." He watched while she tasted the pineapple, his own ice ignored for the moment.

"I can see why they are both in demand. It is impossible to say which is the better. What a delight this is. Following an afternoon spent examining such curious and rare items, it makes a very special day, and I thank you." Her nose wrinkled up in a charming manner as she grinned at him. If he hadn't been enamored before, he would tumble this moment. Not that he believed in love. But he did feel attracted. Of course, his primary reason for pursuing Priscilla Herbert was because of her respectable background. However, it was agreeable that she was also attractive with a pleasant disposition.

"Are you to rest at home this evening, or do you venture out to some gathering?" He still hadn't learned if there was an employee of his that was well acquainted with one belonging to the Herbert household. He might not always be able to inquire directly. Perhaps he might persuade his groom to pay attention to the little maid. Felix hadn't missed their exchanged glances.

"I believe we are to attend a musical evening at a Lady Pringle's house. I look forward to it, as we rarely have talent of any measure at home. I do enjoy good music."

"As do I. Why do I not take you both in my carriage as I plan to attend as well? It is a shame for your aunt to order hers out when I will be going. Do you think she might approve?"

"Yes, my lord." Her gaze was gently reproving. Surely he must know that no woman in her right mind who had a marriageable young woman in her care would refuse his escort. Priscilla might not be *au courant* with the latest in London news, but she knew that much.

"Excellent. I enjoy fine music and Lady Pringle is exceptional in obtaining superb performers. Some are foreign, some English. Whatever they are, they are talented." He relaxed against his dainty chair, looking almost smug.

Priscilla decided she must have imagined his smugness, for there was nothing in the least to be smug about! She observed that several of the women in the little shop eyed them with what appeared to be enormous curiosity. Whispered conversations and darted looks in their direction made her wonder if the gossip was good or bad. That it was gossip she had little doubt, she had seen enough of it when at home. After all, people were the same no matter where.

She placed her spoon beside the empty dish, sighing with satisfaction at the taste that still lingered on her tongue. "That was positively delicious. I shall have another occasion about which I can write Mama. She is interested in all that I do while here."

"I should imagine she is. How good it is for you that your aunt decided to bring you out. All of London welcomes you."

He smiled into her eyes with a warmth that set her heart to beating far too fast. What was happening to her? Priscilla could feel the heat rising to her cheeks and wished she wasn't so inclined to blush at a compliment.

"Thank you, my lord." In an effort to alter the subject, she said, "This is a charming little shop. It certainly is well patronized. May I ask if you know any of those women on the far side of the room? It seems to me they have been staring at us ever since we entered."

"The one in gray is Mrs. Renshaw, Chauncy's mother. Lady Bolsolver is at the next table. You must recall that young woman we encountered just before we left the museum. Her mother." He continued to list the few others he recognized. "Gunter's is a popular place for women to take tea and ices or cakes in the afternoon. Sooner or later nearly everyone shows up here."

"I believe your friend, Mr. Renshaw, is entering now." She gave him a pleasant smile as he approached their table.

"We were just about to leave, Chauncy. You know Miss Herbert, of course." Lord Latimer rose from his chair to clasp his friend's hand in greeting.

Priscilla rose as well, standing composedly by their sides while aware she was being even more avidly studied by the Society women not far away. Lady Bolsolver in particular stared at them, whispering to her companion in covert snatches.

"Pleasure, Miss Herbert. Trust your aunt is well, and all that?" His cravat was so high it was difficult for him to turn his head, but he managed a creditable bow.

"Aunt Mercy is quite well, thank you. Ah, I believe your mother is trying to capture your attention, Mr. Renshaw." If frantically waving a handkerchief at him was any indication, Mrs. Renshaw was desirous of his company.

Chauncy gave her a twinkling smile before looking to where his mother sat impatiently awaiting him. "Indeed. I've come to fetch her home. She enjoys her outings, not to mention the ices and cakes."

Priscilla peeked again to note that Mrs. Renshaw was what Mother would call comfortably plump. She looked to be a cozy woman with a pleasant disposition—like her son.

"We must be off, old chap."

"You going to White's later?"

"Actually, no. I shall attend the musical evening at Lady Pringle's."

Chauncy gave them a horrified look before backing away, as though their musical evening was a disease that might be catching. "Good grief."

Lord Latimer nodded. He placed his hand under Priscilla's elbow, escorting her from the tea shop with the utmost care. She considered it was like she was a fragile parcel. She was very aware those women continued to watch, and she wondered about it. Of course, it was because the earl was with a nonentity, a woman none of them knew. It was not the least surprising that they were curious. It was just like at home when a stranger turned up in church on a Sunday morning. All curiosity was aroused!

"I suspect your friend does not care much for music."

"Renshaw? Never considered it before, but I daresay you have the right of it." He assisted her into the carriage and joined her in a trice.

They left the attractive square behind, setting a fast pace on their return to Aunt Mercy's house. Priscilla had enjoyed herself enormously, excluding the unpleasant encounter with Miss Bolsolver. That was a mystery Priscilla would eventually solve. But had he cared for

Anne Bolsolver at one time, then the relationship broken? There must be a reason for his frozen politeness and her animosity, not to mention the unpleasant looks from Lady Bolsolver.

They had reached the corner where they would turn off Brook Street to cross to St. George Street, when her escort gave a start. An older gentleman was waving at him from the pavement, attempting to get Lord Latimer's attention. He was quite ignored.

"That gentleman wished to catch your eye, I believe."

"I know. I do not wish to catch his, however."

"You know him?"

"Actually, he is my Uncle George. We rarely see eye to eye on anything." Lord Latimer's voice had turned as cold as the ice from Gunter's and much less welcoming.

"I see," Priscilla replied, not seeing at all. Why would he not wish to greet his own uncle? She decided Lord Latimer was a complex man, with a number of little mysteries.

"Let me see—we attend Lady Pringle's this evening. I believe I can get us into the British Museum tomorrow. Would you like that?"

"I should indeed. I would not have you think I expect you to dance attendance on me every day, my lord. You must have a goodly number of things to do of greater importance." She hated to point this out to him, for she had enjoyed his company very much. But better that than to have him feeling put upon! Being with him gave her a sense of being wrapped in caring regard.

"There is little that would keep me from your side, my dear Miss Herbert. You must have gathered by now that I am quite serious in my intentions."

Priscilla swallowed with care. Could he mean what she thought he meant? If so, he was amazingly quick in his decisions. They had scarce met. He *must* have meant something else, and she wasn't sufficiently *à la mode* to grasp that intent. However agreeable the thought of marriage might be, she had best put this in the back of her mind. Not to be forgotten, just warily contemplated.

He turned away when he had to pay attention to his horse. However, the image of his uncle attempting to hale him lingered in the back of her mind. What could separate an uncle from his nephew? Money? She knew Lord Latimer was far from poor. And she was also aware that in London gaming was a temptation many men could not resist. Perhaps his uncle wanted a loan? That could account for his desire to avoid the man.

The groom helped Lily from her seat, a matter that caught Priscilla's attention. The flush on that young person's face caught her eye, a budding interest?

"Perhaps I had best speak to your aunt about this evening." Lord Latimer took her arm, tucked it next to him, and walked her the short distance to the front door.

Priscilla responded to the query in his voice with a nod. "I know she would be pleased to see you, my lord."

And so it proved. Miss Herbert took note of the way Lord Latimer hovered at her niece's side, and agreed at once to his scheme. "We shall be delighted to attend Lady Pringle's with you as our escort. I vow, we will be the envy of every woman there." Her smile was roguish!

Priscilla blinked. Dear Aunt Mercy was flirting with Lord Latimer.

"On the contrary, I will be the envy of all the gentlemen present to have two such beauties on my arm."

He bowed and left them with a reminder of the time that he would pick them up.

"How odd," Aunt Mercy mused. "I do not recall seeing him at Pringle's before. But then, I have missed on occasion. Now, tell me all that occurred, my dear."

"I will, but first, can you tell me more about Miss Bolsolver? We encountered her at the museum, and she was extremely rude. Later, we saw her mother at Gunter's, and she stared quite boldly at us. I thought her nearly as ill-mannered as her daughter."

"I fear I cannot. I have not met the woman often in my excursions into Society. She cannot be of the highest *ton*, my dear, else I would know her. But to please you, I shall attempt to learn what I can."

With that Priscilla had to be satisfied. She spent the remaining time relating her viewing of the museum, followed by the excursion to Gunter's Tea Shop. She almost mentioned the remark Lord Latimer had made about his intentions, then thought perhaps that she had read too much into his words and remained silent. She casually mentioned the matter of the earl's uncle, and the evident estrangement between them. "I thought it odd that Lord Latimer would not stop to greet his uncle."

"Perhaps it was merely a matter of business the earl thought could wait until later? Uncles do not always think of the convenience of a discussion." She seemed about to say more, then apparently changed her mind, clamping her mouth shut.

Priscilla frowned, thinking that it didn't seem the case here, but since she knew nothing of the matter she remained quiet. Shortly, she escaped to her room to pen a brief letter full of her news to her mother and sisters.

When Lord Latimer came to collect them, he seemed pleased with Priscilla's appearance. At any rate, he ran what appeared to be an approving gaze over her.

Madame Clotilde had delivered a gown of pale rose-colored patent net over a cream satin slip. It was trimmed with blonde lace in a clever manner unlike anything Priscilla had seen. In her cheval glass she noted her Roman slippers revealed neat ankles, something for which she must be thankful. It seemed gentlemen set much store by a neat ankle!

Lily had dressed Priscilla's hair high on the back of her head with a few curls teasing her ears. At the earl's intent regard, her hand crept up to touch the simple strand of pearls at her neck.

Although she knew better than to believe the earl, heir to a marquessate, would select the daughter of a rector for a wife, she confessed she certainly enjoyed his company, not to forget his admiration. As to what he meant by his intentions being serious, she dismissed any thought of marriage. Perhaps he merely intended to remain a good friend? Marriage was too good to be true.

"Well, now, I believe we are ready for the evening!" Aunt Mercy exclaimed. Her richly hued shawl draped about her, she led the way down the stairs, followed by Priscilla and Lord Latimer.

Priscilla's shawl fringe caught in one of the banister decorations, a lion rampant. She paused to untangle the fringe.

"Allow me," Lord Latimer murmured close to her

ear. He quickly removed the offending fringe from the lion, then with what Priscilla thought was exceedingly tender care, positioned the stylish shawl around her shoulders.

She had observed his attire when he entered the room. His midnight-blue tailcoat over cream breeches was dignified, and that cravat with a sapphire discreetly tucked in an intricate fold was a masterpiece. To be seen at his side must be the supreme satisfaction for a young woman set upon storming London—which she was not, but it was still agreeable.

But upon studying his face once they had settled in the town coach, she decided his lordship had something on his mind. She didn't think it was her, considering the way he frowned. She was about to inquire whether he might be under the weather or something of that sort when they arrived at Lady Pringle's home.

The house was a neat affair, typical of London town houses. The rose brick was accented by attractive shutters at the windows and a splendid black door that possessed a plain knocker. It was opened at once, and soon Priscilla found herself in a spacious drawing room filled with those uncomfortable gilt chairs that seemed to appear at every function. She recognized a few faces and was relieved that the gossipy Lady Bolsolver was not to be seen.

"I am afraid I must disappoint you regarding tomorrow," Lord Latimer said at last when they were settled and the program had yet to start. His voice was low and soft. Her aunt couldn't have heard his words.

"What a pity. I trust it is nothing serious?" She wondered if she might venture there on her own. Or was that another place where a young woman must have an escort? Maybe her maid would suffice? How tiresome it was to *always* be on her toes, remembering the strictures of Society.

"I've been called to my country home—a problem that must be dealt with immediately. When I return I promise you we shall do the British Museum thoroughly. I hope you will not forget me while I am away?" He cocked a brow at her, half smiling, yet she thought his eyes held a serious light in them.

Priscilla decided that had to be the silliest remark she had heard since coming to the city. "I daresay I shall be able to recall you, my lord." She smiled easily at him, but wondered what the pressing problem might be. He didn't see fit to confide in her—which she supposed was only suitable. They were hardly close enough to warrant a confidence—yet he *had* paid her particular attentions from the moment they had met at the school.

"Good. I took the precaution of asking Renshaw to escort you about, that is, if it meets your approval. He is an agreeable chap, you know, for drives in the park and that sort of thing. I am not certain how long this business will take." Lord Latimer looked anything but pleased to be called away from London at this moment.

Priscilla repressed a grin that longed to burst forth. Was he setting her up with his good, spaniel-eyed friend so that someone would keep an eye on her? That was even sillier than she forget him while he was gone. Yet, she thought that perhaps she might learn a thing or two from the very open Mr. Renshaw.

"My Cousin Rawlinson has promised to take me to some ball. Other than that, I am free. I imagine I am not supposed to say such a thing, but I abhor evasion and deceit. Honesty is always the best policy my papa says, and he is right." She wondered why he shifted in his chair as though uncomfortable with her words. But then, the hard seat reminded her that the chairs were less than cushy.

"Fine. Renshaw will be in alt."

Whatever she might have replied to that nonsense was not to be said. Lady Pringle bustled forth to the front of the room to announce the first performer, an Italian singer of imposing girth. The tenor possessed a fine voice and entertained them with a polished selection of songs. Priscilla relaxed as much as possible against the carved back of the dainty gilt chair and simply relished the music.

Truth be known, she was delighted that Lord Latimer had been able to remain so as to escort her this evening. She sensed that those present were of Society's *crème de la crème*. Perhaps there was a mother on the hunt for a girl well suited to wed her second or third son, or something of that kind. Priscilla was gifted with household management.

She could keep the books, knew how to economize, and in short thought she would make some less-than-blessed-with-worldly-goods son a capable wife.

Lord Latimer might have been paying her a lot of attention, but she was far too sensible to read much into his interest. Her brother was wont to shift his attentions from one girl to another with the change of seasons. His lordship might speak of his intentions; that didn't mean he meant a betrothal.

When the evening entertainment concluded, they didn't linger. Aunt expressed a desire to return home at once, and Lord Latimer hustled them from the Pringle home with less than flattering speed.

He likely intended to rise early, or perhaps he had no wish to chat with those attending? Either way, they were off in a trice, having bestowed gracious thanks on their hostess for such a splendid evening.

Lord Latimer didn't tarry when his carriage stopped before Aunt Mercy's house. It was easy to see he had something on his mind, and she didn't think it was her.

Once the door had shut behind them they could hear the clip clop of his horses as the carriage proceeded down the street.

"I trust there is an explanation for his lordship's hasty departure?" Aunt Mercy took a firm grip on Priscilla's elbow as they walked up the stairs.

"He received an urgent message to go to his country home, wherever that may be. He will leave first thing in the morning, I believe." Priscilla chuckled. "He informed me that he requested Mr. Renshaw to escort me whilst he is away—quite as though I were a parcel he didn't wish to be unclaimed."

"I have a feeling that Lord Latimer is entirely smitten with you, my girl. I realize it has been but days since you met, but he shows all the signs. Had he remained in Town, I imagine he would have declared himself."

Priscilla gave her dearest aunt a wry look. "We shall wait to see what happens."

The time for afternoon callers brought Mr. Renshaw to the drawing room. He looked a bit ill at ease, but when Priscilla made no attempt to flirt with him, in fact treating him just like her brother, he relaxed.

"I was, er, wondering if you might enjoy a drive in the park, Miss Herbert?" he inquired at last. He had stayed a bit longer than usual for callers. Did he prefer to ask about a drive when the other callers had left? There had been a satisfying number of ladies, their daughters, and, in two cases, sons, who had called upon Priscilla and her aunt this afternoon.

"I should like that very much, Mr. Renshaw." She raised her brows in inquiry as to a possible time.

"Oh, er, five of the clock, if you please." He grew faintly pink in the face. Priscilla wondered if he was accustomed to inviting young ladies to drive, then speculated if perhaps his hesitancy had something to do with Lord Latimer. Anything was possible.

He took his leave, clattering down the stairs as though Priscilla might change her mind.

"So, Mr. Renshaw is fulfilling his promise to his friend." Aunt Mercy exchanged an amused look with Priscilla.

"Apparently so." She checked the time on the delicate mantel clock before jumping to her feet. "If I am to be ready and waiting for him, I had best hurry. Lily fusses over my hair, and insists that every fold of my gown must hang precisely so." She grinned, waved at her aunt, then ran lightly up the stairs to where Lily and her room awaited. By some mysterious means, it seemed the servants anticipated an amazing number of things—like her drive in the park with Mr. Renshaw. Perhaps he had said something to Simpkins? Like he would return at five of the clock?

A periwinkle-blue carriage dress that buttoned down the front went on quickly once her morning gown was removed. Lily brushed her hair, and checked to be certain all was proper before releasing Priscilla from her care.

"I wonder how I ever managed without you?" she murmured to the maid after slipping into a silver-gray pelisse. She was pleased with what she saw in the looking glass. She'd not embarrass Mr. Renshaw should his friends see them, especially with her new silver satin jockey hat.

They set out at a sedate pace, entering Hyde Park just as many other members of the *ton* sought their airing.

"So, Lord Latimer has gone to the country?"

"True. His father summoned him, although what for, I can't imagine. They see little of each other as it is."

"Perhaps he wished to query him regarding his plans?"

"That might be." Mr. Renshaw gave a decided nod. "And I should think Felix might take satisfaction in telling the old man that at last he intends to wed."

"Really?" Priscilla felt a cold band clutch her heart. This made no sense in view of his attentions to her . . . unless his father had ideas of his own? "Do you know who the young lady is?"

"Course I do—it is you!" He sounded almost indignant.

Priscilla reeled from the news so calmly imparted. "How . . . fascinating. Tell me, whatever made Lord Latimer decide to wed me, in particular?"

"He vowed he would marry the most respectable woman he could find. Miss Herbert, you suit his needs to a tee!"

"Why respectable? That is a curious requirement!" Priscilla thought she just might trounce Lord Latimer when she next saw him . . . if she saw him.

"Was turned down because of his ramshackle family. *You* are to make his family respectable again, you see. Thinks highly of you and your aunt. So does his archdeacon cousin. Just the touch of propriety the family needs."

"Good grief!" Priscilla muttered, quite in shock. She was as angry as she had ever been in her life. And yet the scheme was ridiculous. Could Mr. Renshaw be believed? "I should like to know more about his family, if you please."

Chapter Six

"*H*ave you ever heard of anything so outrageous? Dear Aunt Mercy, what shall I do?" Fists clenched, Priscilla took another turn about the drawing room, pausing now and again to shake her head and cast an angry look at her aunt. "I cannot marry a man simply to make his family respectable! Why me? The entire notion is ludicrous. Surely he must see that?" Never mind that marriage to the aristocratic Lord Latimer appealed to her. If he thought marriage to her would have any effect on his family one way or another, it was just plain nonsense.

"It is unusual, to be certain. Of course, had you an arranged marriage you would likely have a predicament not too unlike this." Aunt Mercy tilted her head in a considering way. "Only in this case the gentleman has decided you are the perfect answer to his wishes. In a way, it is quite flattering. He is not wedding you for a fine dowry or a title. It is his wish to improve his family's reputation."

"Wish! *His* wishes! Suppose I said *no* to his proposal? He would sweep me into marriage just so he can make his family respectable? I find it very hard to believe what Mr. Renshaw told me. I think it decidedly deceitful and certainly lowering. He wants my company merely because I am respectable? Faugh!" Priscilla stamped her foot, her Roman slippers making a thump on the carpet.

"I confess it is a trifle unusual, dear. But, come now, surely it is not all that terrible? I should say that most men prefer a respectable bride." Aunt Mercy glanced up from her embroidery of an altar cloth to study her niece. "What man would want to marry a hoyden? And you must admit that Lord Latimer is a fine figure of a man, not to mention possessing a handsome fortune, excellent prospects, and a country home to rival the finest. He also has superior manners; he would never cause you to be disgraced by *his* behavior. I believe that were you to marry him, you would lack for nothing, and I suspect you would be treasured just as you deserve, my dear."

Priscilla replied with an angry sniff to that bit of wisdom. Her aunt *might* have the right of it; it was simply so . . . outrageous. To be treasured would be agreeable. If it happened. One must be sensible about these things. A daydream could easily turn to a nightmare.

"After all, my dear, he is an earl and in due time will inherit the marquessate. There are few women who would turn him down, no matter what the pretext for the marriage might be. If such a one existed, she would be an utter fool." Aunt Mercy placed the altar cloth in her lap, folding her hands atop it while observing the blush Priscilla could feel rising on her cheeks.

"I believe I would like to meet these dreadful relatives of his," Priscilla said in an effort to steer the conversation in a different direction. "I would see for myself just how terrible they are. Mr. Renshaw mentioned an aunt. Do you know who she is? Anything about her? I am determined on this," Priscilla concluded.

"Oh, dear," the elder Miss Herbert murmured. "I pay little heed to gossip. But I do recall that many years ago Lady Beatrice Sutton eloped with her brother's tutor, a Mr. Aston. It was a nine-day wonder and caused quite a scandal. I believe he was from an impoverished family of decent standing—gentry. Not too unlike your brother would be. But still, she was a considerable heiress and nearly everyone believed he wed her for her money. After all, thirty thousand pounds invested in funds is a tidy sum."

"And Uncle George? What about him?" Priscilla sank down on the chair close to the fireplace, where a neat blaze warmed her chilled person.

"Lord George Sutton lost his wife some years ago."

Aunt Mercy's eyes took on a faraway look. "Since then he has become a gamester, or so I have been told. I do not wager on cards or anything else for that matter, so I am not well versed on these matters. However, that said, I do not think he gambles to excess. What else there is to know about him I cannot say." She studied her niece with a faint frown on her brow. "What is in your mind, dear?"

"Why, not a great deal. But I do think it behooves me to meet these relatives. Wouldn't you agree?" Priscilla bestowed a sweet smile on her aunt, one her mother would instantly find suspect.

"I suppose so," Aunt Mercy replied after some hesitation and a questioning look at her niece.

"I will not do anything scandalous, mind you. But I will ask around, find out how to locate these various relatives and see for myself just how bad they are."

Priscilla flashed a defiant grin at her aunt. The effect was lost because Aunt Mercy had returned her attention to the exquisite altar cloth on which she worked delicate stitches.

Simpkins brought in the tea tray at that point, ending Priscilla's outburst quite effectively.

She poured for both of them, then sank back against the chair to consider a plan. She knew Lord Latimer's Uncle George was in Town. She had seen him. Surely a discreet query would elicit his location, how she might find him. Perhaps a request to meet him would not be out of line? And pigs might fly.

"How can I meet his Uncle George?" Priscilla uttered the words before thinking of possible ramifications. "I saw him walking along the pavement while out with Lord Latimer only the other day. He must be in London in that event."

"Well, one thing for certain—you cannot seek him in his usual haunts—the gambling clubs." Aunt Mercy set her cup down with a gentle click, then gave Priscilla a cautious look.

"Do you think he would come here if you invited him to take tea with us?" Priscilla observed her aunt blush as a young girl might, and wondered at the surprising reaction to her suggestion.

"I suppose I could if you truly wish it." Aunt Mercy shifted her gaze to the altar cloth at her side, avoiding Priscilla's watchful eyes.

"But you do not? Of course, it was a harebrained thought." Priscilla sipped her tea, ignoring the plate of biscuits that normally would have tempted her.

"No. Not at all. I will do so." Her aunt acquired a strange expression on her face. "It is for a worthy cause." She took a large gulp of tea and nearly choked.

Priscilla plunked down her cup and dashed around to thump her dearest aunt on the back. "Do not do that!"

Once Aunt Mercy had regained her usual aplomb, she gave Priscilla a regal nod. "I shall send him a note this very day."

Priscilla eyed her aunt with misgiving. What on earth was she getting the pair of them into with her mad scheme? She began to pace before the fireplace, wondering if she was wise to proceed. Then Mr. Renshaw's words returned. That any man would seek to marry her for the sole reason of bringing respectability to his family name was outrageous. Not that she wished to be a hoyden or a disreputable woman such as she knew existed— far from it. Her parents had reared her to be a proper lady. But to be wed for such a reason!

She wanted to be wed because she was loved—and loved in return.

Later that day, in a small but elegantly appointed apartment, a gentleman of advanced years stared with disbelieving eyes at the note just handed him by his man-servant. Mercy Herbert invited him to take tea with her on the morrow? Why? Polite society hostesses had shunned him for aeons. Why would one of the highest sticklers in London Society seek his company? By Jove, he'd go just to find out what was on her mind!

He had fancied her once upon a time. He wondered if she had changed and how much.

He rose to stare into his looking glass, studying his reflection with a critical eye. He would dress with care and exert caution in his speech. He had been away from the refined ladies for much too long. He sent his acceptance at once.

* * *

When Lord George Sutton marched into the Herbert town house, he still had no notion as to why his company was sought. He followed Simpkins up the stairs into the fashionably furnished drawing room with eager steps. At last the little mystery would be solved. At the doorway to the drawing room, he paused.

Miss Mercy Herbert might have grown older, but she was still a stylish and attractive woman. She had definitely fared better than he had. The years had been kind to her, whereas he had lost some of his early looks. Late nights and too many bottles of claret accounted for that, he supposed.

He bowed to her, crossed the room to where she stood before the fireplace and placed a kiss on her hand. Then he noticed she was not alone. He'd only had eyes for Miss Herbert when he entered the room.

"Lord George, how good of you to come on such brief notice. I would have you make the acquaintance of my niece, Miss Priscilla Herbert. She is my older brother's daughter and my own goddaughter. I thought to give her a taste of London life." There was a pregnant pause before she continued. "She has met your nephew."

"Not Alfred! By Jove, I'll crown the lad if he has done a thing out of line." Lord George's round cheeks turned a mottled red. His gray locks concealed some of his forehead, but the frown was undeniably impressive.

"Not Alfred. Lord Latimer—Felix, your other nephew." Aunt Mercy gave him a reproving regard.

"You don't say!" Lord George looked as astounded as he sounded. "Felix? My word! Not that he don't favor a beautiful young lady, or one that is proper, mind you, but, well, you don't say." He actually looked a trifle dazed.

Priscilla withstood his examination and reaction with equanimity. She gestured to a chair. "Won't you be seated, my lord? Simpkins will be in with the tea shortly."

Once she saw him safely seated and his color more normal, she went on. "I saw you not long ago while I was driving with Lord Latimer. You hailed him. I gather he did not wish to stop, for we continued on our way."

Lord George gave her a sapient look. "Aye, I recall the occasion. Wanted a word with him, but I expect he thought I wanted to borrow some money. Don't do that any more, you know." He gave her, then Aunt Mercy a reassuring smile. "Made an investment on the 'change. Done very well for myself. Only play cards for the pleasure of it now, although I don't say anything to a soul. Odd thing is now that I don't truly need the money, I win more often."

"He said nothing more than you are his Uncle George."

"Interested in him, are you?" Lord George tilted his head, again studying her with a knowledgeable eye. "He's a handsome lad. Can quite understand if you are."

Priscilla did not have to answer his awkward query as Simpkins entered bearing a tea tray followed by a maid with a tray of delicacies such as Priscilla had never seen before. Evidently Lord George was to be impressed.

"He said you like to play cards, gamble." She picked up a cup to place it on a saucer. "I wish I knew how to play cards. I am impossible. I doubt anyone could teach me to play, much less win." Priscilla gave him what she hoped was a guileless smile before pouring out the tea for him.

With Aunt Mercy's nod, Priscilla set about pouring tea for her and offering of biscuits and little cakes.

"Do you ever teach, my lord?" Priscilla ventured to ask after a time of sipping and munching and small chat.

"Teach what?" He gave her a narrow scowl.

"How to play cards." Priscilla placed her cup precisely on its saucer, held a macaroon in one hand, and waited. "You know, give lessons."

Aunt Mercy gasped. Lord George stared at her with a quizzical expression.

"I thought it would be interesting to know. How to play at cards, that is." She took a bite from her macaroon and waited.

"Teach a young lady from a highly respectable family how to gamble? For that is what you want, is it not?"

"Indeed, it is. Not that I would *ever* enter one of those gaming houses! No, but I would like to know how it is done. One never knows when something of that sort will come in handy." Priscilla popped the rest of the macaroon into her mouth and again waited.

Lord George stared down into his teacup for a time before draining it dry. Priscilla offered more, poured the tea at his nod, and plopped in a small lump of sugar.

"There." She clasped her hands in her lap, deciding that Lord George couldn't be all that wicked if he refused to teach her how to play cards.

"I would come here?" He looked to Aunt Mercy, who nodded vigorously. "Say, every day for a time, until you are proficient?"

"Yes!" Priscilla cried in delight. She could scarcely believe it, the gentleman was agreeing to teach her. And in return, she would get to know one of Lord Latimer's relatives. She shifted her gaze to her aunt, who appeared to be in a trance. "Aunt Mercy? This is agreeable with you? I'd not displease you for the world."

"It is just fine, dear. Quite fine. Come, have another cup of tea and do try the macaroons, Lord George. I seem to recall that you once enjoyed them very much."

"Don't mind if I do. My cook ain't much for macaroons and such. I confess I have missed them." He smiled into her aunt's bemused eyes with what Priscilla considered was a fond regard.

She wondered if it was simply the macaroons he had missed. She didn't fail to notice the way he gazed at her aunt. He resembled a hungry lad at a bakery-shop window.

"I think it will prove to be a highly entertaining time." Aunt Mercy nodded her head while studying her old acquaintance. "I believe I shall sit in on these lessons. I never was allowed to play cards as a girl, you know. My father and brother thought it improper. I have no doubt it might prove to be most agreeable."

Priscilla quickly shut her mouth after it had dropped open too far. What had she done! Aunt Mercy learning to play cards? What would Papa say if he heard of that?

But Aunt Mercy would never let a word of this seep out. Would she? No. There was something else afoot here, unless Priscilla missed her guess. Aunt Mercy had blushed when Priscilla suggested they invite Lord George to take tea with them. It would bear watching.

Teacups were set aside as the time for the lessons was decided. At last Lord George rose from his chair, bowed low over Aunt Mercy's hand, looking courtly and rather handsome—for an older gentleman. Priscilla thought she detected a family resemblance to Lord Latimer.

"I look forward to these lessons. Wonder what Felix will say to this?" He cocked a brow at Priscilla, a slight smile curving his lips.

Did he guess her reason for wanting him to teach her how to play cards? Undoubtedly Felix, as he called him, would have a royal fit! "I believe he is at his family estate at present. His friend Mr. Renshaw mentioned that he had been summoned by his father." Priscilla figured that he ought to be made aware of his nephew's whereabouts.

At her words, Lord George sent a sharp stare at her. "Was he now? Curious. I suppose my brother wants to urge marriage again. He is convinced that his threats and cozening will persuade Felix to do his bidding."

"Mr. Renshaw seemed of the opinion that Lord Latimer had made up his mind as to a bride. But perhaps there was something else that required his attention."

"Possible, quite possible." Lord George did not look the least convinced this might be so.

"Priscilla, would you be so kind as to fetch my rose shawl from my room?" Miss Herbert got up, supposedly to speed her guest on his way.

Rising to her feet at once, Priscilla agreed and promptly left the room.

When her footsteps could no longer be heard, Miss Herbert said, "She is a fetching girl, is she not? I think your nephew Felix is quite taken with her. Once they met, he was underfoot from that time on. If we went to the theater, he appeared there as well, joining us in our box. When we attended a musical evening, he escorted us, and I have never seen him there before. He squired Priscilla to Bullock's Museum, if you can believe that! And next he plans to take her to the British Museum, as well as private collections, Miss Linwood's Gallery, simply everywhere she longs to go. This is *not* a mere infatuation. For one thing, he is too old for such nonsense."

"Where *did* they meet?" He gave her a perplexed look.

Miss Herbert gave him a demure smile. "Why, at the charity school I help fund. He came while we were there. Had his cousin Archdeacon Pallant with him! Showed some stereopticon slides of *Cinderella, or The Glass Slipper* to the children, who adored it as you might well imagine."

"Do you think she is the girl Renshaw believes Felix wishes to marry?" His lordship glanced at the door, then back to his old acquaintance.

"I do. And her fondest wish now is to get to know his family. Will you help?" She placed a gentle hand on his arm, her touch, feather light.

"By teaching her to play cards!" His brows rose to disappear beneath his gray curls.

"By showing her what a fine man you are. I have never believed the gossip about the Sutton family. Lady Beatrice was always a darling, and the only thing truly wrong with Alfred is that he is horse-mad and . . . and he dresses outrageously."

Lord George gave a crack of laughter at her assessment of his sister's boy. "True, too true." He gazed at her with skepticism in his eyes. "Never thought the worst of us all, did you?"

"Never. Now, will you conspire with me to see that Priscilla gets to know the real Sutton family? Not the one painted black by nasty gossips."

"I can do this by teaching her to play cards?"

"And to win."

"By Jove, I'll do it. Seems a clever chit. Must be to capture Felix."

"As to that, I heard a rumor that he had asked another young lady to wed him and was refused by her father because of his family's scandalous reputation. The mother is not above dropping little nasty remarks that a simpleton can figure out. Abominable creature! Felix is well rid of that family—reeks of the shop."

Priscilla's slippered footsteps on the stairs could be heard from the hall. She hurried into the room with an armful of rose paisley.

"Sorry, I had trouble locating the shawl." She tenderly draped it around her aunt's shoulders.

Miss Herbert gave Lord George an inquiring look.

"I shall be here tomorrow with a fresh pack of cards. Think about which game you want to acquire and we will begin to learn the intricacies of it."

"Thank you, dear sir. I will look forward to it."

"And where do you go this evening? If I may be so bold as to ask." He remained standing close to her aunt.

"The theater. Would you care to join us?" Miss Herbert tilted her chin up as though daring him to accept.

Priscilla listened with amazement to the challenge in her aunt's voice.

"I should like to, but I think it best if I don't." He bowed over her hand once again, thereupon striding from the room without a backward glance.

"Well, did you have a pleasant visit?" Priscilla had stalled as long as she could in her search for the paisley shawl. It was obvious to her that her aunt wished to speak privately with Lord George. Priscilla wouldn't attempt to guess what might have been said.

"Indeed. Pity he wouldn't join us this evening. It would surely set the cat among the pigeons if he did." She fingered the fringe on her shawl with an absentminded touch while gazing into the embers of the fire.

Priscilla wasn't sure what her aunt meant, but assumed it had something to do with the notoriety of the Sutton family. Could it be that her aunt also wished to restore the Suttons to respectability? "Never mind. We will enjoy ourselves anyway. I believe Mr. Renshaw is to escort us. I must say that he is very conscientious in his duty to his friend." If there was a touch of irony in her voice, her aunt made no comment on it.

"As a good friend ought to be," Miss Herbert said with emphasis. "We will not disappoint him. Don that lilac silk again, my dear. Even if Mr. Renshaw has seen it before, it will do no harm for the dress to have another wearing."

"I should hope not! I am not one of those females who believe a dress can never be worn more than once." Priscilla strolled across the room to stare down at the street below, wondering what Lord Latimer was doing in the country and who the girl might be his father would urge him to marry.

So, after a dainty dinner for two, they met Mr. Renshaw in the entryway and proceeded to the theater, where they viewed an insipid play with inferior performances.

Perhaps it was only because Lord Latimer was absent that Priscilla found the play wanting. She could not deny that he had enlivened the previous theatrical production considerably. Miss Bolsolver was absent as well; an omission Priscilla found more than agreeable.

At the family country estate Felix found his father's demands tiresome. He would not give him the satisfaction of letting him know the proper girl to wed had been found. With his dear parent's charm, he'd likely try to win the girl for himself. Although to be fair, he had sought the company of older women to date.

Felix longed to return to London and Priscilla. He could only hope that she was sheltered from unpleasantness and that Renshaw guarded her from those other chaps.

Then his father claimed his attention in regard to the estate, and Felix left off his musing.

The following morning at ten of the clock, a time when many fashionable women are still in bed, the three met in Miss Herbert's drawing room. A table had been set close to the bay window and three comfortable chairs stood ready for the players.

"Ah, I must say this is splendid! For one who does not play cards, you have done all correctly." Lord George rubbed his hands together after placing his pack of cards on the table.

"I look forward to this, you know." Priscilla gave him a laughing look. "If I am sufficiently capable I shall try a game while at a ball or some entertainment where cards are offered. So . . . do your best, sir."

"Excellent. Your butler knows to deny entry to any and all who seek you?" Lord George glanced at the doorway.

"We shall be totally private." Aunt Mercy gave him a cool look, gesturing to the chair in the center.

He smiled, his eyes twinkling with amusement. "It has been a long time since I have heard such words from a beautiful woman."

Priscilla observed her aunt's blush was a lovely thing, a pink tint to her cheeks, and very becoming it was, too.

"So," he declared after seating Aunt Mercy and noting Priscilla's businesslike manner at the table, "what game is it to be first?"

"Piquet." Priscilla thought she had heard this game for two people mentioned more often than any other game. Huge bets were placed on the outcome of many card confrontations between gentlemen. Her request was met with a short nod.

"Very well." Lord George was all business in his approach. He removed the cards lower than a seven and set them aside. "Each card has a different value. An ace counts eleven points, ten for all court cards, and the face value for the remaining cards. The aim of the game is to score points for certain combinations of cards held, and for tricks taken. I will deal us each twelve cards and set the remaining eight for a stockpile."

He did precisely as he said. Priscilla picked up her cards with trembling hands. She had been gifted with an excellent memory, but would it serve her here?

He continued on to explain about a carte blanche. "You can claim ten points if you are dealt a hand containing no court cards."

Priscilla could see at a glance she didn't qualify for that. She listened carefully as he went on to illustrate how the exchange took place and how the declaration was made.

"In piquet you must concentrate on making points as non-dealer, for it is while you are not the dealer that you have the dual advantage of first exchange and the opening lead. And note that it is always best to exchange the five cards allowed—unless it would seriously damage your potential combinations."

Priscilla exchanged the five cards allowed, showing them to Lord George as he suggested. He explained how she was to play, what the possibility of her hand could be, then played his cards. He also explained why he played as he did. They continued this way for several deals until he felt that she might attempt to play without his guidance.

At the end of six deals, both their points were over a hundred, much to her satisfaction. However, Lord George had the higher score, so merited the one hundred-point bonus and won the game.

"You did very well, my dear. You have a clever mind. I believe that in no time at all you will be winning handily."

"Perhaps I can persuade Aunt Mercy to play with me. I shall need practice."

A roguish grin lit his face. "I should like to see Miss Mercy Herbert playing piquet." He turned to Priscilla, studying her a moment before inquiring, "Is there any other game you wish to learn?"

"I suppose whist is a common game. I have watched it played but do not understand it."

"Why not? We ought to have four players. Perhaps we can convince Mr. Renshaw to join us?" Lord George leaned back against his chair and rubbed his jaw as he waited for Priscilla's reaction to his suggestion.

"I do not know how well that would do. Perhaps your other nephew—Alfred, I believe his name is—would serve?"

This brought forth a chuckle. "I can ask him. If I could hint it is to thwart Felix, nothing would hold him back."

"I would not want to cause animosity between them." Priscilla gave him a puzzled look. "The cousins do not deal well together?"

"You might say that. If I can convince him to join us—say next week—perhaps you will see the difficulty."

It was agreed that Lord George would be there the next morning. Again he bowed low over Miss Mercy Herbert's hand, speaking quietly to her as he did.

Priscilla rose from her chair to walk to the window. From here she could see there was no carriage awaiting his lordship. Apparently he had walked, which was not really an indication of his wealth or lack of it. It simply told her that conventions didn't matter to him.

She bid him a polite farewell. Once he had departed the house, she turned to face her aunt.

"Well, it is so bad?"

"Actually, I think it might be rather good. I listened carefully, and if you are agreeable we will try a set of piquet following our luncheon."

"Oh, good. I need all the practice I can get. I suspect Lord George is an excellent cardplayer. I couldn't have chosen a better man to teach me."

"True." Miss Herbert wore a secret sort of smile, and stared off in space for a time until Simpkins announced their lunch awaited them.

Chapter Seven

That evening instead of going out, the two women remained at home to enjoy several hilarious games of piquet. With each game, Priscilla felt her confidence grow. It lasted until Lord George faced her over the card table one fine morning.

He did not merely beat her, he totally annihilated her.

"What did I do wrong, sir?" Priscilla said with a chagrined grimace. "I thought I played my cards properly."

"You were not so bad. I played better!" He proceeded to explain what had happened in the game, how his discards had tripped her up. Then he settled down to once again lead her through her paces, correcting her discards, judging her plays with no mercy shown.

When it came time for him to depart, he paused. "By the by, Felix has returned to Town. I shall attempt to avoid seeing him. But I'll wager he will show up here. What shall you tell him?" Lord George wore a peculiar expression, one Priscilla couldn't interpret.

"I see no need to offer any explanation. Who knows that you have been here? And if someone might have seen you enter the house, would they not properly assume that you came to visit my aunt? I cannot believe the loftiest sort of scandalmongers would find the slightest hint of impropriety." She smiled at his seemingly grudging look of respect.

"He will learn of this. Never fear on that score. I would suggest you think of a good answer."

"Rubbish," she declared most roundly.

He raised his brows, then nodded ever so slightly. "So be it. Tomorrow?"

"If you think I will allow your nephew to dictate my doings when we have no, ah, close association, you are far off the mark, sir." She lifted her chin in a challenge. "I will be most pleased to accept your tutelage on the morrow. I think I should like to try a game of vingt-et-un."

"Ah, that is a game of probabilities. I believe your mind is capable of grasping the nuances of that most clever diversion." He bowed to Priscilla, then to her aunt. "Until tomorrow."

Priscilla watched him leave, then went to the window to see that again he elected to walk.

"Do you suppose Lord Latimer will actually learn that his uncle has been spending some hours with us?" There was a thread of worry in her aunt's voice.

She turned from the window to study her aunt. "I cannot see how. I doubt he will know a thing about it. Care to make a small wager?" she concluded with a mischievous wink.

"Priscilla Herbert! You know full well I would never do such a thing." She paused slightly before adding, "Shall we say five shillings?"

Catching sight of the echoing impishness in her aunt's eyes, Priscilla curtsied. "You are on, I believe the saying goes. Am I leading you astray, dearest aunt?"

"I doubt I am led. Perhaps rebelling?" Her aunt gave her a rueful smile, before patting a pillow on the sofa to perfect plumpness.

Upon that they left the drawing room to partake of a modest luncheon, commenting on how the days had flown by. Priscilla had missed Lord Latimer, truth be known. In such a short time she had come to rely on his company, enjoy his conversation, and relish his sense of humor. He was quite a nonpareil. She couldn't believe that such a perfect gentleman of his standing would wish to marry a nobody like Miss Priscilla Herbert.

It was later the same afternoon when the hours for paying social calls had arrived that Simpkins brought up Lord Latimer's card.

As usual the butler had the most impassive expression

Priscilla could imagine, but she thought she detected a slight smugness in his eyes.

"Please, escort the gentleman up at once, Simpkins." Aunt inspected Priscilla so long that she wondered if there was something amiss with her dress.

"Everything is proper?" Priscilla inquired, shifting uneasily on her chair.

"Oh, quite," her aunt whispered back just as they heard footsteps at the top of the stairs.

Priscilla might be angry with the gentleman, but she couldn't fault his attire. The dark brown of his coat almost matched the color of his hair. The cravat tied above his tasteful dark gold waistcoat looked admirable on him—neither too fussy nor too severe. And she doubted another man in Town could better the fit of his breeches. In spite of herself, she admired the way they fit. Shards of afternoon sunlight caught the gleam on his boots, and the cane he carried looked to have a beautiful clouded amber top. He was indeed a very fine gentleman.

But . . . did he truly mean to wed her? In spite of what Mr. Renshaw had said, she doubted it. Why, she and Lord Latimer were barely acquainted. The very notion he would propose to her merely for respectability was preposterous.

She ignored the tales she had heard about marriages proposed after meeting but two or three occasions. So what if his father expressed a strong desire to see his son wed? Did not every father wish the same? Perhaps her own father had not said anything about her brother—he might still nurture hopes.

They began with the usual chitchat found in afternoon calls. The weather was fine, the latest *on dits* were trotted forth, and a polite inquiry was made as to their various enjoyments.

"Actually we remained at home much of the time."

"The play we attended with Mr. Renshaw was dreadfully dull," Priscilla commented further.

"I am glad to know that Chauncy escorted you, however. It is good for a lady to have a gentleman to guard her from unpleasantness."

"I scarce think we need have worried, my lord," the elder Miss Herbert replied. "Others must have been warned of the paltry talents on offer that evening and remained home!"

He smiled. There was a brief silence before he spoke again. "I hope you do not take it amiss if I approach a matter dear to my heart."

Priscilla and Mercy Herbert gave him quizzical looks but said nothing. They both nodded in encouragement.

He took a deep breath before continuing. "I chanced to visit your father before returning to London," he said to Priscilla. "When I asked for your hand in marriage, he gave his consent. Will you marry me?"

Priscilla stared at him in amazement and vexation. Never in her dreams had she anticipated an offer from an earl, no less, and one made in the presence of her aunt.

Before she could reply, her aunt rose from the sofa. "I think I shall allow my niece to give you her answer in private, my lord. But do know that you have my blessing, for what it is worth." She turned to her much-loved niece. "Priscilla, think carefully before you reply."

The earl looked rather taken aback at her speech. When she stepped from the room, he moved to take Priscilla's hand, drawing her to her feet. "This is sudden, you may say."

"True, it is, my lord." She focused her gaze on his hands, now clasped about hers, their grip oddly comforting. Her fury at his assumption ebbed with his touch.

"And yet I did tell you I had intentions. It is what I want, and you? Your father seemed to think you might welcome my advances."

"That is also true. I cannot think of any young woman who would not be pleased to have the attentions from so handsome and polished a gentleman." Her voice was soft and low, intimately husky, masking her pique. She removed her hand from his clasp, taking a step away.

Dash it all, Felix thought, she was not going to reject his offer . . . was she? He dropped her hand to place one of his at her back, the other tipped her chin up so she perforce must meet his gaze.

"Priscilla, I care not for what other young women might like. I want to know what you want." At the confusion he saw in her eyes, he instinctively drew her closer and placed a kiss he intended to be chaste and brief on her lips. Only the kiss did not go as planned. Her innocent response aroused his senses. He deepened his kiss, his ardor unconsciously released.

Now her hands were free, her arms went about him. It was not a practiced embrace, but somewhat awkward as though she was not accustomed to clasping anyone close to her. However, she adjusted her slim form against his, and Felix could find no complaint about her embrace. He would see that she acquired a lot of practice. Marrying to make his family respectable suddenly became enormously appealing.

When at last they separated, she gazed up at him with luminous eyes and a trembling smile. "I trust you do not think me a forward girl, my lord, but I confess I liked that very well."

"Honest—in addition to your other virtues. May I take your response as a positive reply to my proposal?" He found her innocent blush delightful. Those long brown lashes fanned over peach-tinted cheeks were quite enchanting. It was difficult not to kiss those satiny cheeks, stroke her pretty blond curls, and cradle her charming form close to him until she answered as he wished.

"I would have more than polite regard from my husband. I had hoped for love."

"Many marriages are based on liking, mutual regard. Love will perhaps come in time."

She glanced down, turning her face away from him. What thoughts spun in her mind? "Very well, I accept your proposal, my lord." She gave him a troubled look.

Felix let out the breath he hadn't realized he was holding. He again kissed his newly betrothed lady, but lightly so as not to frighten her. From his waistcoat pocket he extracted the family betrothal ring. The arrangement of sapphires and diamonds looked very fitting on her slender finger and complimented her blond beauty.

Aunt Mercy returned at that moment, having judged to a nicety precisely how long it would take for Lord Latimer to persuade her niece to accept his suit. She immediately spotted the refined elegance of the ring.

"How nice, my dear. Simply lovely. I am very happy

for you." Her smile appeared genuine, and there was a gleam of satisfaction in her gray eyes.

Priscilla withstood her aunt's searching gaze, meeting it with resolution. She knew full well what prompted his lordship to propose. She also knew that she wished with all her heart to make it a love match.

They chatted for a time longer, then his lordship properly took his leave, lingering over Priscilla's hand as any newly engaged man might do.

When they heard the door shut behind him, Aunt Mercy fixed a quelling gaze on her niece. "So, he persuaded you, did he? I was not certain you meant to encourage him, much less accept his offer."

"I found I could do no less. I fear he overcame what resistance I had too easily. Yet I shall not repine over my decision. I intend to make it a love match, Aunt Mercy." Priscilla's answering gaze was determined. Her chin went up a trifle, anticipating a reproof.

"I will not scold you, dear girl. Truth be known, I believe I envy you. As will most of the young women making their come-outs. The earl has been the target of every matchmaking mama for a number of years."

"They will likely wonder how a nobody like Priscilla Herbert captured a gentleman of such distinction." She thrust her hands behind her, ignoring the enticing sparkle of the beautiful ring. It seemed to weight her finger; she was conscious of the smooth gold encircling it, sure to draw attention wherever she went and chanced to remove her gloves. She did not think she wished to wear it over her gloves, as she had seen done. For now, it would be private, her secret.

She was thankful her aunt released her from the next round of callers. It was important that Priscilla consider her next steps.

She hurried to her room, where in privacy she could contemplate her future. Could she continue with her lessons from her betrothed's uncle? Clamping her lips together, she nodded decisively. She would. Surely Lord Latimer would not deny her the pleasant company of his uncle! Besides, she had not missed the growing attachment between Lord George and Aunt Mercy. *That* she would encourage.

Her aunt declared they needed an evening at home. She was becoming fearfully fatigued with all the parties and routs, not to mention the theater they had attended, to keep going. "A night at home will not come amiss for you, either, my girl."

Priscilla looked at the ring she wore, its weight still unfamiliar to her. "I would like to adjust to my new position before venturing forth in society again. We go to Lady Smythe's ball tomorrow evening, do we not?"

"That will do well enough."

The next morning, a well-slept and refreshed Priscilla was consuming a breakfast far greater than a young woman in love might be thought to enjoy, when her cousin was announced. He was garbed in splendid finery.

"Cousin Rawlinson, how nice to see you." Her puzzlement at his appearance so early in the morning was reflected in her voice. "What brings you here so early in the day?" She placed her teacup on its saucer, suspecting this was no ordinary family call.

"I came to offer my felicitations. What a coup for you, dear cousin." He waved a morning paper before him.

Priscilla gave her aunt a bemused look. "I trust you will explain what has put you in alt?"

"It is here in *The Morning Post*. Read for yourself."

He handed the paper to Priscilla, who promptly searched the columns for whatever it was that had drawn such a reaction from her normally calm cousin. She found the item at the bottom of the second page. "Oh."

"Is that all you have to say to the announcement of the engagement between you—a provincial nobody—to one of the richer peers of the country? My word! I had not the slightest clue that *you* would prove an asset to the family name." He drew out a chair to seat himself, assured he would receive no censure from his aunt. The footman poured him a cup of coffee from which Lord Rawlinson immediately sipped, seeming in need of restoration.

"The family name? Is that so important then? That I be an asset to the Herbert family? I thought that you and your grandfather did quite well without my pittance." Priscilla tried to keep any tartness from her voice and failed. She could not help but think that if it was so important to dignify the family name, her grandfather could at any time have managed a bishopric for her father! The earl certainly appeared to exert more than a modicum of influence in Society!

"Now, now, cousin, you are overreacting. You must become accustomed to the curiosity of the social world."

"I told her much the same, Aylwin. We both know how those frustrated biddies will cluck over a girl who has stolen the finest of the current crop of beaux from beneath their collective noses." Aunt reached out to pat Priscilla on her hand. "You will wear your newest gown to the ball this evening. I fancy that you will attract a fair amount of attention when you appear."

"Does Latimer escort you?" When Priscilla shook her head, for indeed it had not been discussed, Aylwin smiled with satisfaction. "As your relative I shall have the pleasure, in that event. How gratifying it will be to usher you into the Smythes' ballroom on my arm." He nodded to Aunt Mercy, "And you as well, dear aunt." He studied Priscilla a moment, and she had the fantastic notion he was assessing her potential. "What color do you wear? Not blue, I trust. It is too boring to see a blonde in blue."

Priscilla darted a glance at her aunt before venturing to reply to his query. "I have a new lavender satin trimmed in some blonde lace sent to me by my sister. I believe it to be absolutely ravishing."

"I don't suppose I could see it?"

"No, you couldn't!" Priscilla declared, becoming vexed with the cousin she scarcely knew. "You will have to take my word for it."

He shrugged. "Very well. I shall bring you a posy utterly suited to lavender and blonde lace. You wish to leave on time?"

She thought he uttered the words in the expectation that she would assure him that she wished to be fashionably late. He was to be disappointed if that were the case. "Yes, I would like to arrive early. I have no desire to capture all eyes with my entrance as some young women appear to want."

"There will be a lot of curiosity," he cautioned.

"I have no need to answer any rude inquiries. I have handled such at home, you know. There are always ill-mannered people who want to know what is none of their business."

"Well, you should join us for dinner. Then it will be no hardship for us to leave when we ought." His aunt looked down her aristocratic nose at him, but kindly.

He nodded his agreement, rose from the table, and bowed to Aunt Mercy. "I believe she will do tolerably well. She will not disgrace the family." With that declaration, he left the room after giving Priscilla a polite smile.

When she was certain he had gone, she turned to face her aunt. "What a pompous bore, ma'am. Family, indeed. I have long thought that if they cared a jot about the family, the earl might have made father a bishop. I believe he has one in his keeping.

"It is my understanding that the earl is somewhat self-centered, which might account for his not paying the slightest bit of attention to anyone other than himself or his grandson." Miss Herbert took a restoring sip of cooling tea before turning her attention to the paper left behind. "There is a theatrical production that is likely to draw your betrothed's interest this evening."

"I saw that. There is a new opera dancer who is to be in the production," Priscilla answered dryly. "I can quite see how that will attract the gentlemen. I doubt Lord Latimer will feel compelled to attend me. It isn't as though he is madly in love with me, you know."

Her aunt sniffed in reply before turning her attention to other bits and scraps in the paper. "I see where a 'Miss B' has become a trifle too nice in her requirements and has rejected yet another offer. Do you suppose that might be Miss Anne Bolsolver?" she mused quietly. "Rumor has it that she turned down—or her father did—a handsome peer who sought her hand in marriage."

Priscilla felt the most peculiar intuition hit her. "I expect that it was Lord Latimer who was rejected. It would explain his behavior when he saw her in the park and her acrimonious behavior when we were at the Egyptian Museum."

"I believe you may have the right of it. Her mother has been dropping nasty little barbs about the Sutton family and their scandalous members. I do dislike that woman."

"She is not particularly appealing, is she?"

The two women commented over other bits of news offered in the morning paper before going to Priscilla's room to assess her lavender satin.

"A new hat, I think," her aunt pronounced. "Lavender satin with a touch of lace. Why do we not explore the hat shops this morning?"

Since "morning" could extend as late as three in the afternoon, Priscilla smiled and prepared herself for a grueling expedition. She thought she might as well purchase a new pair of gloves while she was out and about.

"And how providential that we had a reticule made up to match your gown. You will be all the thing, my dear."

Priscilla had learned soon after her arrival in London that to be "the thing" was all a young woman might desire.

When Aylwin came to dinner, he regaled the women with tales of his exploits in Society. Naturally, he was a prominent attendee of Almack's, the most exclusive and fashionable assembly room in London, where every girl making her come-out longed to be. He was a member of White's, as was his grandfather. However, he was not interested in joining the Four-Horse club in their May and June excursions to Salt Hill—he thought it too, too wearying.

Priscilla was far too nervous to add much to his conversation. She had conceived a plan for this evening. She would put her new skills in playing cards to the test. Lord Latimer would not be present to censure her. She could see how she did, how well Lord George had taught her and how well she had learned. She didn't intend to make a habit of playing cards. Goodness, she couldn't afford it.

Thus, she left the table, scarcely aware of what she had eaten. She imagined her aunt attributed her abstraction due to the attention she would inevitably draw as the newly betrothed of Earl Latimer.

She had asked her aunt about his title, to be assured

that simply because he did not have "of" in his title did not mean it was not old or respected. It merely had to do with the original grant. Most earldoms were tied to a piece of land. His was not.

Still in a haze, she entered the carriage her cousin had summoned. She was aware her aunt eyed her with frowning curiosity. She would learn in time what went on beneath the blond curls that her cousin appeared to hold in contempt.

Aylwin had dawdled long enough, so there were a fair number of people present when they entered the ballroom.

Priscilla gave her cousin an amused glance as the haughty butler announced them. Cousin Rawlinson wore the most self-satisfied expression she could imagine. Fancy that her engagement would please him so highly!

Their hostess fluttered around Priscilla and Miss Herbert with gratifying pleasure, no doubt because of what had been printed in *The Morning Post*.

"Dear girl, I must see the Sutton ring. I remember that it was a very fine one. Lord Latimer's mama was always so proud of it, you know."

With a silently resigned sigh, Priscilla drew off her left glove to satisfy Lady Smythe.

"Oh, it is every bit as beautiful as I recalled." The baronet's wife beamed at Priscilla, sighing, a sentimental tear in one eye. "I have no doubt you will put one certain young lady quite out of countenance this evening."

On that note, Cousin Aylwin inclined his head to her, then placed Priscilla's hand on his arm. He made it clear he intended to take his cousin elsewhere.

Priscilla smiled politely, pulled her glove back on, then drifted away on her cousin's arm with great affability. "I had no notion that you would prove so useful, Aylwin. How nice it is to have a viscount cousin who dares do as he please."

He actually reddened at her praise. "Well, I cannot abide those fawning creatures."

"I know about that 'certain young lady' Lady Smythe believes will be put out of countenance, so there was no need to protect me. But I do thank you." Priscilla decided her cousin might have a heart after all.

Before they could discuss anything more, Priscilla found herself besieged with gentlemen who sought her hand for a dance. Her little card was almost full of names before she could think of denying anyone on the off chance her betrothed might attend. He had not said a word about coming here this evening, so she assumed she would be free to bestow her favors as she pleased. She did manage to leave one dance open, but not for Lord Latimer. She had another plan in mind.

Mr. Renshaw approached for the country-dance that came first. She gladly offered him her hand.

"I say, I am surprised to see you with Rawlinson. Thought sure you would be with Latimer."

The pattern of the longways dance prevented her from answering him immediately. When they came together again, she merely smiled at him. "I do not require him to live in my pocket. If he chooses to go his own way, he is still free. As I am." She flicked her lashes at him as she had observed other girls do and had the satisfaction of seeing his eyes grow large.

"I say, Miss Herbert, you are in looks this evening."

Her demure thanks were all that was proper, even if she gave him a flirtatious grin. So Lord Latimer was to marry her to make his family respectable? And Cousin Aylwin thought she would be an asset to the Herbert family? Well . . . she intended to kick up her heels a bit. Nothing scandalous, to be sure. Just a little rebellion?

The fourth dance was free. Priscilla observed that her aunt was safely chatting with Lord George. He absorbed her complete attention, so when Priscilla murmured that she would see her in a short while, all she got in reply was a vague nod. It wasn't done, but she felt defiant tonight.

Lord George gave her a speculative look, but said nothing.

Priscilla had taken note of where the card room was located. She now made her way, drifting along in seemingly aimless direction, but always with that door in mind. She saw Miss Anne Bolsolver in the far end of the ballroom. Thankfully, it was unlikely there would be an acrimonious exchange with her.

At last she entered the card room, taking stock of the

players present. Lord George had commented on quite a few of the London cardplayers, noting who was good, who was a dunce, and who was a shark. She wanted to avoid any sharks, even if Lord George had shown her how to detect cheating.

Since she had done her best at piquet, she found a table where a couple was playing that game. They finished their game just as she paused.

"I am done. No luck for me this evening," One fellow rose from the table, sauntering off to look for his luck elsewhere.

"May I join you?" Priscilla asked the older gentleman who remained seated at the table.

He immediately rose, bowed to her, and saw her seated across from him. He raised a brow, but said nothing.

Priscilla noted that no one seemed to pay them the slightest bit of attention. All were too engrossed in their own cards. That suited her admirably.

He introduced himself, and she recalled that Lord George Sutton deemed Lord Cowell a good player. She could take a chance with him as a partner.

He dealt and they settled down for a hand. No conversation, but she suspected he observed the Sutton ring on her left hand when she removed her gloves to play. She wanted no interference with her tactile feel of the cards. Lord Cowell might be a good player, but if he had a run of bad luck, he might not be above marking the cards.

She won the first hand, he won the second when she dealt. The third she declared a carte blanche and showed him her hand after he had made his normal exchange.

He raised a brow, but said nothing. The game continued in silence, other than the declarations of points scored. "Good" and "not good" could be heard as they continued, with Priscilla declaring "pique" and "repique" more than might be expected. After six deals, she had scored not only over a hundred points, but had a higher score than her worthy opponent. This added his score to hers. She smiled at her victory over a man who had fully intended to beat this green girl.

He leaned back in his chair. "I don't suppose you would give me a chance to recoup my loss?"

"I am promised to a dance, my lord. I would dislike to disappoint my partner." She gave him a demure look.

He pulled out a roll of bills and pealed off several, handing it to a stunned Priscilla with good grace. She had not dreamed the stakes were so high. Thank heavens she hadn't asked, she would have been too nervous to play well.

"I believe your partner approaches now."

Priscilla stuffed the bills into her little lavender satin reticule before drawing on her gloves.

"I am surprised to find you *here*." The gruff voice from behind her was familiar.

"Lord Latimer! Hello." She hoped she wouldn't faint.

Chapter Eight

$\mathcal{P}$riscilla forced herself to walk calmly at Lord Latimer's side from the room where she had played cards with Lord Cowell. "Good evening, my lord. I was under the impression you had gone to the theater this evening." Then she realized that her words were not precisely the best ones she could have uttered.

Her gown swished about her ankles as he whirled her around the corner of the room and along the wall of the ballroom. Her heart pounded beneath the soft satin of her dress, and she nervously licked her lips. She smoothed her gloves over her hands, noting the slight lump where her engagement ring encircled her finger. Would he suggest she return the ring? He certainly seemed highly displeased; his smile was wintry and his clasp of her arm was not in the slightest reassuring.

He nodded to a friend. Priscilla sent a smile to her aunt and Lord George. She did not want them to think anything was amiss.

"Is this what you do when I am not around?" Lord Latimer's voice bit and his manner chided her. "Play cards with a strange gentleman? I believed you to be most proper. When I asked you to wed, I understood you behaved with decorum. I did *not* think you would indulge in gaming!"

He guided her to a slight recess where they were in full view of the assembled guests, yet able to converse somewhat privately—provided their voices remained low.

He seated her with punctilious courtesy. The cold marble was not comfortable, which was probably just as well, all things considered. Comfort might cause her to relax, and she needed to be fully aware. She stiffened her spine.

"There was nothing improper about that game. His partner left just as I paused by the table. I suggested we play one game, and he agreed." She hadn't known what the stakes were, however. "And there are many other women playing cards in there—loo, piquet, and I daresay other games as well—I paid no attention to them."

"He explained the wager? Pound points, I believe is his usual stake." He studied her with an impassive expression. She didn't have to guess to know that he was angry, his ire was revealed in his eyes—now a brilliant green—not to mention his grip on her arm. As to the other women who played cards, Priscilla suspected he cared not in the least what these women did. He was mainly concerned with her caper—if, indeed, he viewed it as such.

Priscilla swallowed with great care. "Ah, actually, I forgot to ask. That shows I am not a gamester." She adjusted the strings on her reticule, shocked at the amount of money she now carried. One hundred and forty pounds was a vast sum for a rector's daughter to gain, in particular while playing cards. She had not thought they played for such a great amount. "It's a good thing I won, isn't it? I mean," she swallowed the sudden lump in her throat, "I would have had difficulty in paying such a loss."

"You did count your winnings, then? Cowell is a reputable man, but he might be tempted to fleece so green a girl." He paused, as though he wanted that to sink in. "Cowell is reckoned to be one of the finer piquet players, and not one to give away a game because he feels generous. He may be kind, but not that kind. Where did you learn to play so well?" He studied her intently, most likely wondering if she would tell him the truth of the matter.

There was nothing to do *but* tell the truth. Priscilla had always found in the past that if she prevaricated, she was invariably found out. "Your uncle George was so kind as to teach me to play piquet. I asked him, you see."

"You did what?" His whisper had a deadly sibilance.

Priscilla forced her gaze up to meet his. "I asked him to teach me. *I* think he is a rather likable gentleman even if you give him the cut direct. He taught me not only how to play the game, but also how to detect cheating and other fine points." She chewed her lower lip a moment before adding, "He came to Aunt Mercy's house to give me lessons. It was all quite proper."

"I suppose if anyone knows about playing piquet, it would be Uncle George." Lord Latimer's voice was dry. "I cannot believe you would involve your aunt in this scheme." He retained his hold on her arm. She wondered if he even realized that he gripped her so firmly. It was not a situation she ever wanted to repeat.

She firmly removed his hand from her arm, bestowing a tight smile on him. "He said he no longer needs to gamble, for an investment paid off handsomely. He plays cards now for the pleasure of it. Oddly enough, now that he no longer depends on his winnings to live, he has found he wins more often. Isn't that nice?"

"Nice does not begin to cover it." He sounded more than a little skeptical. "Did he contact you?" He noticed where she looked and followed the direction of her gaze to where his uncle remained with Aunt Mercy.

"No, Aunt Mercy invited him to take tea with us. It was then I sought his help. Actually, I wished to make his acquaintance." Priscilla's enthusiasm for her scheme to know his uncle better burst forth in a softly worded plea. "You cannot mean to cut him forever. He is a dear gentleman, ever so polite. I do believe my aunt finds him particularly pleasing. And—I think he likes her."

Lord Latimer gave her a frowning look, his gloved hands clenched in his lap.

"I believe Lord George is unhappy about your separation." Priscilla noted the clenched hands, tight jaw, and cold expression. "Do not mind what gossips say about him. What do they really know? At least talk with him. You are missing the company of a very amiable gentleman."

She feared her pleading fell on deaf ears. Lord Latimer sat at her side, his speculative gaze now on his uncle. Was there a faint softening of expression?

"You believe I should seek him out? That I ought to overlook the scandal he has caused our family?"

"Well, think of the Prince of Wales. He has caused enough scandal for ten families." She looked away from his lordship to where his uncle sat in cheerful conversation, if his smile was anything to go by.

"The royal family can do little but hope about the heir to the throne." Lord Latimer turned away from the sight of his uncle to study Priscilla once more. "I suppose you thought you were performing a service—bringing the black sheep into the fold, as it were."

Surprised he should see her motive as clearly as that, she nodded. Glancing at her little dance card, she held it up for him to see. "I have a partner for the next dance, my lord. Your friend, Mr. Renshaw, was so kind as to seek my hand for a country-dance."

He plucked the card from her hand to study it. "There is a waltz after this. You will dance it with me. I'll not have my betrothed waltzing with another chap, particularly Wilson. He is an abominable flirt."

So his lordship was still claiming her as his—even after the debacle with the cards? She wondered at his possessive attitude. Yet it was comforting to know that he cared one way or another, even if his sole purpose was to make his family more respectable.

"Mr. Renshaw approaches. While I dance with him, perhaps you might consider greeting your uncle. He truly is charming. In fact, I can see something of him in you." She beamed a smile at her betrothed, hoping that if all went as she wished that he might come to love her.

Felix was stunned at the brilliant smile bestowed on him by his affianced bride. First of all it made her luminescent, a beauty that shined from within. Secondly, she looked at him as though she thought him wonderful, a defender who could do no wrong. And thirdly, the expression in her eyes made him long to whisk her away from this crowd to a very private place where he could indulge his desires. This engagement was not working out precisely as he had planned. Priscilla Herbert was not what he had expected in a proper young miss! He had thought he would get her safely engaged, then be free to do as he pleased. Not so.

He rose to stand at her side, absently greeting his old friend with a nod and a few polite words. When they left he felt as though a part of him had gone, a very vital part, and he wasn't sure he liked that feeling.

He regarded his uncle, and saw he was deep in conversation with Miss Mercy Herbert. They were laughing. He couldn't recall ever seeing his uncle laugh. He must have done so. Felix simply had no recollection of it.

Without being aware of his reason, he walked around the perimeter of the ballroom to where his uncle and Miss Herbert sat. He bowed to her.

"Miss Herbert. I trust I find you in good health this evening?" He avoided eye contact with his uncle for the moment.

"I am exceedingly well, thank you. And I am pleased to see how splendidly Priscilla is taking. She has danced nearly every dance." Miss Herbert preened a trifle, seeming more than a little gratified at her niece's success.

Lady Smythe was very particular to have only the finest musicians. She and her baronet husband hosted one of the premier balls of the Season. It was a feather in a young woman's cap to be invited. To make a splash was beyond anything wonderful.

Felix let her comment on the dancing go for the time being. He turned to his uncle to see a hint of anxiety in his eyes, a wariness in his attitude.

Could it be that Felix had judged him unfairly? But Uncle George's gaming had been scandalous. Although, to be fair, Felix could not recall one instance where Uncle George had wiped out another's heritage or caused a man to blow his brains out in despair. George had seemed to play with men who could afford to gamble. He appeared to win more often than he lost. Felix considered the past years. There had been no talk in the clubs about his uncle possibly cheating. Of course, no one would have said a word regarding that around Felix.

Still, he would have heard, people being what they are. "Uncle George. You are looking in good health. I imagine all is well with you?"

"Felix, I am doing excellently. Don't play cards as much as I once did." His wariness seemed to increase.

"Rather, you have taken to tutoring green girls." Felix did not hide the animosity he felt at what he conceived as a wrong.

"When I had found a young woman as resolute as Priscilla is, I made it a point to teach her to play the best game possible. She is good, you know." The wariness had fled and determination taken its place.

Felix made a wry face. "I know. She just won one hundred and forty pounds from Cowell. You know what he is like. I suspect it was some moments before he recovered from the shock." He shot a dry grin at his uncle.

"Great heavens," Miss Herbert breathed. She vigorously fanned herself at this shocking news.

No matter how you looked at it, that was a tidy sum of money! Felix guessed that amount wouldn't often come the way of a girl in the rectory.

"That's my girl," Uncle George said with pride in his voice. "She is a rare talent, a person who can recall the rules, know what to play, and keeps cool under pressure. Not many like her, I can tell you, especially women."

"You sound proud of your pupil." Felix twiddled with a fob that dangled from his white waistcoat of finest cassimere. His world appeared to be shaking on its very foundations this evening. Perhaps he should have remained at the opera. The new dancer hadn't been all that much. He lost interest rapidly, thinking he would rather seek out Priscilla's company. When he discovered that Miss Herbert and Priscilla had gone off to the Smythe ball, he had nurtured expectations of an enjoyable time dancing with her. Instead he had been required to hunt for her, then found her in the room set aside for card playing!

"Why shouldn't I be proud of her. She could beat you to flinders, Felix, and you aren't bad at cards. She is better." His uncle's eyes gleamed with amusement.

A reluctant smile tugged Felix's mouth up at one corner. "Truly? I shall have to put her to a test."

"I had no idea she was playing cards this evening." Miss Herbert shot a worried look at where her niece floated through the paces of the country-dance, looking like a dream in her lavender satin gown bedecked with blonde lace. She had been much sought after earlier—before her foray into the card room and the advent of her intended.

"Perhaps she just meant to try her skill?" Uncle George looked at Felix as though to gauge his ill will.

Being essentially a fair man, Felix decided that perhaps he was being too harsh on Priscilla. "I daresay she found it impossible to resist." He pinned his uncle with a look. "Once you had taught her."

Miss Herbert suddenly looked uncomfortable. "My lord, it may not be as you think. Priscilla desired to meet your uncle and devised the card playing and tutorage as a means of doing so. I believe both she and your uncle enjoyed their mornings in the drawing room. I am not the least sorry I invited him to take tea with us that first day. I do not believe for a moment that Priscilla intends to make gambling her minor obsession. I sat in on the lessons, and I believe I could play as well, particularly given a partner as gifted as your uncle."

"Bravo, Mercy," Uncle George said quietly. He took her hand in his to pat it gently, offering his comfort.

Felix bowed to Miss Herbert, sorry he had caused her any distress. He was about to say so when the dance concluded. Renshaw ushered Priscilla into his care with a knowing grin. "Dashed fine dancer. If this is a sample of country grace, I shall have to investigate, find another such as your treasure."

He backed away at the look from his best chum. "Said I wouldn't trespass."

"I believe our waltz is next, my lord." Priscilla sought the feel of the diamond and sapphire ring on her finger. She needed to remind herself she was actually engaged to this man. He inspired awe, and it wasn't merely his appearance—which was certainly impressive. He exuded a sense of power. It was hard to explain what she sensed when she was at his side. It was exhilarating, to be certain, even if she was still angry with him.

He placed her hand on his arm, gave the pair of relatives his nod, thereupon escorting her to where others gathered to enjoy the new dance all London had embraced.

Only the other women couldn't claim this man as their own. Priscilla knew a moment of disquiet when she considered her plans. What on earth would he do when he discovered her intentions with his aunt?

She drifted into his arms, spinning around in the slow whirl, closing her eyes for a moment. Oh, to savor the closeness this dance offered.

"You waltz well, my dear."

She snapped her eyes open, studying him with care. "Thank you. My brother assisted us all in learning. How useful a brother can be when he wants."

"So you wished to meet my uncle. Why?"

"I was curious, mostly. I find it difficult to believe anyone close to you could be so terrible."

"Naive child. There are many fine people who have perfectly vile relatives." He raised a brow at her, firming his mouth.

"True. But Aunt Mercy knew him. She would never know anyone who was vile, much less sigh over him." Priscilla gave her betrothed a cautious regard, not sure how he would react to her words.

"Your aunt *sighed* over Uncle George?" Lord Latimer glanced to where his uncle still sat beside Aunt Mercy. Lord Latimer looked baffled, as well he might. Priscilla did not altogether understand what was between those two, either.

"Indeed. Is it possible she has a *tendre* for him? I mean, he is a charming gentleman. And she never married. She told me once that the man she loved had married another. I wonder if that might have been Lord George."

Lord Latimer looked as though he had been struck by lightning. "But he was married for years. Surely she could have turned her attention to someone else?"

"Mama said there are some women who love but once in their life. She thought Aunt Mercy to be one of them."

Was she one of them as well? Priscilla wondered if by agreeing to marry Lord Latimer she was inviting heartache. Would he come to love her? Eventually? Perhaps and perhaps not. Only time would reveal the truth.

"Somehow it is difficult to see my uncle in the light of one who inspires such passion."

"That is because you do not see him in the proper light at all. He has been divinely kind to my aunt. I believe he thought himself unworthy of her attentions. See what has happened merely because you scorn his friendship. At the least you might acknowledge him."

"I just did," Lord Latimer reminded. He swung Priscilla around so her skirt belled out about her slim form. She felt giddy and wondered if this feeling was related to falling in love. She feared she was. In love, that is. Even with his nasty scolding she would far prefer to be on his arm than with any other man in the room.

"Where would you like to go tomorrow afternoon?"

"Perhaps Miss Linwood's collection? Aunt Mercy said it is very nice." As usual her aunt had used her favored word, but Priscilla thought maybe the collection of embroidered works of art was truly to be admired.

"We can contemplate the British Museum the following day in that case." He gave her a considering survey. "I should like to spend more time with you."

Priscilla gave him a wary look. It appeared that her affianced intended to take up her days. It might make meeting his aunt, Lady Beatrice, a trifle difficult. But since Aunt Mercy had indicated that her ladyship enjoyed early morning rides, that might well be a means of meeting her. Priscilla had always been an early riser at home. It ought not be too difficult to get up early.

She had to admit that staying up late made it unpleasant to rise betimes, but if it was for a good cause she could do it. And pray she didn't yawn while out with Lord Latimer.

"I'd give a monkey to know what is going on in your head just now. If I did not know you are a proper young lady—at least most all the time—I would think you concocting some wild scheme."

How providential the waltz ended at that moment. Really, she had much for which to be thankful.

When Lord Latimer returned her to her aunt, she discovered her cousin Aylwin standing by her.

"I believe I am promised the next dance, Cousin Priscilla. You'll not disappoint me?"

She glanced at her betrothed to see his reaction. Apparently dancing with a cousin was considered to be quite acceptable in his lordship's eyes.

When Priscilla paused at the side of her cousin during the dance, she gave him an inquiring look. It was a mark of distinction that he sought her hand in a dance. Why had he?

"How goes it, Priscilla? I see your betrothed is keeping a stern eye on you. Didn't approve of that card game, did he?" Aylwin cocked a knowing brow, giving her a somewhat sly smile.

"And what do you know about a card game? And what has it to do with me?" Priscilla attempted to don a mask of innocence. From Aylwin's expression, she failed.

"Why, it is all over the room, my dear. You defeated Lord Cowell in a game of piquet. This is a man other men rarely beat. For him to be trounced by a mere slip of a girl is beyond anything astounding."

"Lord Latimer was not best pleased. I did not mean to create gossip. But I have had Lord George Sutton teaching me as a means of getting to know him. He is such a delightful gentleman. I do believe he did well as a teacher for me to defeat Lord Cowell so easily."

"Remind me never to play with you." His voice was dry, although nothing of his inner attitude was revealed in his face. As usual, Aylwin wore his look of bored disdain.

"Well, that is easy enough to do. I do not intend to make a habit of playing at cards with anyone, except, perhaps, Lord Latimer."

"That ought to be safe enough." Aylwin glanced back to where Lord Latimer, her aunt, and his uncle watched.

Priscilla also looked before it was time to step forth in the pattern of the dance, and she lost sight of them for a time.

Rather than return to them, when the dance concluded, she informed her cousin that she would go to the lady's retiring room. "That last gentleman stepped on the hem of my gown, and I dare not let my aunt see the damage. I must have it fixed at once."

Leaving her cousin to make explanations, she hurried along to the pleasant room where she found a maid who offered to mend the slight tear.

A young woman entered the room shortly after.

Priscilla blinked at her appearance, for she wore an amazing gown of silver tissue bedecked with purple ribbons and far too many flounces around the lower skirt.

"You are Miss Herbert," she stated in a breathless voice with a hint of a lisp.

"Indeed, as you say. May I be of assistance?" Priscilla felt wary of the girl, although she had no reason—other than the remarkable apparel.

"Did you really beat Lord Cowell in a game of piquet? It is the talk of the ball." The lisp was definitely in evidence.

"True. I did." Priscilla's wariness increased.

"Oh, would you teach me? I am a dreadful player, and I have lost ever so much money. I must recoup else my mother will be sure to take me home." Her words ended in a wail.

"I fear I am no teacher, miss, er . . ."

"Staples. I . . ."

Whatever she might have said was lost when the door opened again to allow another young woman to enter in a rush.

"I saw you come here. Is it true? Did you win? Oh, I should like to know how to do it. Just once, I would like to beat the flinders out of my odious brother."

Priscilla knew that feeling all too well. However, she shook her head in denial. "I am no teacher, I fear. Perhaps it was mere luck—or a fluke that I won."

"A thousand pounds, I heard tell."

"Hardly," Priscilla replied with vexation. She had never before been the target of gossip and speculation. If this was the sort of thing Lord Latimer had endured, she could well understand his feelings on the matter. "It was a far more modest sum. And I have no intention of gaming again, you may be certain."

The second miss was clearly disappointed that the

amount had been exaggerated. "Who taught you how to play?"

Miss Staples edged closer so not to miss a word.

"I am not at liberty to say without his permission. But he did say it requires concentration, an ability with numbers, and to recall the rules of the game. Study the rules if you can. Also, I was advised never to play for money unless I could afford to lose the amount wagered."

Miss Staples looked utterly crestfallen. The other young woman sniffed and left the room at once.

"And whatever you do, do not go to the cent-per-centers. I have been told that once they have you in their clutches, you will have a nearly impossible time to get out."

Miss Staples blanched, her hand creeping up to a very bare neck. "Oh, dear."

"Quite so."

"I am undone!"

"I suggest you confess all and hope for understanding." She gave the girl a look of sympathy.

The maid finished the repair to the hem. Priscilla took a few coins from her reticule to give her, then left the room immediately.

She felt as though all eyes were fixed on her as she made her way back to her aunt.

"Oh, my dear, you look positively hunted."

Priscilla turned to Lord Latimer. "I believe I know a little of what you complained before sir. I was accosted by two young women demanding to know how to play piquet and win." To Lord George she added, "You could have a lucrative profession going—teaching young women how to properly play cards. I dared not tell them who taught me." She gasped and touched her hand to her lips. "I do hope they don't think it is Lord Latimer."

"That would be an ironic touch, wouldn't it?" he said. He took her hand to place on his arm. "Let us take a stroll. Perhaps we may find a soothing drink or a bit of food." With a bow to the others, he led Priscilla away.

"Thank you. I did not wish to discuss the card game or the teaching or anything else that has occurred this evening anymore. I can quite see how you detest gossip and scandal, my lord."

"You may as well call me Felix."

"Oh, I could not do that. It would scarcely be proper, and you did say you wanted a proper young lady."

Felix looked down at her eyes. They were full of mischief, brimming with delight. His heart acted strangely when he was close to her. Couldn't explain it in the least, but there it was. He had no idea what caused it, but since there seemed no harm in it, he would attempt to forget about it. If he could.

They found the room where the refreshments were set out. Perfectly delicious bites of superb foods were arranged in tempting variety. "I long to taste a bit of everything. One does not find such things while living in the rectory."

After seating Priscilla at a small table the right size for two, he went to heap two plates, nodding to the footman when he offered to pour wine. That was set before them when Felix returned.

She eyed the foods with dainty hunger. "I know a lady is not supposed to admit she is starved. I am. Does that make me less ladylike?"

"Hardly. You are honest in your desires." Felix glanced at her to find her staring at him rather than popping a tidbit into that luscious mouth. He swallowed with care, his gaze centered on her mouth, now slightly open awaiting a bite of fruit. He wondered what she would taste like—pineapple, perhaps? Or peach? Or would there be a hint of wine?

She blinked, then settled her gaze on the plate full of delicious foods. She pierced a morsel of cheese with her fork, then slipped it into her mouth.

Felix chewed thoughtfully. Her desires—what might they be? All at once he found he very much wanted to know. And although they were engaged, he supposed he had no right to ask or find out for himself. Drat.

Chapter Nine

The next morning Priscilla woke early. After a peek out of the window to check the sky, she hastily dressed in a deep-blue merino cloth riding habit trimmed with unusual embroidery. It promised to be a fine day eventually once the mist wore off. She perched her small round hat of fine beaver on her blond curls, checked its set in the looking glass before gathering her Limerick gloves and crop. It was a simple matter to slip quietly from her room. A misty blue sky made her hopeful that the morning would improve.

She paused in the entry to request her horse be brought around from the rental stables.

Her blue kid half boots made no sound as she made her way to the breakfast room. Aunt Mercy was not to be seen. However, that dear lady had discovered that Felix's aunt Beatrice rode in the park at a very early hour—hence Priscilla's determination she would see her there.

Thinking it best to have a substantial breakfast rather than toast and chocolate, she consumed an ample meal. While nibbling on a scone, she wondered how Lady Beatrice would receive her—if Priscilla found her. Would she turn up her nose at being accosted by stranger? Oh, Priscilla devoutly hoped not. She swallowed a sip of tea, then took a resolute breath as she rose from the table.

It was important to meet another of Felix's relatives. She was sure he was having some second thoughts about his dear uncle George. Likely Felix's dislike of them had begun in his boyhood. It seemed to her that as an adult he hadn't seen enough of them to alter his opinion from blameless to scandalous. She wished she knew more, but perhaps that would be revealed all in good time.

She drew on her gloves and picked up the crop. The horse rented from the nearby stable waited at the bottom of the steps when Simpkins opened the front door for her.

As late as it had been when Lord Latimer had brought her home, she was wide-awake, most likely with the excited thought of actually making the acquaintance of Lady Beatrice. If, that is, Lady Beatrice would allow an unknown young woman to be so bold. But then, it seemed to Priscilla that any woman who had the daring to elope with her brother's tutor might be approachable.

Mist drifted across the park in the early morning light. Golden shafts of sunlight pierced the haze that now revealed, now concealed the landscape. Ghostly trees loomed up like ragged giant mushrooms on tall rough stems. It was not really chilly, but she shivered just the same—nerves, most likely.

She searched the path ahead. The parkland lay to one side, with Rotten Row behind her. Where was Lady Beatrice? As time passed, Priscilla began to think her quest hopeless. She walked her horse along the Row, alert for the sight of another rider. There was not a soul to be seen through the mists. She was about to turn back, deciding she would have to try on the morrow, when a distant movement gave her pause.

Off to one side she caught sight of a woman riding alone, just as Priscilla did. It was not the done thing, to slip out without a groom. But with no one to see, what difference did it make? Who was to know?

Priscilla slowed her horse, watching the superb rider canter across the parkland. What marvelous form. She appeared to be one with her horse. Priscilla doubted she would ever achieve that grace, particularly on a horse she rented from the nearby stable.

When she reached Rotten Row, the woman paused, seeming to stare toward Priscilla.

It gave her hope, and she urged her horse forward. Within a few minutes she had come even with the stranger.

"Good morning." The stranger's assessment of Priscilla was cool, not especially promising. "I see there is another who prefers the peace of the dawn to the crush of afternoon." The cultured tones snapped out with precision. Here was a woman who could never be languid, never be impassive. She fairly bristled with liveliness, even sitting still on her horse. She reminded Priscilla of a general who had once visited her father.

Her habit was sharp black, accented by a bishop's blue scarf at her neck and a white pie frill that cascaded over that. A hat of well-brushed black beaver sat precisely on her head. Even her black gloves were perfect and held the reins with equally perfect control. However, upon additional inspection, her face had a kindly look. It was her eyes, mostly. They were an unusual green color with hints of brown, and at the moment they glowed softly, offering Priscilla encouragement.

"Good morning to you, ma'am. Indeed, it is so peaceful you might think you are in the country." Priscilla hesitated a moment, then plunged into speech. "Are you by any chance Lady Beatrice Aston?"

The lady tilted her head to one side, gave Priscilla a half smile, and nodded. "I am. You have the advantage over me. May I know who you are?" She urged her mount, a superb chestnut, to move forward, and Priscilla did the same to her rented horse, an awkward bay.

"Of course." Priscilla felt the heat from her blush rise to her cheeks. "I am Priscilla Herbert, niece of Miss Mercy Herbert and engaged to your nephew, Lord Latimer."

"I saw that Felix was engaged at long last. Amazing. I am doubly pleased to meet you, my dear. What is it you want, for I assume you didn't plan this meeting without a reason." She shot a hasty glance at Priscilla before returning her attention to her horse and the path ahead.

Taken aback at her perceptiveness, not to mention the plain speaking, Priscilla drew in a breath before offering her explanation. "You see, it is like this . . ."

When she had concluded her tale, clarifying her thoughts on the importance for Felix to reexamine his feelings toward his relatives, she came to an abrupt halt, wondering if his aunt would think her mad.

Lady Beatrice smiled, a rather wry twist of her mouth. "You think to change his judgment after all these years? I doubt it can be done."

"I can but try, ma'am. I cannot imagine anything so frightful as being separated from your family."

"A noble endeavor, indeed. *You* obviously have a close family. Come, ride with me; we will discuss what is to be done."

Priscilla gave her nod of agreement. The two set off on Rotten Row at a matched pace, although Priscilla was quite sure that Lady Beatrice held her chestnut back in deference to the slower gait of the bay. Of course, Priscilla had never been accounted an accomplished horsewoman. The rectory ran to her father's horse and another that was used for the carriage as well as the rectory gig. She felt she acquitted herself as well as might be expected under the circumstances.

At the far end of the Row, they wheeled to return to where they had met. Here, Lady Beatrice reined in.

"Call on me later this morning—say one of the clock. Bring your aunt with you. I've not seen Mercy Herbert in ages." She held herself perfectly erect, her face almost regal in its composure. She looked every inch a marquess's daughter.

Priscilla thanked her even as she smiled at one of the clock being considered morning. At home, in spite of the fashionable attempts made by a few, morning ended at noon. In London, it seemed as though morning could last as late as three of the clock, Venetian breakfasts often taking place at that time. At home, her father liked to eat his dinner at four, having a late supper around nine in the evening. London life was at times very confusing.

"I look forward to our meeting. I am to go with Lord Latimer to view Miss Linwood's exhibit this afternoon. I believe he said three of the clock."

"We will have things arranged long before then, my dear." She grinned, an endearing expression on her aristocratic face. "My poor nephew—he will not know what has hit him."

Priscilla wasn't certain if she wanted that reaction, but she thought he needed to be converted from his present opinion of his family. Life was too short to nurture enmity.

Once at her aunt's house, she handed the reins to the footman who had come out to attend her.

Inside, she paused in the entry. "Simpkins, is my aunt up and about?"

"She is in the breakfast room, miss."

Priscilla nodded, and then hurried to her room to change from her riding habit to a proper morning dress of white muslin trimmed in blue riband. Lily brushed her hair before weaving a matching riband through her curls.

Not bothering to check her appearance, Priscilla eagerly raced down the stairs and around to the breakfast room, where she found her aunt absorbed in the morning paper. She looked up at Priscilla's precipitate entry.

Priscilla halted, then with more dignity helped herself to a scone and tea before taking a place at the table.

"I suppose your enthusiastic entrance heralds news of some import." Her aunt's voice was dry as she surveyed her niece.

"Good morning, Aunt Mercy. I must tell you at once. I met Lady Beatrice in the park!"

"We had decided that would be the best place to encounter her. What did you learn? Did she speak with you? She has remained somewhat remote since her marriage, although by all reports she seems content enough."

"We had a lovely ride together and she is the dearest person, quite the proper lady I would expect of one in her position." Priscilla sipped her tea, appreciating its restoring warmth.

"What did she think of your proposal regarding Lord Latimer?" Aunt Mercy folded the newspaper and set it aside to devote her full attention to her niece.

"She was dubious at first, then came around to my point of view. She also agrees that Lord Latimer must have come to regard his relatives as scandalous fairly early in life—perhaps while away at school." At her aunt's quizzical expression, Priscilla added, "Well, he has scarce seen enough of them while an adult."

"That might be true, but he has ears to hear the prattle that comes from every quarter. London is a hotbed of gossip, my dear."

Priscilla mulled that over before shaking her head. "No, I am not convinced that gossip would affect him to that degree. Perhaps he suffered at the hands of mean, taunting schoolboys? Boys can be utter fiends at times. Although my brother Adam is quite nice now, he was a tease as a lad. I have seen far worse in the lads my father tutors in Latin." She frowned. "I think it must be hard to raise a boy to be an intelligent, kind adult."

"I suspect it is equally difficult to raise a girl to be the same. You have been fortunate in your family, my dear. Not all are so happy."

Priscilla glanced at the clock on the fireplace mantel. "Lady Beatrice suggested we call on her at one of the clock. Would that be agreeable with you? She said she looked forward to seeing you again."

"We do not move in the same circles, so it has been a time since we last spoke. Yes, I'll go with you my dear. For one thing, I'd not miss out on your plotting for the world!"

Later that morning the two ladies left the Herbert house in perfect accord, dressed appropriately for a call on the daughter and sister of the Marquess of Silverstone. Lady Beatrice might not move among Society, but she was sure to be aware of her due.

They were ushered into an agreeable town house in the better part of London by a butler who appeared conscious of his position.

Lady Beatrice rose from a gold damask sofa to greet them. A handsome gray-haired gentleman stood by the fireplace, a half smile lingering on his face.

Once introductions had taken place, Lady Beatrice immediately plunged into the discussion of what, where, and how they were to arrange the meeting between her, her husband, Guy, and Felix.

It was Mercy Herbert who suggested a family dinner. After that it was merely a matter of time and place. The menu was left to Miss Herbert.

* * *

Garbed in her pale amaranth round gown and the pelisse of blue wool with the black frog closures, Priscilla met Lord Latimer when he arrived to claim her company. When she had worn it before, she thought he had given her an appreciative look. He did so again.

"I like that bonnet," he gestured to the villager hat she wore.

Her heart gave a flutter at his intent gaze. This was the man she had promised to marry. Could she go through with it? She thought it probable. She had hopes. Her parents approved. Mama had written a warm letter expressing her wishes for her daughter's future.

The relationship with his uncle seemed promising. It would be interesting to learn what it was that prompted his attitude to the family. Oh, she knew about the gambling and the dash to Scotland. She rather liked the quiet Guy Aston. She could understand why Lady Beatrice found him appealing. The nicest thing was that they seemed truly enamored of one another. The little touches, the intimate smile spoke volumes to one who looked for just such gestures.

Priscilla thought Felix's manner now promised a pleasant outing. Clearly he was willing to overlook the gaming incident at Lady Smythe's ball. She hoped so. At least he was smiling at her. That boded well for the day.

"Shall we depart?" He offered his arm after transferring his cane to the other hand.

She wondered at his use of the cane. He seemed not to require it, witness his smooth and effortless waltz of last evening. It must be simply an accessory, like a quizzing glass—which he did not affect. She was glad of that. How dreadful to be peered at through one of those little magnifying lenses as though one were an insect.

His carriage awaited them before the town house. The coachman must have been given their destination as they simply entered the carriage and were off.

"You feel well after the excitement of the Smythe ball?" He sat opposite her. Any change of expression or pinkening of her cheeks would be immediately noticed.

Striving to retain her poise, Priscilla nodded. "I slept well. A ride in the park this morning brushed away any megrims that might have lingered."

"I did not know you had a horse stabled in Town."

"I do not. Aunt arranged for one to be rented for my use." She smiled slightly at the recollection of that horse. The bay might have had shortcomings, but it accomplished what she desired.

"That will never do for the future bride of Earl Latimer. Cancel the arrangement. I shall have a horse from my mews sent over when you wish to ride." He looked down the aristocratic nose strongly reminiscent of his aunt's.

"Well"—she thought a moment—"it might not be convenient for either party."

"I will be glad to accompany you on your park rides, my dear."

Priscilla merely smiled, murmuring her thanks. What a good thing she had previously met his aunt in the park. "When the weather is fine, it would be agreeable to practice my riding. I am far from an accomplished rider, my lord. However, I believe I should like to improve that skill."

"Society considers it a necessary grace for those of the upper strata, of which you will be one."

The words seemed pompous to Priscilla. She might love him, but there were times she could box his ears.

Fortunately she was spared any reply, the carriage having stopped before the entrance to Miss Linwood's Gallery on Leicester Square.

Felix took Priscilla's hand in his, enjoying the delicate clasp so trustingly reposing in his. He would make a point to find her a proper horse suitable for a novice, as she indicated she was. It would be a pleasure to accompany her. He intended keeping an eye on his Priscilla.

He ushered her into the gallery, handing her a catalog so she might refer to it as they wandered along.

They entered the principal room. This gallery, the walls of which were hung with scarlet cloth, was of excellent proportions. Priscilla paused, gazing about her with curious eyes. She turned to him. He thought her blue eyes the loveliest he had ever seen—and he had seen a great number of fine blue eyes. They were clear, perfectly formed, and of sweet expression.

"Impressive, is it not?" She cast her gaze about her

as though not wishing to miss a thing, then nodded to the first of the embroideries.

At her gesture he walked with her along the collection, heeding the watchful eye of the guard. "He stands guard to make certain no one touches the pictures. They are so amazing it is difficult to believe they are wool embroideries, not paintings."

"Indeed," she murmured, seeming to walk close to him without the objectionable clinging he disliked. He enjoyed her being near him. If she would forget what she had learned about playing cards, all would be perfect.

There were sofas and settees covered with the same red fabric as the walls stationed in the window recesses and before the tall pier looking glasses. If one wished, one could sit to study a picture at length. At the end of the room was a splendid seat and canopy covered in red satin and silver.

"What an amazing place this is," Priscilla whispered.

He liked having her draw close to his side so she might whisper in his ear. He could smell the fragrance of her cologne—the spicy scent of carnation. It suited her, for she certainly possessed piquancy. Yet her voice was always gentle, soft and low, nicely refined. He could not recall her once speaking in that high, fluting voice so many ladies had that grated on the ear.

"Come this way. I believe you will find it of interest." He led her through the door near the canopy into a long, dimly lit passage. At the end of this they found what appeared to be a prison cell. Pictured in it was the beautiful Lady Jane Gray, visited by the abbot and keeper of the tower presumably the night before her execution.

Priscilla drew back against him much to his delight. It was a simple matter to place an arm around her to offer comfort.

"Oh, how very sad. The poor woman, knowing that this was her last night upon this earth."

When she appeared to have her fill of Lady Jane he suggested, "Come, perhaps the next representation will be happier."

A little farther on was a cottage. Peering into the interior, one saw an exquisite copy of Gainsborough's cottage children, with chimney and cottage furniture complete.

"I must admit, this is more pleasant, although I shall carry the image of the tragic Lady Jane far longer." Priscilla turned her face up to his, her eyes shining.

Felix heroically refrained from kissing her. There was not a soul around, but that didn't mean one might not come trundling around the corner at any moment. He would brook no more scandal. Were he found kissing a beautiful young woman—never mind they were engaged—the word would whip around the London drawing rooms as fast as it could fly.

Beyond the cottage children they found a picture of a woodsman, also by Gainsborough and given the same arrangement.

"I have never see the original, but this is very fine." Priscilla met his gaze briefly before returning her attention to the embroidery.

Felix thanked his lucky stars that he had offered to take her here. He could escort her around the gallery in surprising intimacy, his arm possessively about her slim form, enjoying her scent and her confidence. It was an oddly heady experience. He was very glad he had asked her to marry him. She seemed the perfect bride.

The lions pictured in the last niche were exceedingly realistic. He could feel her shiver of apprehension at the depiction of wild, raw power. The lioness surveyed them with a warning look that seemed to say, "Beware."

"Here, this way is the main gallery. I think you will like the next picture." Felix guided her through the short hall into the main room, thence to a side room where a copy of a Carlo Dolci painting hung in great splendor.

"This is extremely good. How kind Christ looks as he blesses the wine and bread. My father would like this very much." Priscilla leaned against him in a confiding manner. "I do think it might be a trifle Catholic, however."

"Well, he is Italian, after all."

There still existed a friction between Catholics and the Church of England. No one hazarded a guess when this might be erased, in spite of the attempts to pass the Catholic Emancipation Bill in the Parliament. Most English were distrustful of the Catholics, fearing an attempt to return England to Catholic rule. After years of freedom from the dominion of the pope, it was a thought to be rejected.

They slowly strolled from the Dolci copy to the front of the building where the carriage awaited them.

"You certainly guessed how long it would take us to go through the gallery." She appeared to admire his carriage, and, in truth, it was one of the better ones he had seen.

"I have viewed it before, so I had some idea." He handed her up into the landau, spoke to the coachman, then joined Priscilla in the comfort of the carriage. "I told John Coachman to take us to Gunter's Tea Room, if that is agreeable with you. I seem to recall you rather enjoyed our previous visit there."

Priscilla grinned, an unrepentant grin of impish delight. "That would be nice." She really ought to try avoiding that word. She heard it so often from her aunt it was too easy to have it slip into her sentences.

The day had become so fine they were able to relax beneath the trees in Berkeley Square while a waiter dashed back and forth with their ices. Although he knew it was the custom for gentlemen to leave the carriage to lean against the railings around the square, Felix declined to do so. He far preferred to enjoy the sight of Priscilla savoring her ice.

"This is delicious, quite the nicest way to end an afternoon, my lord."

"Felix," he prompted, liking the way she said his name.

She blushed delightfully. "Felix," she echoed in a soft voice.

Priscilla enjoyed the last sip of her orange ice, placing the dish on the tray brought by the waiter. She wished Felix wouldn't put her to the blush as he did. For all she knew someone could eavesdrop, hear her familiar use of his name. It was not the done thing.

"Does your aunt have plans for the evening? If not, I thought perhaps a concert of ancient music might be to your fancy."

"I did not realize you enjoyed music so much. I do

not know if she planned anything, which probably means she has none. I would like it above all things, my lord, er, Felix," she hastily appended to her acceptance. "Do you know my mother still calls Father 'Mr. Herbert' when there are others around. I find such familiarity difficult."

Felix nodded. "Just so. It would never do for merely anyone, as you well know. But I believe it permissible for us."

Priscilla trembled with the warm look he gave her. Oh, how lovely it would be were they to truly be in love. He was reserved in many respects. She supposed it was caused by his aversion to scandal. For a few moments while they were at the Linwood Gallery, she had thought he meant to kiss her. Foolish thought. He would never do anything so improper! She had confessed she liked his kiss, a naughty admission on her part. Of course she dare not ask for another, but it was a lovely notion.

He behaved with propriety, bringing her to her aunt's house in fine style. He joined Priscilla when she entered, going up to greet Aunt Mercy with his usual good manners.

"Dear Aunt, Felix has suggested we might wish to attend a concert of ancient music this evening."

"You have tickets? Sometimes they are difficult to obtain." Miss Herbert greeted him with an alert expression.

"I have no difficulty, ma'am."

Aunt Mercy nodded decisively. "I should enjoy that very much. They are so close by, just along the Square, that we may walk over there. It is so convenient to have music concerts near us."

He quietly agreed.

"Come, stay for dinner with us. It is foolish for you to go home, then return so short a distance."

"I would be pleased, ma'am."

The time had never flown so fast. They discussed what had been on view at Miss Linwood's Gallery and the delight of fine weather, so to enjoy an ice in Berkeley Square.

Priscilla was content to remain in her amaranth gown, trusting it was not important for her to change merely for the concert. Her aunt disagreed.

"I shall visit with Felix while you change, my dear. It would never do to appear in the concert hall wearing a day dress!"

So not too very long later, Priscilla returned to the drawing room to find her aunt and Felix in a congenial discussion of Bach.

"It is to be a Bach program this evening. I trust it meets with your approval?" Felix smiled at her in a way that made her heart speed up. How strange it was that he had this power over her. No other man had made her heart go wild, her pulse race, her very being ache to be in his arms. She must be a rather wicked girl, to know such outrageous emotions. It was a good thing he couldn't read her mind. The very idea made her cheeks warm.

Felix escorted Priscilla and her aunt down to the dining room on the ground floor. While her aunt's hand rested politely on his arm, Priscilla's more delicate hand scarcely touched him, and he would swear she trembled.

He glanced down at her with an inward smile. Such response boded well for their future if she was so aware of him.

Following an excellent meal, the three set off for the Hanover Rooms, where the *Concert of Antique Music* was held. This Wednesday the director in charge of the evening's selections had chosen his favorite Bach pieces, something for which Felix was most grateful. He didn't think he could have tolerated a Handel oratorio after such a pleasant day with Priscilla. The oratorios were reserved for Lent, thank goodness. Many a gentleman had enjoyed a good snooze at them.

After greeting the peer who directed the program selections, they immediately settled on chairs, prepared to enjoy the evening.

Priscilla studied Felix's profile while the rich tones of the first Bach piece enveloped her. He had folded his arms across his chest, vaguely smiling, as though the music pleased him. It pleased her, and what's more, she nurtured hope that all would go well. She had yet to inform him of the dinner that had been planned.

Chapter Ten

Priscilla woke early the next morning. The *Concert of Ancient Music* had not gone on to the wee hours, so they were all able to retire at a respectable hour. She had slept well, not permitting her qualms to keep her awake.

One glance out of her window revealed that it was going to be a pleasant day. When Lily came in with early morning hot chocolate and rolls, she agreed to help Priscilla into her habit at once. Hastily downing her chocolate and nibbling at a roll when she could, she slipped into the blue habit.

"My half boots, please, Lily." Priscilla put on the blue kid half boots, then whisked her beaver hat from the dresser to plop on her head, not bothering to check her appearance. She was ready to hurry off to her morning ride.

Her gloves and crop in hand, she lightly ran down the stairs. Lily had alerted Simpkins that her mistress intended to ride out once again. He opened the front door with a stately flourish.

Priscilla eyed the bay standing at the bottom of the front steps with misgivings. However, since it was too soon for Felix to send a horse for her to ride, she was limited to the bay. She offered the hack a lump of sugar, then mounted with the footman's assistance.

Again, she ignored the dictum that a single lady riding alone ought to have a groom in attendance. She wanted no one to report her meeting with Lady Beatrice if such occurred.

The day might look fine, but the temperature was chilly. Priscilla shivered, then urged the horse into a fast walk. Once in the park she broke into a canter.

The morning mists had risen. The air was crisp and clear, but the sun had little warmth to it. Priscilla feared she might be too late to meet Lady Beatrice. Her worries were for naught, for well along Rotten Row she again saw the elegant figure of the older lady heading her direction.

"Miss Herbert, well met," Lady Beatrice cried in her well-bred tones.

"Lady Beatrice, I hoped to see you again today."

"Did you enjoy your outing to Miss Linwood's Gallery yesterday?" Lady Beatrice fell in beside Priscilla, and they amiably walked their mounts side by side along the Row.

"Indeed, it is an amazing collection. After we viewed it, we went over to Gunter's for an ice. The temperature was far more pleasing yesterday!"

"How was Felix?" Lady Beatrice tilted her head in inquiry, her unusual eyes not missing the flush Priscilla could feel on her cheeks.

"He was in fine fettle. My aunt invited him to remain for dinner, after which we attended a concert at Hanover Hall. The *Concert of Ancient Music* was devoted last evening to Bach rather than Handel as usual. Felix said that the director for the evening may be fined for having music too modern." She flashed a grin at her new friend.

"Oh, I wish I had known. I do enjoy Bach."

"As do I. I believe it is somewhat restrictive for the program to be confined to music composed prior to twenty years past." She paused before continuing in a different vein; she gestured to the horse she rode. "Felix insists he will provide me with a mount, but I have no idea when."

"The hack you are on would not take any prize, but it is not a bad horse for all that. Tell me, have you given more thought as to what evening we should plan for this dinner?"

"What about three days hence? I will ask your nephew about his plans when I see him later today. He is to escort me to the British Museum this afternoon."

"Excellent. As soon as you know, send a message to me. Shall I have his cousin Alfred come as well?" This suggestion was made in a lower, hesitant voice, quite as though Lady Beatrice expected Priscilla to reject the idea at once.

She suspected Felix nurtured no more love for his cousin than for the rest of his scandalous family, but still there ought to be harmony established. "I imagine that might be acceptable."

Lady Beatrice chuckled, sounding pleased. "Alfred is an absurd lad, addicted to betting on horse races and wearing the most outrageous garb he can find. I fancy a large part of it is trying to best his cousin. Felix is so top of the trees that Alfred thinks he can't possibly compete with him—hence his inclination to go the opposite direction. Or at the very least appear as different from Felix as night is from day. I imagine that one day he will come to realize it is not necessary to compete with his cousin. Certainly nothing *I* say has any effect on him."

"I see," Priscilla responded politely, not sure she did. Her brother always dressed with restraint.

They proceeded the same as the day before, cantering to the far end of Rotten Row, wheeling about to return to where Lady Beatrice parted ways with Priscilla.

"Mind, do not forget to send the note."

Priscilla nodded, gave a wave of her crop, then cantered as far as the Stanhope Gate. From here she made her sedate way to her aunt's town house. It was so early that as yet there were few people out and about in the more genteel area of Mayfair.

The rest of the morning was spent conferring on a menu for the planned dinner. By the time Felix was due to arrive, all had been settled. All, that is, but inviting the one for whom it was being given!

Felix nodded to Simpkins upon entering Miss Herbert's town house at half past one o'clock. The museum ceased to admit viewers after two, so it was necessary to be prompt. Retaining his hat and gloves, he followed the butler up the stairs to where he found Priscilla awaiting him. How gratifying it was to have a future wife who did not believe in keeping him dawdling while she did whatever it was women did while they kept their hopeful beau in the drawing room. She had excellent manners.

"Good afternoon, my lord," Priscilla said, offering a curtsy that was not only graceful but impressive as well. There was something about the girl that appealed to his eye, the fluidity of her movement, the delectable line of her figure. She held her head with pride, walked with an enchanting charm, and her voice was alluring—low and soft, inviting, and yet possessing a vibrancy that caught the ear pleasantly. She entranced him without so much as trying.

"Hello, my Priscilla." He was taken aback for a moment. Where had that come from? Of course she was "his," but it was an intimate greeting for unmarried people.

She blinked, but made no reply.

Miss Herbert entered the room in a flurry. "I believe you have a nice day for the museum. It has become rather nasty out, the wind having risen and all."

"Yes, it could scarce be better for our purpose." He turned to Priscilla. "Could we depart? I have the carriage waiting for us, and time is of the essence."

"And we do not wish to keep the horses standing. Of course." She gave her aunt a kiss on her cheek, tugged on her gloves as they walked down the stairs, and gave that stiff butler a fine smile as they left the house. She probably had all the servants in the house at her bidding if she smiled at them in such a fashion. Felix was thankful that his butler and footmen were all somewhat older. It would never do to have a young footman mooning over his mistress. It was nice to dispense with the maid for once.

He assisted her into the landau, the top of which had been raised in view of the mounting wind. Once the door had been snapped shut, he rapped on the ceiling and they set off.

"I hope you enjoyed the music last evening?"

Her smile was radiant, sending a warmth shooting through him. "Indeed. I do enjoy Bach. Although—it is a pity their list of composers is so limited. I would like to hear some of the newer works by Beethoven."

"For that, we shall attend a concert by the Philharmonic Society at the Argyll Rooms. It is a pleasant way to spend an evening by all accounts."

She nodded, but appeared to sink into contemplation. He studied her a few moments before inquiring, "Something is on your mind?"

"Er, no, that is, yes. Would you come to dinner two nights hence?" She bestowed a hesitant regard on him.

As an invitation it was rather abrupt, but perhaps she was more accustomed to writing them out. He raised a brow. "I believe that would be agreeable. A special day? A birthday or something of that sort?"

"No, merely the pleasure of your company, my lord." She smiled at him again, looking even more winsome if such a thing was possible.

"We do seem to get along well, do we not?" Felix crossed his arms before him. It was either that or move to the other side and take the delectable Priscilla in his arms. Egad, but she was a seductive armful in her prim pelisse, one he'd not seen before. Apple-green wool hugged her fetching figure with a ruff of fine lace cascading down around the neck. Apples and cream, luscious, delectable, good enough to eat bite by slow bite.

"I have truly looked forward to the British Museum. My brother came up from Oxford to see it and told me that under no circumstances should I miss it."

"I gather he is of a scholarly bent?"

"He is. Does that mean that most of the museum is only of interest to scholars?" She frowned, chewing at her lower lip probably in vexation.

"We shall see. There is an assorted collection of books, but there are many other items of interest." How he wanted to soothe that lower lip, kiss away her frown.

She turned her head to look out of the window at the passing scene.

Felix watched her, wondering how soon he could persuade her to marry. St. George's just down the street off Hanover Square was convenient. He might just purchase a special license. Her father had told him her middle name, and he had his written consent to the marriage. A special license was usable for three full months. If he couldn't accomplish what he wished in that time, he wasn't as persuasive as he thought. However, his pursuit went well.

Indeed, it would be a good step forward on his path of redeeming his family name. She seemed the answer to his quest, his desire. How could he possibly find a woman more suitable and at the same time so desirable? He had not thought to find respectability so attractive.

At this point they had arrived in Great Russell Street, halting before a large and impressive house. Felix promptly got out, then handed Priscilla from the carriage. He placed her hand on his arm, thus keeping her close.

Priscilla studied the archway through which they were to enter the building. Felix walked near her, a surprisingly comforting thing. "It certainly is imposing."

"I believe it is said to be in the French style, something like the Tuilleries. We won't bother with the first floor, it is all books. Rather, we will go up to the upper floor."

With her at his side, they slowly ascended the grand staircase.

"This is more like a public building. I cannot imagine it as a private residence. How imposing this staircase is, and what a lofty ceiling!"

He nodded agreement, but made no comment on her remark. Then he guided her into the first of the display rooms.

Priscilla found the case full of miniatures displayed entrancing. She went on to study the cases with interesting china, but offered no observation on them.

The collection brought back by Captain Cook, she thought very curious, particularly the examples of clothing. "I'd not want to wear anything so barbaric." She gestured to the woman's garment that would reveal far more than proper. The collection of idols she found quite as revolting as her brother Adam had cautioned.

Felix whisked her through the rooms containing various manuscripts, for which she was thankful, not being of that bent. Although she enjoyed seeing the Magna Carta from the Cottonian collection.

In the room holding the collection of minerals, she found the domed ceiling of greater interest. It was covered with a gorgeous painting depicting the birth of Minerva. She turned to Felix to exclaim over it and held her breath at the expression on his face.

"You are enjoying this?" He gazed at her with an intensity she could only wonder at.

Could she capture his appearance, particularly the warmth in his eyes, she would have that painting placed so that she might see it upon first arising and before she went to sleep. She drew closer to him, searching his face, his eyes, wishing she knew his thoughts. His expression was much like the time he had kissed her. She would welcome another kiss, but not, she thought, in the middle of the British Museum!

They continued through the various rooms, viewing the pictures and stuffed birds. When they reached the rooms devoted to the Greek and Roman antiquities, Priscilla gave Felix a broad smile. "I find these of far greater interest than the South Sea Island things, or the minerals and assorted rocks, much less the eggs and birds someone gathered. There is something sad about stuffed birds."

"You would like to visit Greece and Italy?"

"Indeed, I would. To see such beauty *not* in the confines of a museum, but all around you in the natural setting would be of all things to be desired. Can you not imagine the abode where these beautiful vases and urns were found? Think of olive trees rustling in the sea-scented breeze and the hot Italian sun beating down its warmth from an intense blue sky to bless the marble with a particular glow."

"We shall go there."

Priscilla found it impossible to speak for a few moments. She stared at him, utterly overwhelmed with the enormity of his promise. "Thank you." She wanted to kiss him, but there were people about them intent upon the various curiosities.

"I suppose you will wish to see Egypt as well," he commented as they viewed the mummy donated by the king.

She shook her head. "I am not drawn there as I am to Greece and Italy. Perhaps it is the thought of so much sand and heat?"

"Possibly. We shall not venture there if it is not to your liking."

"I had not thought of traveling. Do you enjoy seeing new sights and places?"

"I believe I would with you at my side."

He seemed about to say more, then several others joined them and the moment was lost.

They left the building promptly at four as required. Priscilla chatted amiably about the things they had viewed. For the most part Felix remained silent. And she wondered why.

Felix left his bride-to-be to head for Tattersall's. He had promised Priscilla a horse, and nothing in his own mews was appropriate for her.

Chauncy hailed him as he neared Hyde Park Corner and Tattersall's, the site of the well-known horse auctions.

"What ho?" Chauncy inquired as he joined Felix in his carriage.

"I pledged Priscilla to find her a horse for her rides in the park. I don't have anything suitable, goodness knows."

"Heard that Lombard is selling his grays. And Paul Northcomb has been forced to part with his chestnut."

"Is that so? Northcomb's chestnut?" Felix leaned back against the squabs, staring out and seeing Priscilla's face as she had gazed up at him. It had been a moment to prize.

"Imagine so," Chauncy replied.

They drove in silence a minute or so before Chauncy casually asked, "How does your pursuit of the fair Priscilla go?"

"Well. She wears my ring, and other than that one incident of piquet at Lady Smythe's ball, she has been the epitome of propriety." Felix rubbed his chin in thought. She had been so close to him this morning that he could almost hear her thinking. And he would bet anything he owned that she had wanted his kiss as much as he had desired hers. And wouldn't that have been proper in the middle of the British Museum!

"I saw her this morning, returning from the park on that bay she has rented. She looks to be a fair equestrian. Good posture and all that. The bay is typical of what you expect from a rental stable, but she controlled it well."

Felix mulled over that bit of news in silence. Priscilla had said nothing regarding any early morning ride in the park. Of course it might be that she did not wish to remind him of his promise to obtain a horse for her use. She was a thoughtful girl, likely not wanting to embarrass her betrothed. Another example of good manners.

After giving his coachman instructions to head for his mews, Felix joined his friend. They strolled into the famed horse establishment, going at once to the arena where the horses for sale were brought out for showing. Not being the day for an auction, they continued on to the loose boxes, where they might view the offerings.

"That chestnut of Northcomb's seems a fair one. I believe I'll make a bid on it tomorrow morning."

Chauncy pointed out several other possibilities, all of which had to be examined before the pair of them left the establishment in favor of looking in at White's. Here they settled for a glass of wine, listening to the gossip that floated about them like petals in the sea.

"Saw your cousin Alfred earlier."

Felix raised his brows but made no reply. What he might like to say was better left unsaid. He might detest the fellow, but he was still a relation.

The following morning he successfully bid on the Northcomb chestnut, sending it off to his mews with his groom.

The following days after the outing to the British Museum, Priscilla and Aunt Mercy spent preparing for the dinner. It wasn't that her aunt or she had much to do, it was more of a mental exercise.

The invitation, written precisely as Aunt Mercy dictated, had been sent to Lady Beatrice and Guy Aston, and included Alfred. When Priscilla had suggested that they also invite Lord George Sutton, her aunt agreed, but appeared very thoughtful.

"You do feel this is the proper thing to do?" Priscilla asked anxiously. "I am having second thoughts, you know."

"I am as well. What if it goes amiss, that Felix misunderstands our intent?" Aunt Mercy shared a worried look with Priscilla.

"Well, short of canceling the dinner, it is too late to change our minds. I pray he will take it well, give his darling aunt a chance. She truly is a delightful person."

"By all accounts she has managed her inheritance with skill, investing it wisely. Those who knew about it were scandalized she retained control of her fortune. But she and her husband are comfortably fixed. When you saw them, you must have been aware they married for love. He is a faithful and pleasant companion—which is more than you can say for a great many gentlemen of the *ton*."

"So I understand." Priscilla considered some of the gossip she had heard and wondered how she would fare. Just because Felix was attentive now, didn't mean he would be later. There was always a new opera dancer to fascinate.

By the time the evening for her dinner arrived, Priscilla was a bundle of nerves, only diminished by knowing that her seemingly calm aunt was no less concerned.

As agreed, Lady Beatrice and Mr. Guy Aston with a curious Alfred in their wake arrived first. Lord George Sutton shortly followed them. Although Priscilla had thought to invite a young lady to partner Alfred, Aunt Mercy declared it unnecessary.

"This is a family dinner, unless you have a sister convenient for us to ask."

"No, ma'am," Priscilla replied with a rueful grin.

Priscilla clasped her hands tightly together, wondering if Felix would take one look at his supposedly scandalous relatives, turn on his heel, and leave. She truly did not know him all that well. It was strange that she could agree to marry him, yet know so little about him. She would learn, sooner or later.

When Simpkins announced Earl Latimer, Priscilla rose from where she had seated herself to wait for him. She had enjoyed a pleasant conversation with Lady Beatrice. Now every eye was focused on the doorway as Felix entered the room.

He stopped dead, his expression of greeting frozen. He might have been carved from ice.

"Felix, I have no need to introduce you to your aunt and uncle or your cousin Alfred," Mercy Herbert declared with composure. "In honor of your engagement, I thought it nice to have all your family here. Alas, your father remains in the country and could not join us."

Nice? Priscilla thought if ever a word was misused it was at this moment. *Nice* was obviously about as far from the occasion as one might get.

Excellent manners overcame any inclination to behave otherwise. Felix slowly crossed the room to accept his aunt's hand. He bowed over it just enough so as not to be insulting. "Aunt Beatrice, this is indeed a surprise." He turned to her husband, who had once been young Lord George's tutor. "Uncle Guy, I am all astonishment."

"I fancy you are," Guy Aston replied with decided reserve.

Priscilla got the immediate impression that Guy Aston would take great umbrage at any slight paid to his beloved wife. It warmed her heart to the quiet gentleman.

"Well met, cousin," Alfred uttered, uncommonly sedate in his garb for the evening.

Priscilla appreciated that it must have given him a pang to arrive for dinner wearing a plain but well-made dark blue coat over a canary-yellow waistcoat and buff breeches. True, the waistcoat was embroidered in brilliant colors with various birds, but from all she had heard, it was mild compared to some other garments he had presented to Society.

Felix took in the attire his cousin wore and nodded, a ghost of a smile briefly touching his lips. "Well-done, Alfred. I am amazed all over."

Since Felix wore a rich gray wool coat over a simple cream waistcoat of superb design and pale gray breeches, he outshone his cousin. But from all Priscilla had gathered, this was not an uncommon occurrence. She doubted that Alfred would ever acquire the ability to wear a cravat tied in the complicated, yet stunningly effective, manner his cousin managed to create.

She smoothed one trembling hand down her rose sarcenet gown, her other playing with the foaming lace at the neck of her demure bodice. She had thought to pacify Felix by wearing a modest evening dress. She doubted he had even noticed it.

For long minutes no one spoke.

Simpkins chose to enter the room at that moment with a tray bearing delicate crystal glasses and a bottle of champagne.

"A toast to your betrothal is in order, I believe." Lady Beatrice moved forward to stand before her nephew. She took a glass, allowed Felix to pour the liquid, then gestured for the others to follow suit. The bottle was emptied in no time.

It was Guy Aston who proposed the toast. "May you know the felicity I have known the many years married to your lovely aunt, the finest woman I have ever met."

"Hear! Hear!" Alfred cried with enthusiasm. Whether it was for the toast or the excellence of the champagne was not known.

Felix darted a look at Priscilla. She felt it as though it had actually pierced her.

He was furious. This was far worse than her playing piquet at Lady Smythe's ball and winning a game from Lord Cowell. Felix had not wanted to confront his Aunt Beatrice and Uncle Guy, much less see his Uncle George again. Alfred was another kettle of fish, for he was everywhere seen and impossible to avoid.

What a blessing Felix had the distinction of having not only beautiful manners, but also the grace to behave as he ought when he probably felt as though he would rather leave at once.

"Thank you, Uncle Guy."

Priscilla could see that any conversation would be heavy weather. She exchanged a glance with Aunt Mercy, who promptly gave a nod to Simpkins.

The taciturn butler cleared his throat, then announced, "Dinner is served."

Everyone placed their crystal on the nearest table, then joined their hostess in a parade down the stairs to the dining room.

Felix managed to separate Priscilla from the others by the simple means of holding her back.

Her eyes were wary, as well they should be.

"This was your idea." He wanted nothing so much as to leave at once. His manners stopped him. He would never let his family see how much he disliked them.

"I thought if we are to have a happy marriage, it would be well for you to make peace with your relatives. You see, from all I can discover, they are not so terribly scandalous. And I do enjoy them. Your Aunt Beatrice is a darling, and what she did was surely not beyond the pale. I mean, other women have eloped in the past and will undoubtedly do so in the future, things being what they are. Are they not eventually forgiven? And there have been other men who have gambled. Your uncle George only plays for pleasure now. Surely that is not so bad?"

"Perhaps." It was as much as he was prepared to admit at the moment. "Uncle George does indeed seem a good sort."

She reached out to place a tentative hand on his arm. "Try—that is all I ask, dear Felix." She astounded him by rising on her tiptoes to place a butterfly kiss on his cheek.

He was at a loss following such a surprising act on her part. "Heaping coals of fire?"

"Never, you are not my enemy. Come, to use one of Aunt Mercy's favorite words. They will wonder what has happened to us." She took his hand to lead him down the stairs and into the dining room.

Feeling like a fish out of water, he joined his relatives at the table. The evening would be a trial, but he could see that Priscilla had taken a strange liking to these people. He supposed the least he could do was be civil. He admitted he scarcely knew them.

Yet he remembered the taunting over their various doings that he had endured while at Eton and Oxford. He had hated it then, and that feeling had persisted. Had it merely become a habit? He wondered.

"The soup, my lord," Simpkins said, offering a tureen of cream of asparagus.

"Please."

And the dinner proceeded awkwardly but without the feared fireworks.

Chapter Eleven

*F*ollowing a dinner unlike any Priscilla had ever known and never hoped to know again, they returned to the drawing room. Felix walked up the stairs at her side, silent and withdrawn. She had seen his eyes. Anger glowed deep within them, lighting golden fires in their dark green depths. The skin over his cheekbones was taut, his jaw clenched, his posture rigid. It was clear this scheme was not to his liking. He was not one to be prodded into reconciliation.

What had she done? Was it so terrible to want to heal the breach in his family? She had told him she was not his enemy. Did he believe her?

Once seated in the drawing room, she attempted to draw Felix into the discussion about the music they had heard at the Hanover concert, to no avail.

He answered in monosyllables or nods. He seemed inwardly frozen. It was like looking at someone through a windowpane—you could see him but you couldn't touch him.

Conversation was strained for a time until Lady Beatrice addressed her nephew. "I have missed seeing you, Felix, visiting with you over the years. Do you suppose that our separation could at last come to an end? Have we not yet paid the dues for our transgressions?"

Priscilla gasped even as her hopes rose. This was plunging to the heart of the matter with a vengeance. She fixed her gaze on Felix—from the corner of her eyes without obviously turning her head. How would he react to his aunt? He sat quietly, hands knotted, body stiff.

He said nothing.

To put it mildly Felix was stunned at his aunt's question. He gazed at her, the woman he had shunned for so many years, and wondered if it was possible to tamp his feelings down to a tolerable level. The taunts of schoolboys echoed in his head. Memories of the fights he had waged over his family's peccadilloes ached in his hands. The sly digs from the Oxford chaps who had sniggered when stories of his father's amorous adventures were mentioned rang in his memory. It was this last trial that had been the hardest to bear. Why had he been beset with a father whose success with various women was legendary?

After the death of his mother, his father had remained in the country for barely a year before he was observed escorting a woman of questionable virtue about London. From then on he flitted from one beautiful creature to another—widows, spinsters of loveliness if not wealth. At least he had the decency to refrain from enticing married women into his arms and bed. That much Felix had to grant him.

Oddly enough, the women besieged him, almost begging to have the distinction of being in his company. The Marquess of Silverstone was indeed renowned for his taste in the feminine graces as exemplified by these women. It seemed that to be one of his chosen was a measure of prestige.

The worst had come when a few fellows had begged him to afford them introductions to his father, with the hope he might introduce them to his castoffs!

At least his father wasn't here this evening. It was quite enough to see Aunt Beatrice and Uncle George at the same time. He gave them a considering look.

"Do you remember how as a lad you would go riding with me?" Uncle George said, his eyes crinkled in a half smile. "We had some rare times, we did. I took you to your first horse race."

Felix well remembered the event. He had seen his father with not one, but two enchanting women on his arms. He'd had no time for Felix then, even less later on until he decided it was time for his son to wed.

"Yes, I well recall the event." He also remembered

the gambling in which his uncle had engaged. He had bet on anything and everything, from raindrops on a windowpane to geese crossing the road. Every race, whether at Epsom or Derby, Ascot or Newmarket, saw his presence. The boxing at Fives Court often found him watching, wagering. Ah, indeed, those lads at Oxford had also sought to know his Uncle George. The devil of it was that his uncle won far more often than he lost. He had a gamester's genius.

Felix gazed at this uncle, recalling the mockery of the young men who implied his uncle cheated, for who could win so often if playing by the book? Unconsciously Felix rubbed his knuckles. He had fought a few battles over that as well. No one, he'd asserted, would cast aspersions on his family. Yet was he in truth any better? Had he not done the same thing? Condemning them out of hand?

Earlier, about the time his father had married, Lady Beatrice had dashed off to Scotland with Guy Aston, his uncle's tutor. True, Aston had been young and handsome then. He still looked fit, with scarcely a bit of gray in his hair. Pity Alfred was such a loose screw.

"I hardly know what to say, Aunt Beatrice. It has been a long time." His reply was inadequate, he knew, but the best he could manage in the shock of the moment.

Society had neither forgotten nor forgiven Lady Beatrice for marrying so far beneath her on the social scale. Aston might have come from worthy gentry stock, but he was not suitable for the marquess's daughter, who possessed a fortune in her own right. After all, there were any number of peers who would have welcomed her riches, as well as the lovely Lady Beatrice, into their homes.

Felix turned his head to look at Priscilla. His marriage would be no misalliance. She was of excellent status, kin to the esteemed Earl of Stanwell. Her cousin, Viscount Rawlinson, was among the *crème de la crème* of Society and everywhere received. Felix had been surprised to learn from his cousin, Archdeacon Pallant, that Priscilla's father was much published in the religious field. Respectable. Honorable. Well thought of among his fellow ministers of the cloth. Just what Felix wanted.

Felix turned his attention back to his aunt. He didn't know what else to say to her. The ravine that existed between him and the rest of his father's side of the family was great. Could it be crossed?

The strained silence was broken by his uncle reminiscing with Guy Aston on a few races they had seen. Although one had been the tutor and the other the student, they were not so very far apart in age and had obviously had a bang-up time together.

"Felix," Priscilla said quietly at his side, "I should enjoy getting to know your lovely aunt better. I have ridden with her on occasion and must say I admire her ability. I thought to ask her for help—goodness knows I could use a few pointers on my riding."

She sounded diffident, offhand in her manner, yet he sensed she truly admired his aunt. The proper Priscilla and his aunt? Together? Felix could not believe his ears. She must have known he would not approve of her meeting with his aunt. Still, since he and Priscilla were not wed, he had no right to forbid her rendezvous with Aunt Beatrice.

"I meant to tell you that I have a horse for you." Felix hoped to avoid offering advice, much less agreeing to have her ride with his aunt!

"What? You found a horse at Tatt's? Which one?" his uncle queried. "I looked them over just yesterday."

Forced to be polite, Felix replied, "Northcomb's chestnut."

His uncle gave him a sagacious nod. "Prime animal. I'll wager you paid a fancy sum for it."

"No need for a wager, Uncle. Sufficient to say it was fair." Felix wondered, not for the first time, if everything in life was a gamble to his uncle.

"I would enjoy coaching Priscilla, although I think she does quite well as it is." His aunt smiled at Priscilla, whose cheeks pinkened slightly at the tribute.

"I do not have your address, ma'am." Priscilla grinned back at his aunt with gallant spirit.

"That comes with time, my dear." Aunt Beatrice gave Priscilla an approving nod.

Felix wondered how the conversation had slipped into riding and training.

"I'll bring the chestnut over in the morning. We shall take a ride in the park. I shall see for myself how you do." Felix turned his attention to Priscilla.

"Oh, dear," she cried in mock dismay. One slender hand crept up to her cheek, and she truly looked dismayed. Surely she didn't fear his censure! The most he would do is perhaps make a mild suggestion.

The others thought her consternation amusing. Their laughter seemed to break the icy barrier that had existed.

Guy Aston tilted his head, fixing his gaze on Felix with intensity. "We are planning a birthday ball for Beatrice. I trust you will join us? There will be a family dinner beforehand, of course. George has promised to attend. I believe your Cousin Pallant has agreed as well."

Felix felt cornered. If the Archdeacon graced the ball with his presence, it would be a signal to Society that past follies had been forgiven. Felix knew that whether he liked it or not, he must attend as well. Perhaps, along with marrying Priscilla, this event would help to restore his family in the eyes of society? It was possible. Anything was possible at this point.

"Priscilla? I'll not consider attending without you at my side." Felix turned to view the nicely composed girl. That she could remain so calm in the midst of an admittedly strained situation spoke well for her coping with Society matrons.

"As if you needed to ask, my lord. I would be honored to attend a birthday ball for Lady Beatrice." She gave his aunt a warm smile like he hadn't seen from her this evening. Although he vividly remembered her light kiss on his cheek as they were to go down for dinner. It had been an incredible surprise, but a warmly welcome one. He now wondered if she had saluted him because he had refrained from flinging words at his relatives or because she hoped he would continue his good behavior. She had said she wasn't his enemy—what was she?

"And you as well, Miss Herbert," Guy persisted.

"As to Mercy Herbert, I'll escort her to the ball, the family dinner as well," Uncle George declared roundly, giving Miss Herbert a stare that dared her to challenge his claim to her company.

Priscilla's aunt looked somewhat taken aback, but agreed gracefully—more gracefully than he had, Felix acknowledged.

Alfred had remained silent, relatively withdrawn for the most part during the tense conversation. Now with the obvious strain abated, he wandered over to chat with his Uncle George, seeking his advice on some horse race.

Priscilla rose to join her aunt Mercy and his aunt Beatrice. They fell to discussing bonnets, of all things. Felix, not wanting to be left out of a conversation, sauntered across the room to join his uncles and cousin.

He couldn't begin to describe how he felt, conversing with these men he normally avoided. He'd proceed with caution, but always with good manners.

"That's a fine chestnut you got Priscilla, Felix. I must say, I heard there was some spirited bidding." Uncle George clapped him on his back, giving a nod of approval.

"The mare is worth all I paid. I pity Northcomb for needing to sell her." Felix met his uncle's gaze without flinching. Was there a hint of apprehension there?

Uncle George gave him a judicious look, a glimmer of amusement in his eyes. "Heard he lost it all on a wager."

"So I was told," Felix responded.

"Fool. He ought to have known better than to bet with Armbruster. The man is a cheat and a fraud. That is one thing you could never say about me, Felix. I have never cheated a soul in my life. I learned to play cards because my allowance was too small for me to live in the comfort that I liked. Winning at cards required that I sharpen my skills, improve my memory, and play only where I knew there would be fair dealing." He then mentioned the sum he had invested on the stock exchange that now enabled him to live as he pleased.

Felix suspected his brows rose as high as they might. "You have done well, Uncle. Very well, indeed!"

"Yes, I have, if I do say so. High time I took me a wife, I suppose. Never do to have my nephew wed before me!"

Would there be no end to the shocks this evening? Felix smiled, as he supposed his uncle intended. "It would keep you out of trouble, sir."

"So Guy tells me." He glanced to where Miss Mercy Herbert perched in animated conversation with his sister and her niece. "All the same, I may."

"You believe the lady is willing?" Guy inserted, his gaze following to the lady his uncle eyed.

"Don't know. Hesitant to put it to the test."

Alfred, who had been silent for a time, added, "Be sure to tell her of your investments. That ought to reassure her if nothing else does."

The men chuckled.

Felix relaxed. He would leave as soon as he might. But he acknowledged the evening had gone far better than he expected when he first caught sight of his relations as he had entered the Herbert drawing room. Perhaps . . .

Simpkins brought in the tea tray loaded not only with the teapot and all that went with that, but dainty pastries as well. From the sideboard he brought a tray with bottles of fine canary, claret, and Madeira wines in the event the gentlemen preferred an alternative to the tea.

Felix accepted a glass of excellent claret, then watched Priscilla pour tea for the aunts. She was very graceful, pleasing in her manner. His heart swelled with pride that he would have such a worthy addition to the family.

He forgave her for her meddling. After all, how could she possibly know what he had endured? He had never told a soul about it. Perhaps an intuitive person might have guessed. He had no way of knowing.

It was a relief when the Astons and Uncle George decided it was late and they best return to their homes.

Before he left the house, Felix made arrangements to meet Priscilla in the morning. She could look forward to riding a horse that encouraged her skill as a horse-woman.

The following morning Priscilla joined her aunt in the breakfast room. She was not disappointed in the conversation or her food.

"I think all went well last evening," Aunt Mercy said

after putting *The Morning Post* aside. "Although I must confess I had a number of qualms to begin."

"As did I! The expression in Felix's eyes nearly undid me." She exchanged a contrite glance with her aunt.

"I trust you smoothed it over in that event, for he behaved in a becoming manner for a man who is faced with relatives he has shunned since boyhood. I doubt it will be an easy situation, but the ice has been broken now. Each meeting will be a trifle easier."

"I suppose you have the right of it." Priscilla poured herself a cup of tea, then heaped her plate with scones and a helping of buttered eggs and bacon.

"He is to be here soon." Aunt Mercy glanced at the mantel clock, then back to Priscilla.

"As you see, I have my riding habit on and I put my gloves and hat along with my crop on the hall entry table. If Felix has his own horse as well as the one I am to ride in hand, he will not appreciate being left waiting."

"I believe you are quite clever to view things that way. Were I a betting woman, I would wager he is of the same mind. Who would not be? Do you know, I think there are a vast number of stupid women in this world. They think it is dashing to keep a man waiting for them."

Priscilla, her mouth full of buttered eggs, nodded her head in agreement. When she could speak, she added, "So my mother always says. She thinks it quite rude."

The remainder of the light meal was spent in speculating what they should wear to the birthday ball. That it would be a grand affair, they had no doubt. They had best place an order for their ball gowns soon before the mantua makers became deluged. At her aunt's suggestion Priscilla agreed that a gown of delicate pastel aqua satin would do nicely.

Aunt Mercy declared she would have rich naccarat in silk sarcenet. "That sort of tangerine-ish color will bring a bit of color to this pale face of mine—and it is so popular now."

"I am glad Lady Beatrice has decided to take the initiative," Priscilla declared. "Society will be compelled to reckon with the sister of the famous Marquess of Silverstone! Her past will be buried once and for all. Perhaps Lord George will return to the bosom not only of his family but also to Society?" She placed her napkin on the table and eased her chair away.

"Perhaps," Aunt Mercy said in a firm manner that brooked no questioning. "I doubt Lord George seeks to be placed with those dandies who grace the balls and parties of the *ton*."

"But what about quiet dinners and parties with those whose company he enjoys?" Priscilla persisted.

"I expect he has that now, or almost." Aunt Mercy fell into a contemplative muse that Priscilla was reluctant to interrupt.

She rose from the table after a glimpse of the clock. "The time," she murmured. After bestowing a kiss on her aunt's cheek, she left the room.

That lady made no response, and Priscilla wondered what had drawn her into such deep reflection. Priscilla pulled on her riding gloves, checked to see her hat was straight, and then gathered her crop so she would be prepared.

When Simpkins opened the front door to Lord Latimer's imperious knock, Priscilla at once spotted the beautiful chestnut.

"What a beauty! Does she have a name?" Priscilla sailed from the house to offer the mare the lump of sugar she had taken from the breakfast table.

"Not that I was told. What shall you call her?" Felix led the horse forward so Priscilla might walk around to the other side.

"Why, Beauty, of course." She gave Felix a cautious smile.

"I should have known." He shook his head, but his expression was pleasant.

Relieved that he didn't think her silly for choosing such an obvious name for the mare, she relaxed. Allowing him to give her a boost to the saddle, she arranged her skirts, waiting silently while he mounted his own horse.

"I forgot to ask . . . your horse . . . what is his name?"

"Beau." He met her look of incredulity with his own of amusement.

She chortled softly as they clattered down the street. "How appropriate, Beauty and Beau. Pity there isn't a beast. They would make a splendid trio."

She glanced over at him to see a frown on his face. Best not to make any more remarks along that line. Obviously he was not in a humorous frame of mind this morning.

The weather had improved, the temperature being slightly warmer today. The exercise brought a warmth to her cheeks, and she felt better than she had since she had come to London with Aunt Mercy.

She was coming to terms with life in London, so very different from her life at home. The prospect of a future with Lord Latimer was a little different. She was unsure what to expect. She had always hoped for a marriage that contained love. More and more it seemed to her that he just wanted to add respectability to his family rather than join in a marriage that held love and mutual respect. He appeared to have selected her as a suitably proper mate, not because he was in love with her. He certainly obtained no monetary gain from the marriage, as her dowry was barely passable. Perhaps she could persuade him that love was feasible? For she had tumbled into love with him not long after they met, to her misfortune. Could there be anything more disheartening than loving someone only mildly fond of you?

Felix made no comment on her riding skill or lack of same. They rode on in silence until they reached the part of Rotten Row where she had previously met his aunt.

They were in luck. Lady Beatrice came riding across the green with an impressive expertise, greeting them with a serene smile. "Good morning to you both." She studied Priscilla's mare with a knowledgeable eye.

Beauty took exception to her ladyship's mare, and Priscilla had a time quelling the animal's high spirits. Felix leaned over to give the horse a touch with his crop, immediately stopping the nonsense.

Lady Beatrice made several suggestions as they walked forward. They all made sense to Priscilla, who felt herself somewhat a neophyte compared to her ladyship's perfection.

At Lady Beatrice's urging they set off at a canter. She

dropped back slightly. Priscilla supposed that she wished to check Priscilla's posture. She made an effort to sit as straight as she might. It was not difficult to manage the sidesaddle. Indeed, it was surprisingly comfortable. But she wanted to improve her horsemanship. The *ton* seemed to set great store by riding. Felix did as well. She wished to please him—at least in something!

"My dear, all you need is a bit more practice. You have a fine mount now, better than the bay rented for you." Lady Beatrice rejoined them, and they continued to canter to the end of the Row.

Here they came to a halt when Lady Beatrice positioned herself across so that Felix and Priscilla had to stop as well.

"I wanted to explain without the others listening why I wish to have my ball."

"It isn't necessary for you to explain your actions to us, Aunt Beatrice." Felix looked uncomfortable, as though a burr was lodged under him.

"I want to, Felix. I have been thinking about this for weeks. I decided it is utterly foolish to allow Society to dictate my life for me. I intend to invite everyone who has said a kind word to me in the past years. It is a small way to repay them."

"Why invite me?" Felix asked quietly. He wore a tight expression that Priscilla guessed hid a very strong emotion, although she didn't know quite what.

"You are a part of my family."

"As is my father. Will he be there as well?" Felix said without the belligerence Priscilla suspected he felt.

Lady Beatrice looked away down Rotten Row before returning her gaze to Felix. "I have no idea. I must invite him, you should know that. If there is to be any reconciliation, all of us must be together, present a united front to those who have in the past maligned us." At his start she nodded. "Indeed, I plan to ask those I consider my enemies as well."

"Well, that should give them pause. They will scarce know what to make of it." Felix gave her a reluctant grin.

"Turning the other cheek, as it were," Priscilla added. "How disconcerting that will be for them. I suspect most of Society is accustomed to having people bow and scrape, terrified lest they lose status by not following some unspoken rule set forth by someone who was likely being spiteful."

"Will they come?" Felix wondered aloud.

"Society loves novelty. They will be curious . . . and they cannot bear to miss out on such a novel event." Lady Beatrice flashed a quick smile.

"Well, we shall stand resolutely as your side, dear ma'am." Priscilla touched her crop to her riding hat in a gesture of salute. "No one shall be cruel or unkind, not if we have anything to say about it."

"I do like your chosen lady, Felix. She will be a welcome addition to our family."

Priscilla blushed at the kindly spoken words. Felix admired her color, for it spoke of modesty and propriety.

"I believe that plain speaking has been a hallmark of Sutton speech for many years," Felix said, more rueful than amused.

The horses were even less amused at being kept standing. Priscilla's mare fidgeted, and even Felix had to signal his horse to mind his manners.

"Come, we had best be on our way," Lady Beatrice cried. She lightly touched her horse, then cantered off down the Row.

With a questioning look at Felix, Priscilla did the same. He was beside her in an instant.

Aunt Mercy had sent a message to the mantua maker, requesting she bring samples of the fabrics in the colors they wished, along with suggestions for the design of the two ball gowns.

Priscilla was awestruck at the sketch presented for her approval. Never in her life had she thought to own such a beautiful gown. The pale aqua crepe was ornamented with a deep border of tulle embroidered with shaded aqua silks and chenille. The full short sleeves were also trimmed with tulle, with tulle around the neck as well. Her pearls would be perfect with it, though she'd need matching slippers.

Aunt Mercy selected her fabric and sketch with what appeared to be delight. "That neckline is daring and the gown is excessively modish, but I shall be on display and wish to do Felix's uncle, that is, the Astons, proud."

"Knowing Lord George, he will be pleased that you look fashionable. You have the means, why not?" Priscilla had been slightly taken aback when her aunt explained the source of her income, not to mention how generous it was. She would never have dreamed of inquiring, it wasn't done. But at least she had the satisfaction of knowing the lovely wardrobe purchased for her had been well within her aunt's means. Indeed, it probably scarce put a dent in it!

Once Aunt Mercy and the mantua maker had wandered off to discuss the trimmings for her aunt's gown, Priscilla went to the drawing room, thinking to play the pianoforte.

Simpkins met her in the hall. "There is a gentleman to see you, miss."

Priscilla beamed a smile at the stately butler. "Lord Latimer?"

"No, miss. Mr. Alfred Aston awaits you. You wish to be at home to him?"

"When I marry Lord Latimer he will become my cousin, so I expect I best see what it is that he wants."

Under the butler's approving eye, she marched down the stairs to the small sitting room, where Cousin Alfred awaited her. "Mr. Aston. This is certainly a surprise. To what do I owe this pleasure?"

"I thought that since we are to become relatives, we ought to become better acquainted."

Suddenly wary for no reason at all, Priscilla sought time by gesturing to a chair. Once he had seated himself, she offered him a glass of canary, which he readily accepted. At last she took a seat opposite him on the sofa.

"You enjoyed the dinner last evening? I found it a pleasure to get to know Lord Latimer's relatives a bit better." She pleated her skirt with nervous fingers. The door was open, he was a relative of her betrothed, yet she was not certain she entirely trusted him.

"Exactly why I'm here." He studied the pale yellow wine before shifting his gaze to her.

"Well," she replied, searching for a means to find out

what was on his mind, "I thought last evening auspicious."

"True, true." He sipped the wine before giving her a look she could only think was a trifle cagey. "I wondered if perhaps we might spend a little time together. Uncle George put me on to a good thing in a race out at Epsom. Have you been there? It's just south of Richmond."

"A horse race? Me? You wish to take me to a horse race at Epsom Downs? Why?"

"If you've not attended one, it is high time you did."

"Oh." Perhaps it would be a good thing if she went along with Alfred. Anything to heal the breach between the families. She didn't much care for him, but surely it would be acceptable. "Very well, I shall go."

Chapter Twelve

Alfred seemed immensely satisfied with Priscilla's agreement. "It is not far," he assured her. "A mere ten miles or so south of Richmond, and that, you know, isn't far out of Town."

"Not far?" she cried. "That should take us perhaps two hours to reach!" She had suspected it was some distance, but not that far away.

"That's nothing on a fine day. Uncle George said I might use his carriage for so worthy an excursion." He grinned at her in obvious jubilation.

Priscilla's concern faded some when he mentioned his uncle. Surely if he sanctioned it, the outing ought to be acceptable. Although she did wonder why Alfred didn't have his own equipage. Surely the only son of Lady Beatrice and Mr. Aston should be able to manage something decent, or even use something that belonged to his parents. It struck her as being slightly odd. However, in an effort to bring about peace and harmony—if such could be achieved—she would not badger him with questions.

"I'll be here first thing in the morning. Nothing like an early start to begin a good day." He gave her a satisfied smirk. "Nothing like it."

"Just how early is early?" Priscilla gave him a dubious look.

"Oh, perhaps eight of the clock. The horses will be fresh and eager. I'll have a groom along." His expression was as cautious as she felt. Best not tell Felix about this absurd scheme. He would be certain to squash it instantly.

Priscilla wondered if she was mad to agree to Alfred's urging. "I am not certain if I ought to go with you. Perhaps I should consult with my aunt." She rose from the sofa, thinking to hunt out her aunt. Surely she ought to be finished with the mantua maker by now?

"You think she will object to your going with me? A cousin to Latimer? Son of her dear friend Lady Beatrice?"

Priscilla at once felt a bit foolish. "Oh, of course she won't mind. And you will have a groom along."

Alfred nodded with obvious relief. "Keep it under your hat. I don't want my cousin spoiling the fun."

At once Priscilla got suspicious. "If this is so innocent, why can't I tell Lord Latimer?" Not that she had planned to inform him, but why didn't Alfred want his cousin to know about it?

"Ah—he would want to come along with us. That wouldn't do. Why he would win all the bets and then where would I be?" The innocent expression sat ill on his face for some reason. It reminded Priscilla of the boys in her father's Latin class when they plotted to get out of an assignment by fair means or foul.

"I don't know. Where would you be?" Priscilla almost smiled at his reaction.

He gave her an exasperated look. "Nowhere, that's where."

She gave up, not in the least comprehending his talk. She would go along to bring peace to the family and helping to heal the falling out that had occurred over the years.

"What is appropriate wear for a race?" she wondered aloud, clasping her hands before her as she slowly walked to stand by the fireplace.

"A sensible pelisse. If you have a velvet bonnet, you might wear it along with a muff. Never know how it will be like on the road."

"I thought the races at Epsom didn't begin until June." The recollection had popped into her mind, something her brother had remarked on some time ago.

"This ain't a regular race. This is a private race just between two horses—both of them prime goers. There is a prize of fifty pounds for the winner. Sure to be some spirited betting as well."

She frowned in puzzlement. "You are going all this distance to watch a race between two horses? It would seem to me that you might do that much closer to home."

He didn't say a word—just gave her a look of disgust.

"All right, all right, I shall say no more." She stood staring down at him, pinning him with a stern look. "Just promise me I shall not come to grief over this."

"I don't see how you could." He rose at that and, within minutes, had left the house.

Priscilla went to the window, watching as he made his way along the street, again wondering if she was utterly mad to agree to his scheme.

When she met her aunt at the table around noon in the morning room where a light meal was set out for them, she at first made no mention of Alfred's visit. Then she realized that it would be necessary to explain why she would be away the following day. She mulled over just how to phrase the excursion.

"You have something on your mind. I can tell by the little frown you wear. Come, is it anything I may help you with?" Aunt Mercy inquired solicitously.

"Alfred popped in this morning to invite me for a drive tomorrow." She prudently omitted just how long a drive it was to be.

"How nice. Did he say where he wants to take you?"

"He mentioned Richmond." That was true enough, for he'd reminded her that Epsom was south of that area.

"Well, I think it very nice indeed that he wants to improve the friendship between the two families." Aunt Mercy nodded emphatically. "You ought to have a nice time."

"May I remind you that we are not quite related as yet." Priscilla wondered if she was becoming as devious as the Latin students. She knew she truly did not wish to equivocate regarding the outing tomorrow, yet she suspected her proper aunt would quibble regarding a race meeting. She walked a fine line between truth and falsehood.

"What will you wear?"

Thankful to avoid any additional discussion on the outing destination, Priscilla murmured something about her blue pelisse. "I thought a velvet bonnet with that fur muff you bought me. Do you think my brown velvet bonnet will go well with the blue pelisse?"

"I think a deep blue would look better. Come with me after you finish nibbling on that sandwich you constructed. We are sure to find just the right sort of thing."

Priscilla met her aunt's fond gaze and felt utterly dreadful. Yet her aunt approved of her attempt to mend fences, as it were. The details of the matter were the source of her dilemma.

They shortly left the little morning room to fetch their bonnets and reticules. Priscilla donned a fine dark plum spencer over her morning dress, satisfied she looked well enough to brave the inspection of anyone they met. Anyone meaning Felix, of course.

They found the precise deep blue velvet bonnet to go with her pelisse in a little shop on Oxford Street.

"That bonnet is lovely but is a trifle plain. What do you say we look in at Botobol's shop for a small feather to add a finishing touch?"

When they entered the plumassier's shop, Priscilla was struck anew by the fanciful collection of feathers and plumes of every hue imaginable that were offered for sale. After buying two little clusters of tinted feathers, Miss Herbert studied some cream plumes of great distinction.

"Those are the sort of plumes you must wear when you are presented at court following your marriage to Lord Latimer." She lightly touched the nearest one.

"Must I be presented at court?" Priscilla quaked in her slippers at the mere thought of such a thing.

"The countess of Earl Latimer, the future Marchioness of Silverstone, *must* be presented at court, my dear. It would be shocking if you were not."

Priscilla thought that she might tolerate shocking a few Society matrons to avoid the ordeal of a court presentation. She had heard tales of young ladies tripping on their gowns, or falling while attempting the deep curtsy required when being presented to royalty. It was not a pretty thought to contemplate. And the court gowns were utterly ridiculous, reminding her of the dome of St. Paul's Cathedral, only far fancier. How much better to wear a suitable evening gown.

"I shall be happy to tutor you in the art of the court curtsy." Aunt Mercy sighed deeply. "It seems like a long time since I was presented."

"I believe Mama mentioned it." Actually, Mama had regaled her daughters with the story of their aunt's presentation a number of times in the past. The queen had favored Miss Mercy Herbert with conversation!

"Of course, as the grandniece of an earl, you would be able to be presented now if you wished. However, you might as well wait until you are married. It would be a far greater distinction."

Priscilla wondered if marrying Lord Latimer was going to be all she desired. He had yet to say he loved her. He'd told Chauncy that the main reason he wished to marry her was because she was so respectable. Decent. Proper. If he knew what she intended to do on the morrow, he would probably inform her that her position as his wife was no longer required!

But he had kissed her. Of course she had shamelessly responded. She had confessed that she liked it quite well, and he hadn't seemed shocked at her admission. But then, what did she know of men and their feelings?

"Come, dear. We must return to the house in time to rest. We are to attend the Price-Fothergill ball this evening. The baroness always offers such delightful entertainment."

"I met her daughter." Priscilla opened the door.

"Did you? Such a pity, that poor child. It would be difficult to find any woman with looks less presentable than hers." Aunt Mercy marched out to the pavement.

"She needs different colors, simpler gowns."

"She's a trifle plump, true." Aunt Mercy summoned a hackney, urged Priscilla to enter, and then joined her after giving the jarvey their direction.

Priscilla stifled a chuckle. The girl was a dumpling, and to face a come-out ball! Poor thing, indeed.

"No one of whom my mama would approve." Priscilla attempted to look coy and failed. She chuckled instead, thus further endearing herself to him.

"Have you given any thought to my aunt's upcoming ball?" He wished he might toy with the golden tresses wreathed about Priscilla's head. She wore a silly, but fashionable, aigrette composed of rose-tinted feathers in her hair. He could brush them against her cheek, across the delicate skin of her sensitive . . . He stopped his wayward thoughts. That way lay danger.

"We ordered our gowns this very morning. Aunt said we must be prompt less the mantua makers are besieged with orders and we cannot have them in time." She gave him a very conscious look, and he wondered what in the world might cause that.

"And did that take all day?" he probed.

"Ah, no. After our lunch and aunt's rest we went shopping. I needed a new bonnet and some feathers."

Felix succumbed to the desire to touch her hair. He stroked the little aigrette with a gentle finger, lingering to feel her curls as well. "I fancy this might be a part of your shopping?"

She blushed adorably. Confusion filled her eyes for a moment, then she looked away from him. "I think I should like to dance again."

Felix was only too pleased to take her in his arms for a waltz.

Eight in the morning came all too soon to please Priscilla. Upon waking, Lily brought her the early morning chocolate and rolls favored by the ladies of Society.

Priscilla gulped the chocolate, then gobbled down the rolls while she hurried into a simple ivory day dress trimmed with plum ribands. The new bonnet went on after she had donned her blue pelisse. She was swallowing the last of the rolls while she pulled on her gloves as she tiptoed down the stairs. Reticule and fur muff in hand, she awaited Alfred in the little room off the entry.

She traced the pattern of the rug with the toe of one plum leather slipper. She supposed she ought to have worn half boots, but nothing she owned would look right with this dress and pelisse. How vain she was becoming.

At home she'd have worn the half boots and not minded a bit.

The clock was striking eight when Alfred presented himself at the front door garbed in a pair of colorful Petersham trousers and an even more colorful coat.

She whisked herself around to the door. "Hush," she cautioned as she opened it. "I'd not disturb my aunt."

Simpkins materialized from the rear of the house to close and lock the door behind them.

Priscilla entered the curricle with apprehension. She knew nothing about Alfred's driving skills. Would he be as good as his cousin? She rather doubted it. Few could match Felix in anything, particularly driving. However, the groom now perched up behind them had looked capable.

They set off. Priscilla watched his handling of the ribbons with a wary eye, then relaxed. He might not be as gifted as Felix, but he wasn't ham-fisted.

The traffic was light, understandable given the time of day. Still, she was thankful when they left Knightsbridge behind and headed in the direction of Richmond. "You drive well, Alfred."

"Uncle George showed me a few tricks. He wouldn't let me borrow his curricle unless he thought I could handle his pair."

That explained his treatment of the horses. "At least the weather is decent. I was so afraid it might rain and ruin the trip." That wasn't quite true. Actually she had not given any thought to rain at all. She had slipped into daydreams of her waltz with Felix last eve, and Alfred's demand for an early departure had intruded on them with unseemly rudeness.

"Jolly good not to have rain."

"You'd not have gone in rain . . . or would you?"

"What's a bit of water? The hood on the curricle helps, and we have a waterproof folded up at our feet."

Priscilla studied the oiled denim and wondered how effective it would be to ward off rain. Even if you covered up your legs and lap, there was still the upper body exposed. She said nothing, but devoutly prayed those clouds in the distance were going the other direction.

They stopped to change horses, then continued on their way. It was after ten of the clock before they reached the grounds where the race was to be held. Carriages and horses and people were everywhere.

She examined the other women perched in the various vehicles and decided she would remain where she was. With any luck at all, she could stay in the carriage and not be required to speak to what she strongly suspected were members of the *demi-rep*.

"The view will be better from here," she explained when Alfred wanted to assist her from the carriage. She edged deeper into the shade offered by the curricle hood and averted her gaze from the gaudily garbed women.

"Dawson will keep an eye on you." Alfred hurried off to join his friends.

Dawson tended the horses, ignoring her completely.

Priscilla fumed in silence. Why had Alfred invited her to this stupid race if he had no intention of spending any time with her? He certainly had no conversation to offer while they drove here.

She scrutinized the area. At last she spotted the two horses that were obviously the ones to be raced. The young men who were astride the horses looked rather insignificant to control such great beasts. While she watched, one gentleman in a black frock coat held up a pocket watch and cried out for the race to start.

The horses dashed off, and within seconds she had lost sight of them from where she sat. It was just as well; she truly did not care much for watching horses race. It seemed boring to her way of thinking. Of course she wasn't betting on the race, either.

When the horses returned there was much shouting, jumping up and down, and excitement in general. From where she sat it looked as though the race was a tie.

One horse was pronounced the winner.

"You lie! My horse was the winner! You cheat!"

The shout came from a man who probably owned the losing horse. It would be logical. She stood up, the better to see what was going on. The owners were arguing. One obviously challenged the other to a duel. She could see them pace off with the crowd urging them on. A pistol gleamed in the sunlight. She shuddered at the sight. When they were at the precise spot, they turned and took aim.

Bang! Bang! Two shots were fired into sudden silence.

The gunshots startled Priscilla, and she sank down on the cushion with a thump. She had known they would come, yet she wasn't prepared for the sound. The carriage horses fidgeted, and the groom had his hands full controlling them.

"Good grief!" Duels were illegal. She wished she were anywhere but here. If the duel wasn't bad enough, a gentle, if persistent, mizzle began to fall. Hastily, she pulled the waterproof up over her lap and retreated under the cover of the hood as best she could. Closing her eyes she wondered if anything else would go wrong.

Felix had begun his day with his tailor. Upon leaving this establishment, he strolled down Bond Street until he chanced upon his uncle George.

"Felix! I am surprised to see you in Town. Alfred said you were bound for Epsom to watch the race." His uncle leaned on his cane to survey Felix with raised brows.

"I had no desire to go, although I did hear about it. Why would Alfred think I was bound for Epsom?" Felix stepped to one side to permit a young lady bound for Hooker's lending library—her maid close behind—to enter the shop.

"He borrowed my curricle to impress your Miss Herbert. I figured you must intend to ride there on Beau."

Felix gave his uncle a startled look. It wasn't so much that he knew the name of his horse, it was that he would even consider that Felix would allow Alfred to escort Priscilla anywhere, let alone Epsom.

"I had no intention of permitting Alfred to squire Miss Herbert to Epsom or anywhere else, for that matter. What maggoty notion has the boy got in his head?"

"Who knows." Uncle George shook his head in puzzlement. "The way my knee is aching, I would say we are due for a rain. Let us hope it holds off until they return. He took the curricle, you see."

Felix saw all too clearly. Alfred had remained silent at the dinner, and after that Felix had been lulled into thinking the rivalry between them had faded into the past, as it well deserved. If his little cousin had run off with Priscilla merely to plague him, he would cheerfully wring his neck. Felix had a fair notion what sort of women might be found at Epsom today. They would not be the sort with whom he wished Priscilla to associate. She was such an innocent she would probably make friends with them. He shook his head.

"What are you going to do?"

"What else, rescue Miss Herbert."

"Good. And give Alfred a punch in the nose for me. I was of a mind to say no, but he implied I'd be doing you a favor, so I gave in to the lad."

Felix nodded before hailing a hackney. Within minutes he was headed for his home on George Street off Hanover Square. Once there, he ordered his traveling carriage brought around, then went up to change. He also requested a small picnic lunch to take with him, not knowing how long this all would take. He did not wish to expose Priscilla to public notice if unnecessary. He hoped she had the sense to keep away from the crowd.

Slowly winding his way through the thick traffic, he headed toward Knightsbridge, then on to Richmond. At least one ostler recalled the curricle with the young fellow and the pretty gal with the "yaller" hair.

It was now hours since his sighting. Felix urged his team forward, driving himself to better his time. John Coachman tended to be a tad too cautious.

He spun into Epsom just as it began to mizzle. He lost a bit of time hunting out the curricle. They tended to all look alike. Then he spotted a rich deep blue bonnet in the recess of one of the carriages. If that wasn't Priscilla, he would eat his hat. He guided his team as close as he could, handed the reins to John Coachman, and scrambled down. He dashed to the curricle, his greatcoat swinging about him.

"Priscilla," he said in an urgent voice when he got there and saw he'd been right, "come with me."

"Felix?" Her voice was nothing more than a squeak. With no more than a hasty glance about her, she jumped into his arms, allowing him to hold her close a moment before they hurried to the coach.

"In you go." He leaped in behind her and rapped on the ceiling to signal John Coachman to get going. He was certain Dawson had seen them depart and would report it all to Alfred when he finally came to claim the curricle. He wanted no confrontation with his cousin in his present frame of mind, not to mention the increasing rain.

"Oh, Felix, I was never so glad to see anyone in all my life. What a horrid day this has been." She burst into tears, only to mop them with the square of linen Felix offered her. "Sorry. My brother says men hate to be around sniffling females."

"I would say you have been strongly provoked." Felix took his temper in hand to manage a civil inquiry. "What prompted this excursion to Epsom, if I may ask?"

"Alfred popped in to beg me to go with him to some race at Epsom. I agreed reluctantly, you may be sure. I thought it would help bring the two families closer if we were all on better terms. I ought to have been more suspicious—and I was to a degree. It all seemed a trifle smoky, you see." She offered Felix a beseeching regard.

"I can well imagine. Thank goodness I arrived when I did." Outside the traveling coach the rain was now a steady downpour. "You would have been soaked to the skin in no time."

"Alfred was so certain it wouldn't rain. I had my doubts, however. I wish I had paid attention to my initial hesitancy to go along with his scheme. He did not wish me to say anything to you. That was a clue that something wasn't right. I should have told you last night when I saw you at the Price-Fothergills."

She gave Felix such a woebegone look that of course he had to slip to her side of the carriage so he might offer comfort. And if his comfort tended to be in the nature of exquisite kisses, who was to know?

Priscilla wasn't about to tell anyone.

The picnic basket sat on the floor quite ignored by both of them.

Chapter Thirteen

*U*pon their arrival at the home of Miss Herbert, Priscilla uneasily stepped from the traveling coach once Simpkins hurried forth with a large red umbrella to shield her from the heavy rain that continued to pour. Rushing into the house, she waited in the entry for Felix to follow her. He hurried inside, stamping his feet before handing his greatcoat to Simpkins, who had set the umbrella to dry.

She eyed Felix with curiosity and perhaps a little misgiving. What would happen now? How amusing that she was already engaged to the gentleman. She would have been compromised beyond redemption had they been seen—a marriage would have been a foregone conclusion. As it was, the coachman had dealt with the change of horses while Felix and she had remained protected within the coach.

"Come, we had best tell my aunt all that has happened. She is wise and will assuredly have sound advice for us." Priscilla led the way up the stairs to the drawing room.

Simpkins had followed them, crossing at once to light a fire to take a chill from the room.

"Please inform my aunt that we have returned." Priscilla wondered what her aunt would say once she learned of all that had transpired this morning. It seemed incredible that so much had occurred in such a short span of time.

Priscilla and Felix were left alone upon the butler's departure. She surveyed her betrothed with a wary gaze.

He seemed equally cautious, maintaining a discreet distance between them. She would have welcomed the comfort of his embrace about now. Alas, that was scarcely possible. The kisses shared in the carriage had been so marvelous. Would it not be good when they might kiss when they pleased?

What gossip would sail about Town if this day's events became widely known! Felix's desire for a proper and circumspect wife would have evaporated like a puddle after the rain once the sun comes out.

Aunt Mercy entered in a bustle of muslin skirts. She surveyed the couple in her drawing room, before directing her gaze to Lord Latimer. "How curious. Priscilla leaves for a drive with Alfred and returns with you. Explain, please!"

It did not take long to give the description of the morning's disaster.

"I thought your cousin had more sense that to try such a foolish deed." Aunt Mercy appeared horrified at his disclosure of the race and subsequent rain, especially Alfred Aston's desertion of her niece, leaving Priscilla open to discovery and gossip.

"Had I discussed the proposed scheme with Lord Latimer I would never have gone with Mr. Aston, Aunt Mercy. His lordship would have advised me of his cousin's likely motives." Still somewhat bemused by the breathtaking kisses Felix had given her while they returned from the disastrous trip to Epsom, Priscilla sought to abate her aunt's justified annoyance.

"I fear my younger cousin and I have always been at odds, Miss Herbert." Felix shifted positions on the sofa, looking ill at ease.

"So I understand. Your aunt informed me that the rivalry between you is of long standing." Aunt Mercy compressed her lips and looked even more angry.

"What shall we do now, Aunt Mercy?"

Priscilla wondered if Felix had realized the enormous impropriety of their slightly scandalous drive from Epsom to London. They had been alone within a closed carriage the entire time, and to boot, he had kissed her nearly senseless. True, they were engaged, but she had heard that many couples had less contact after an engagement than before.

"It is a problem." Her aunt studied the pair sitting so properly side by side on the sofa.

"I have no idea how many people noticed me in the curricle that Mr. Aston borrowed from Lord George," Priscilla worried aloud. "For the most part they were paying attention to the horses to be raced, not those attending. This was especially true after the charge of cheating arose." She omitted any mention of the duel. Her aunt would have an attack of the vapors if she knew of that.

"However, it is possible someone recognized you." Lord Latimer rose from the blue-striped sofa to pace back and forth before the fireplace. His dark gray coat fitted him superbly, his buff pantaloons equally excellent. Even his boots had but slight stains from the rain. Priscilla admitted that he certainly was a handsome creature, one any woman could desire. But he had taken risks!

"Before you whisked me away in your traveling coach." Priscilla gave him a steady look, wanting to chide him for his improper conduct when he was the one who insisted on proper behavior for her. Or did that only apply to others? She was miffed at him in spite of the kisses. Those kisses could be assigned to propinquity.

"You think in the excitement caused by the duel you escaped unnoticed?" He paused to study her, his gaze seeming concerned.

"Duel? You failed to mention a duel." Aunt Mercy clutched her throat in distress. "I trust no one was killed!"

Priscilla gave Felix a disgusted look. Really, the man was dim-witted—he ought to know better than to mention the duel. "There was a disagreement regarding the race outcome. One man accused the other of cheating and was challenged to a duel. They paced off the distance and shot."

"Good heavens!" Her aunt gasped, and groped for her vinaigrette.

"Do not worry, I did not see a thing, there were too many people in the way. Not that I wished to see someone shot, mind you. I merely observed nothing from where I sat. Then during the confusion, the beginning of the rain, the throngs of people swarming toward the site, Lord Latimer arrived and swept me away."

"That does sound hopeful," Aunt Mercy said in a fading voice.

"I repeat, what are we to do now?" Priscilla ignored the look Felix sent her. With all those kisses, he had not said one word of love. She realized it after they arrived at her aunt's house. Could she, she wondered, continue with this betrothal? Her parents, her aunt, his relatives all seemed to think a marriage between them to be a fine thing. Felix behaved as though she was an answer to his prayers. But he said not one word of love to her. Could she hope he would come to love her in time? It would require some consideration. Without an avowal of love, she did not know where she stood with him. Kisses were fine, but what did they signify? She could only proceed with firmness of mind.

"We must attend a gathering this evening, some public function where we would be seen by a vast number of people." Her aunt frowned in thought.

"The opera or Drury Lane perhaps?" Felix suggested.

Priscilla, thinking of the opera dancers of whom she had heard, said, "Perhaps the theater? Do you know what play is on for this evening?"

Her aunt sniffed. "Does it matter? We shall attend in any event. It is important that as many people as possible see you both this evening and that you look as unruffled as innocents can. Is that clear?"

"What about Mr. Aston?" Priscilla turned her attention to Felix, wondering how he would handle his worm of a cousin.

"I shall take great pleasure in confronting him." He thought a moment, then added, "Perhaps it might be well if he joined us this evening. At least we would have him under our noses, so to speak. Who knows where he might go or what he might say if he is on his own." He ran his gaze over Priscilla in a manner that guaranteed her opposition.

"Oh, very good," Priscilla exclaimed dryly. "He is the last person on earth I wish to see."

"Precisely why it might be a good idea to have him

with us. What do you think, Miss Herbert?" He swiveled to face her aunt, appealing to her in a manner designed to obtain her instant approval.

"I see what you mean. If he is with us, people who may have heard of the Epsom affair won't know what to believe. If the rivalry between you is as well-known as you say, the appearance of both of you should put paid to conjecture regarding Priscilla. As well, it might give rise to speculation that the rift between you and Mr. Aston is healed."

"How I wish I had shown him the door when he first requested I join him," Priscilla remarked with some bitterness. "Here I thought to make peace. Peace!"

"No sense crying over spilt milk, my dear. Come, we will allow Felix to arrange our seats—prominent ones, I believe—for this evening." Aunt Mercy rose and gestured to Priscilla. "You and I will retire to our rooms and inspect our wardrobes. We must outshine our previous appearances." She offered her hand to Felix, who bowed low over it.

"You have my profound respect, ma'am. I will first seek out my cousin while I send my man to obtain the tickets for us. I will make certain the box is a conspicuous one."

"Precisely." Aunt Mercy nodded regally.

Priscilla watched Felix exit the room with masculine grace that few men attained however they might long for such.

"Sometime I wonder about him, Aunt Mercy. He doesn't love me, you know. I am merely a means to an end for him."

"Rubbish! If you believe that I can see why you fell for Alfred Aston's stupid plot." She touched Priscilla on her arm, nodding toward the stairs.

Priscilla followed her up to her room. It was just possible she could—with the help of Aunt Mercy's dresser—concoct a ravishing creation from something she owned. That her aunt believed Felix cared for her would be carefully thought about later.

"Ah," Aunt Mercy declared as she drew a pale rose confection of silk jaconet from the wardrobe, "this has possibilities."

* * *

Felix found his cousin at his rooms not far from where Uncle George lived. The mews were located in between the two places, so it was possible for that curricle to be reposing neatly where it belonged by now.

Alfred's man let Felix in with an ingratiating bow. "My lord, it is a pleasure to see you. Mr. Aston is in his bedroom repairing his appearance after a drenching of this morning. Will you wait here?"

"No, I think not." Felix entered the small sitting room and looked about him. "I shall see him immediately. Don't bother to announce me, he is expecting me unless I am badly mistaken." There was nothing out here to give a clue as to how the morning had been spent.

When he opened the door to Alfred's bedroom, he encountered an amusing spectacle and laughed.

Alfred pulled a clean shirt over his head and glared at Felix. "And what do you find so amusing, cousin?"

"You. This room looks as though a whirlwind struck it. I understand you were drenched this morning. Pity, that." Felix twirled his sword cane about, strolling slowly to the center of the room, all the while keeping his eyes fixed on his cousin. He hoped he made an impressive figure in his many-caped greatcoat, beaver hat, and cane.

Alfred focused on the sword cane and gulped. He swiftly tucked his cambric shirt into his breeches, then sat down to pull on a pair of boots. Off to one side a sodden pair could be seen discarded, ready to be tossed out. On the floor a well-soaked pair of Petersham trousers lay in a colorful heap. The peacock-green jacket on a nearby chair would never be the same again. Thankfully.

"Well, yes, went to Epsom to see that race everyone was talking about. Stupid fellows dueled in the drizzle. They both fired in spite of the rain."

"Anyone killed?" Felix asked with supreme casualness.

"Just winged. Egad, there was a bother about the whole thing. You would think a simple race between two horses would be no matter at all." Alfred pulled on the second boot, then rose to stomp his feet.

"I understand you borrowed our uncle's curricle.

Why?" Felix placed the tip of his cane to the floor, then leaned slightly on it. He continued to stare at his cousin, a thing he knew full well would make him nervous.

Alfred shifted about, giving Felix a wary inspection. "It's nicer than mine."

"Was there a particular reason you wished to have a nice vehicle? And I want the truth, Alfred, if you are acquainted with such." His voice might be soft, but Felix inserted a note of menace in it.

Alfred gave him a sullen glare. "So . . . I took Miss Herbert to Epsom. She wanted to see a horse race."

"Strange, that does not quite match what I observed or heard," Felix said in a silken tone.

"Don't tell me it was you who disappeared with her! I hunted all over the place; sure she had taken refuge from the rain. All I got for my pains was a soaking." He gestured toward the sodden Petershams and the peacock coat, his air belligerent.

"I have no intention of telling you anything. But a slight problem has arisen. It requires your attendance at Drury Lane this evening." Felix strolled about the room, inspecting it without seeming to.

"Why Drury Lane? Besides, I am busy. Have things to do. Must collect on the bet I made with Armbruster."

"I thought you knew better than to bet with him. He never pays, you know." Alfred gave Felix such a look of horror, it was almost enough to make him laugh. "Tell you what—I'll go with you to his place so you can collect your winnings, then you shall come with me to our uncle's chambers to explain to us what motivated your trip to Epsom with Miss Herbert. It was the merest luck I was able to arrive in time to save her, you know."

"I would have brought her back to London," Alfred muttered, his manner even more sulky than before.

"Really!" Felix mocked.

"Yes, really." Alfred pulled on a coat of shocking mustard color that clashed with his French gray breeches to a distressing degree.

"And do put on your greatcoat. No one should have to endure that sight." He gestured to Alfred's garb with a disdainful sigh.

Intimidated by his older cousin's reputation of *ton*nish

behavior and dress, Alfred mumbled dire words, but obeyed.

That evening the quartet that entered a prominent box at Drury Lane Theater was the focus of considerable attention.

First of all Alfred entered wearing an amazingly subdued attire consisting of a dark green coat, cream breeches, and a waistcoat of dull gold and cream weave. If that was not sufficient to capture attention, Miss Mercy Herbert entered at his side, although not holding his arm some noted, wearing a delicate lavender gown with the prettiest silver design and silver ribbons, her costume completed by her evening hat of silver and lavender. She looked very handsome in her ensemble.

Many women and even more gentlemen who could see the box watched as a vision in delicate rose jaconet with a silver tissue overdress entered on the arm of her betrothed, Lord Latimer. Whispers dashed around the theater as Priscilla was tenderly ushered to her front seat. Her smile up at her escort was the sort to make other females gnash their teeth and gentlemen sigh with envy—the pale rose with the silver over it made her look like Aurora rising from the sea.

She was utterly gorgeous.

"I believe we have garnered a bit of attention," Felix dryly remarked when one gentleman ignored his companion to gaze at Priscilla with his glasses, seeming intent on inspecting Society's newest diamond.

"That was our intention, was it not?" Priscilla tartly rejoined, looking uncomfortable at being the target of so many eyes.

"It is certain that there will be some curiosity about Priscilla, not to mention the peculiar instance of Mr. Aston being with us. We are an oddly assembled quartet, my lord." Miss Herbert fixed him with her gaze, then shifted her attention to Priscilla. Her expression softened as she studied her niece. "Although Priscilla does me proud this evening."

"Well," her niece answered, "I'd be a mere nothing without the assistance of your dresser, Rose. How clever of her to put the silver tissue we had set aside for a gown over this rose jaconet."

"My dear Priscilla," Felix said, quite enjoying the view he had standing just behind her and gazing over her shoulder, "it is not the gown or the décolleté that charms, but the woman who wears that gown and has a décolleté worth the viewing that matters."

The most gorgeous creature in the theater blushed, and did so quite adorably to his mind. He noted the perfection of her dress, how her simple pearl earrings were set off by the twist of silver tissue in her golden curls. She was a goddess. And she was his!

Whatever the production offered that evening, it went by the wayside for most of the patrons. There was a huge amount of to-ing and fro-ing from one box to another. Fans were employed to such a degree that Felix thought they lowered the temperature by at least several degrees.

And the gentlemen came to get a closer look at his silver goddess. Felix allowed them into the enclosure, but never very near her. He stood guard as it were. And if his smile was a trifle smug, he was certain that his friends and acquaintances would forgive him. Even Chauncy would understand. How thankful he was that he had used the stereopticon that day at the charity school. He might have missed the bewitching woman who would soon bear his name.

At the interval he suggested she might appreciate a stroll in the corridor. "I feel certain that there are any number of women who are simply dying to get a closer look at you as well as that creation you are wearing."

She flashed him an admonishing look. "Why do I think you have an ulterior motive, my lord?"

"Perhaps because I do?" Felix offered his arm, and she gracefully rose to accept it. "You realize that you are the premier attraction here this evening. I doubt if the escapade with Alfred will be recalled tomorrow when the tabbies prattle over their tea. The latest *Diamond of the First Water* at Drury Lane is bound to prompt a great deal of discussion. I have no doubt that Rose could set up shop as a mantua maker when it is learned she played a part in your gown's creation."

"Good grief, my lord," Miss Herbert declared firmly, "do not let her hear that. I shall increase her pay and hope it is the end of the matter!"

They left the box Felix had engaged to join the parade of those who wanted to see or be seen.

The first person who sought their company was Viscount Rawlinson. "Dear cousin!" he gushed. "How delightful to meet you here this evening. I must say, you are in first looks, my dear. I would scarce call you a country cousin!"

"I am glad to see you as well." She looked about them to see that for the moment they were sufficiently apart from others so they could be somewhat private in speech. "Tell me, have you heard anything about that race at Epsom today?"

"Yes, of course I have," he replied importantly. "It was all over White's. Abingdon claimed that Tallbrook had cheated in the race, and of course that couldn't go unchallenged. Abingdon is now recovering from a shoulder wound. I understand Aston was there. What do you know of it?" He looked at Alfred. "Rumor hath it that you were hunting for your missing mistress. Lose her, did you?" He sniggered discreetly into a cambric handkerchief. "I would wager you got a fair soaking in the process. You had better be more selective when it comes to choosing a bit of calico, Aston. Find one who doesn't mind the damp!" He chuckled at his crumb of humor.

Alfred opened his mouth only to snap it shut when Felix trod on his foot.

"Then nothing is known of the woman?" Felix asked in a lazy, almost indifferent manner.

Unlike Alfred, the viscount was exceedingly sharp. His gaze darted from one member of the group to another, before returning back to Felix. "I see. I won't say a word. What do I know? I was not there—although I would hazard it became interesting." He raised a brow in inquiry.

Nothing more was said of the matter, for several of the gentlemen who had come to the box now sought them out again. As she was introduced to the few who had not come to the box earlier, Priscilla curtsied and smiled until she thought her face would congeal. When she left the village, she certainly had not dreamed she would be in such a position as this!

There was a lull in the conversation so that the remarks of a nearby girl could be clearly heard. "I do so wish to meet her. I wonder how she captivated such an elusive creature? Although he is not above making an offer, I wonder how he came to offer for her! A mere nobody!"

Priscilla turned her head just sufficiently to see Miss Anne Bolsolver drifting toward them. Her usual court was around her. Priscilla would be the first to admit she was a pretty girl, even if her mouth wore a discontented droop. However, her gown of silver tissue was of high style and became her well. She fetched up before Priscilla, giving her a haughty stare.

"Good evening, Miss Bolsolver." Priscilla was prepared to be gracious and even generous, though heaven knew she scarce felt like doing so. Felix sought propriety, and she would behave so until she was no longer required to present this facade of respectability. Not that she wasn't respectable. Felix wished her to be perfectly so. She drew comfort from her cousin, Viscount Rawlinson, Alfred—such as he was—and Felix all hovering about her. Even those gentlemen who had sought her earlier had not left. Aunt Mercy remained close to her side as well.

"You can talk!" Miss Bolsolver beamed a patently false smile. "How clever. I thought perhaps Lord Latimer would have to speak on your behalf. So many country girls have a dreadful accent and cannot be at all understood." She giggled, one of those annoying twittering sounds that could drive a person wild.

Making an effort to sound her most mellifluous, Priscilla said, "Lord Latimer has been all that one could wish—so dashing and dear." She conferred a caressing look on him. "I am indeed most fortunate to have captured him, as you so quaintly put it. You see? I cannot only speak, I also have excellent hearing and even better manners." She smiled benignly at Miss Bolsolver, who appeared to be at a total loss for words.

The unmannerly twit grumbled something that was lost in the noise of the throng. Her friends nudged her away.

Priscilla let out a deep sigh of relief.

"Well-done, cousin. That foolish girl has long been asking for someone to put her in her place." Viscount Rawlinson gave Felix a sympathetic glance.

Felix wondered if the viscount knew and how he knew that Felix had in the past requested Miss Bolsolver's hand in marriage. While he was now thankful to have been rejected, at the time it was a distinct blow to his pride.

"I believe it is time to return to the box," Miss Herbert declared. "I know none of you are paying the slightest attention to the play this evening, but it is amusing. In fact, it is almost as amusing as what is going on here." She serenely turned, clamped her hand on Alfred's arm, and marched off in the direction of their box.

The crowd slowly retraced their steps to wherever it was they sat. That a considerable number of them watched Priscilla didn't appear to bother her. She walked with her usual refined bearing, slipping her hand next to his side as they reached the stairway. Only then did he realize that she trembled slightly.

"Take heart, we should be able to leave before too long. Unless your aunt wants to see the end of the production?" Felix drew Priscilla close to him as a man came racing down the stairs.

"I wonder if it might not be best to remain until the end. We want no speculation as to where we go or what we do." She wore a thoughtful expression, as well she might.

Felix nodded his agreement. "I'd not thought of that. Speculation of any sort is the last thing we wish."

"From what my cousin said, it would appear that no one remarked on the woman who accompanied Mr. Aston."

"That is a blessing, although what you must have thought of Rawlinson's mention of my cousin's supposed bit of muslin, I can't imagine."

By this point they had rejoined the others in the box. Alfred turned his head upon their entry and caught the last remark Felix made.

"I say, I declare that Miss Herbert is a trump. You are a lucky man, Cousin Felix." Alfred's smile was approving. "A lot of women would have been caterwauling fit to wake the dead over the trip to Epsom, much less being mistaken for a bit of muslin. That was enough, but to be subjected to that rain was worse. I do hereby apologize."

Priscilla blinked her eyes, wondering if she had heard correctly. "How very kind you are, sir."

"Especially after I trod on your foot so heavily," Felix added, a smile lighting his eyes an iridescent green.

Alfred grimaced. "Well, I forgot and almost spoke out of turn."

"See that it does not happen." Felix smiled, but Priscilla observed that Alfred looked rather shaken by it.

"I promise to reform, really I do."

Since no one believed him, there was no reaction to his assurance.

While they waited for the play to conclude, Priscilla studied the people she could see. She discovered Miss Bolsolver. She was not directly across, but slightly to one side. Although Priscilla would never say so, the girl was a spiteful cat. It was a good thing she hadn't sunk her claws into Felix. What a dreadful marriage that would have been! But then, what sort of marriage might she have with Felix? Tolerable? She had hoped for better than that.

At the conclusion of the play, they waited until there was a lull, then took their departure, not wishing to remain for the second performance of the evening.

Felix tucked her arm next to him, commenting on the probable success of their stratagem. "You mentioned you would like to see a panorama. How about going with me tomorrow to view Barker's? It is in Leicester Square, not far from Miss Linwood's Gallery."

"And we would be out and about, prepared to be seen and noted." She spoke without bitterness. After all, this was what he had told his friend Chauncy that he wanted. "I shall wear my apple-green pelisse and the new bonnet. It is an unusual garment, so may be recognized."

"Clever girl."

Priscilla wondered just how clever he expected her to

be. She wasn't given to knowing what he expected beforehand.

"Tomorrow, then. Perhaps two of the clock? We can view the panorama, take tea at Gunter's, and perhaps a drive through the park when all is done?"

Priscilla stifled the desire to tell him all that was on her mind and quietly agreed with his suggestion for the morrow.

"Fine," he declared, little understanding that all was not fine.

Chapter Fourteen

Sunshine greeted Priscilla when she rose from her bed the following morning. She sat on the dainty chair by the window to sip her morning chocolate and nibble a roll before she dressed for her morning, enjoying the sun.

First of all she took a ride in the park with Felix's aunt Beatrice. Priscilla had a few questions she wanted to ask her. In particular, she wished to know more of Felix's father. In the past few weeks she had heard snippets, a phrase here, a few words there, and none of it kind or good. But then, gossip was rarely kind or good.

What intrigued her was that whenever the speaker realized a young lady was within hearing, the gossip halted, sometimes in mid word. Whatever the gentleman had done that was scandalous was truly deemed unfit for her tender ears. All of which made her long to know more.

After her hasty snack, Priscilla left the house with a groom trailing behind her. That Felix had hired him either for her, or possibly as someone to tend the horses, she didn't know. But he had brought the horse from Felix's mews and now followed her with determination.

Knowing she looked well in her blue habit with the jaunty hat set just so, she headed for the park and Rotten Row, hoping that Lady Beatrice would not fail her.

Priscilla had about abandoned hope when she was hailed from a distance. She halted, waiting. Looking behind, she noted a distressingly familiar figure.

Miss Anne Bolsolver came dashing up to where Priscilla sat warily waiting and watching. "Oh, good. You heard me."

"I should think anyone in the vicinity would have heard you call. You wish to speak with me?" Priscilla resolved to remain cool and distant. She did not trust this girl in the slightest. She had exhibited inferior manners whenever they met, particularly last evening.

Miss Bolsolver indicated they should continue riding rather than keep the horses standing. Priscilla nodded agreement that it would be best and kept an uneasy distance from the chatty girl and her fidgety mare.

Priscilla's curiosity was gratified when at last the girl apparently got to the matter she wished to impart.

"I wondered if you were aware that Lord Latimer had asked for my hand in marriage first." There was a complacent cat-in-the-cream-pot note in her voice.

Priscilla caught the sly gleam in the young lady's eyes and decided she was being baited. "Obviously you rejected his suit. Although why, I cannot imagine. He is handsome, polished, from an old family, and quite rich. That wasn't enough for you? You dislike handsome gentlemen?" She managed a serene expression, just barely. She disliked Miss Bolsolver, finding it difficult to be so much as civil to the girl.

"Actually, I have no feelings one way or the other. I shall marry the man my father believes most suitable." The pomposity in her voice was scarcely tolerable.

"How nice." Priscilla borrowed her aunt's favorite word with delight. It was so fitting. She devoutly hoped that Lord Bolsolver would betroth the girl to someone worthy of her charms—a "nice" man.

"I must admit it would be lovely to become a countess." The wistfulness in her voice was perceptible. Yet there was also a note of uncertainty. "But to overcome his past . . . that I cannot do."

"I cannot say I have considered that aspect of wedding Lord Latimer. He is a fine man from well-bred ancestry." Priscilla endeavored to seem detached, calm. Actually she would have enjoyed paddling the girl. What nonsense was she about to pour forth for Priscilla's benefit?

"You do not mind the *scandal* in the family? I have

heard it mentioned any number of times." She sounded sweetly informative and somewhat patronizing.

"Find me a family of the peerage that does not have a bit of scandal in their history." Priscilla left it at that. Better to permit Miss Bolsolver to get off her chest why she had sought out Priscilla. There had to be a reason beyond defaming the Sutton family—who had likely held their title long before the Bolsolver barony existed.

They rode on side by side for a time, talking of inconsequentials—things they thought of interest in the city. Although Priscilla would wager it annoyed Miss Bolsolver that her tattle hadn't provoked Priscilla to a round defense of her betrothed—rising to her bait as it were. One did not respond to execrable manners.

"I understand Lady Beatrice and her husband are to give a ball." Miss Bolsolver uttered the words in a manner designed to perplex.

"True." Priscilla longed to tell her to save her performance for someone more appreciative—like the manager of the Drury Lane Theater.

"You shall attend, I suppose?" How sweetly she asked.

"I have been invited, yes. It is only natural, seeing that I am betrothed to Lady Beatrice's nephew." Priscilla frowned in puzzlement. What was this girl getting at?

"Everyone is talking about it. Almost everyone I know has an invitation." There was a sad droop to her mouth, and her eyes held a woeful expression. Oh, she did know how to act quite well. She was definitely worthy of Drury Lane.

"I see." And Priscilla did see. Miss Bolsolver and her parents had not been invited, not being friends *or* enemies of Lady Beatrice and her husband. "But you think it would be interesting to be present at this ball?"

"Umm, well, it might be. Just to see the decorations, possibly the gowns." She bestowed a condescending smile on Priscilla. "I doubt many of the *ton* will attend."

Priscilla bit back the urge to laugh. "If and when I do see her ladyship, I will mention your desire."

"Thank you." They rode in silence a bit longer before Miss Bolsolver spoke again. "I would make a far better countess, you know," she confided sweetly. "I attended the *Academy for Young Gentlewomen* near Bath. You must have heard of it, for it is highly esteemed. And besides which I have a very large dowry." She tilted her nose in the air and assumed a virtuous pose that nearly set Priscilla to giggles. Bad manners compounded by overweening pride!

"I do hope you achieve your goal, Miss Bolsolver. There must be any number of peers who would be happy to have that dowry. And you as well, naturally." Unable to tolerate another moment of her company, Priscilla edged away from her. "I am meeting a friend. Excuse me." And without waiting for a reply from Miss Bolsolver, Priscilla dashed off to where she had spotted Lady Beatrice up ahead.

That lady turned to greet Priscilla with a broad smile. "Hello. Lovely day, is it not?"

"Oh, my lady, I am so very glad to see you."

"I thought that was you. There was a young woman with you. I didn't want to intrude." Lady Beatrice scanned the Row behind them. "She is leaving. You enjoyed a chat?"

"It was quite a revelation. I have been informed, ever so bluntly, mind you, that Miss Bolsolver would make a far better countess than I. *She* attended a fine academy near Bath and has the additional benefit of a large dowry. Of course, *she* will wed whichever gentleman her father selects for her, but I suspect she thinks that now Lord Latimer is to become respectable it makes an enormous difference. To her future, at any rate."

"I did not think to invite the Bolsolvers to the ball. Should I? If they made Felix unhappy, I doubt he would wish to see them." Lady Beatrice gave Priscilla a doubtful look.

"I would think it might be rather amusing, my lady. Felix can turn his nose up at them and let Miss Bolsolver stew in her presumptuous assumptions. I doubt I have ever longed to paddle a girl as much as I did just now." Priscilla gave her ladyship a grim look.

Lady Beatrice chuckled softly, then turned to the matter of the upcoming ball. She wanted Priscilla's opinion on several things—flowers and the motif.

When they had discussed the ball from beginning to end and reached satisfactory solutions, Priscilla dared to make her inquiry.

"Has Felix's father agreed to attend? I am looking forward to meeting him."

Lady Beatrice shook her head. "I've not heard a word from my brother. He is the most vexing creature alive. I daresay he will pop up just before the ball, assuming that *I* would take for granted that he would attend."

"Miss Bolsolver made much of some gossip regarding him. I suppose that has about as much substance as Miss Bolsolver?" Priscilla kept her gaze on her ladyship, watching the play of conflicting emotions on her face.

"As to gossip—indeed, there has been far too much gossip about my brother. The Marquess of Silverstone has always commanded attention, and mostly when he did not seek it. It is my belief he eventually decided to offer what the public sought—scandalous behavior. He isn't perfect, but he is an honorable man. He has not beggared the estate, has made it profitable instead. I know he loves his son very much, yet it is difficult for him to communicate his feelings to Felix." Lady Beatrice sighed.

"I understand many men are like that—reserved and seemingly unconcerned with their offspring. My own father is somewhat remote, yet I am sure he is fond of us."

"You know that Lady Silverstone died giving birth to Felix's sister? The infant didn't survive the difficult birth, either. It utterly devastated my brother."

"And Felix?" Priscilla was beginning to understand some of the reasoning behind Felix's behavior and thinking.

"I do not know how Felix felt. He bottles things up inside him, I think. Never have we spoken of it. Perhaps that is something you may do." Lady Beatrice gave Priscilla a questioning look.

"He is taking me to see the Barker Panorama this afternoon—the one at Leicester Square." Priscilla was not prepared to discuss her future life as Countess Latimer. It did not seem real to her, more like a vague dream.

"You will like that excessively. It is an amazing display of perspective." They turned back, and when they reached the point where they parted ways, Lady Beatrice said, "I will send an invitation to the Bolsolvers if you think it ought to be done."

Priscilla heard the query in her voice. "It is hard to say whether it would be better to let her fret at being excluded from the most important ball of the Season, or invite her and risk her nasty tongue."

"I shall invite her. It will be delightful to squash her pretensions." Lady Beatrice gave Priscilla a naughty smile.

"I suspect you might be rather good at that," Priscilla concluded, admiring the regal air her ladyship possessed when she wished. After a final farewell wave, Priscilla headed for home, the groom trotting behind her.

There was much to consider. She handed Beauty over to the groom, then entered the house in a pensive mood.

She found Aunt Mercy waiting for her in the breakfast room, where an array of luncheon dishes were set forth. Priscilla plumped down on one of the chairs to have a little chat.

"You had a nice ride, dear?"

Priscilla smiled. "I suppose you might say it was 'nice.' I certainly had an interesting time. I intended to meet Lady Beatrice, as you know. Instead I first was accosted by none other than Miss Anne Bolsolver! Dearest aunt, she informed me that she believes *she* would make a far better countess than I would." A mischievous smile hovered over Priscilla's mouth, and her eyes danced with amusement.

"What? How dare she? The very idea! And to say such a thing to you, of all people!" Miss Herbert was obviously very incensed on behalf of the Herberts, not to mention the Suttons.

"Too true. However, she also wanted to procure an invitation to the Astons' ball! It seems we neglected to put the Bolsolver family on the list!"

"Rubbish! What did you tell her?"

"What could I say? I said I would mention her desire to Lady Beatrice when next I saw her." Priscilla pleated the linen napkin that was folded next to her empty plate.

"You saw her this morning. What was her reaction?"

Miss Herbert's hand lingered by her teacup, intent upon what her niece had to report.

"She has decided they will get an invitation. While they are not her enemies, they are Felix's and as such warrant the invitation. The ball will be a just punishment to them, if you ask me. When they see how Society comes flocking to the Aston ball, they will be more than a little depressed. It isn't every day a father whistles down the wind a fortune, a handsome gentleman, and a future marquessate. I shall enjoy seeing the expression on his face!"

"I believe I will as well." Aunt sipped her tea, waiting to hear the rest.

"Miss Bolsolver smugly informed me that Felix had asked for her hand and that her father had rejected him—too much scandal in the family. What a stupid man Lord Bolsolver must be. However, I should think Felix would soon have been exceedingly sorry if wedded to that silly chit."

"Goodness, what a depressing thought."

"Lady Beatrice has not heard from Felix's father yet. She said she'd not be surprised if he just pops up at the last moment." Priscilla helped herself to a bit of food.

"Lord George will be there, as will you and I."

"Do not forget the Archdeacon Pallant!" Priscilla reminded.

Aunt Mercy twinkled a smile. "I doubt if anyone could if they wished. Actually, I think he is rather nice."

Priscilla smiled at the Archdeacon being described as "nice." He was impressive, eminent, and certainly lofty. Somehow "nice" left something to be desired.

"What time will Felix be here?"

"He promised about two of the clock. I shall change into my leaf-print dress and the apple-green pelisse. My new bonnet goes so admirably with them. I do like that clutch of feathers you bought for it. I must thank you again, dearest aunt. You have been more than generous to me." Priscilla fondly bestowed a quick kiss on her aunt's scented cheek.

"Well, I have yet to find a way to take my money with me. And I enjoy spending it on you. You do pay handsomely for dressing, dear girl. Most rewarding, indeed. I hoped that you might find an eligible husband while in London. I never dreamed you would find an earl!"

Priscilla ate a sandwich she put together and drank a cup of tea before heading for her room. She wanted to rest prior to going off with Felix. The thought that she wasn't yet married to that earl her aunt admired lingered in her mind. There was many a slip . . .

Her smile was a wry twist of her lips. She promised to wear the apple-green because people would recognize her in it. Odd, most women would balk at being known for a certain ensemble, and here she was making a point of it.

When she arose from her bed, not having napped but feeling rested, she donned the leaf-print dress, and sat down to do her hair.

"Allow me, miss." Lily had slipped into the room and took over the problem of the blond curls. In a trice she had tamed them into a modish style. Priscilla wished she might have a pair of cameo earrings, but she'd not repine, she liked her simple peridot ones. Her bonnet was all a girl might ask for in fashion, as was her dress and pelisse. Felix would have no cause to bemoan her appearance.

She went down to the drawing room to await him, too restless to stay in her bedroom. Gloves in hand, she spun around for her aunt's inspection.

"I must say that is a nice pelisse, my dear." Her aunt looked up from her ever-present embroidery to survey her niece.

Priscilla's smile was genuine, for she dearly loved her aunt, "nice" and all. "All thanks to you." At the sound of steps on the stairs, she slowly rotated to face the doorway.

Simpkins entered with the earl immediately behind him.

"Is there anything you wish, ma'am?" the staid butler inquired of his employer.

"Nothing, Simpkins. So, Lord Latimer, it is a fine day outside, I believe. Priscilla rode in the park this morning. Met your aunt. She also met a Miss Bolsolver."

Felix crossed the room to take one of Priscilla's hands in his. "What did *she* want?"

Priscilla offered a cool look. "I think she has changed her mind about you. She informed me that she was far more suited to being a countess than I am. After all, *she* attended the select *Academy for Gentlewomen* outside Bath, and her dowry is huge." Priscilla tilted her head, offering a roguish smile. "Shall you be sorry, my lord?"

"I suppose in some eyes that is sufficient. I should think breeding and ancestry are more important."

"Pray, do not forget manners, my lord," added Miss Herbert in her most elevated way. "I believe a wife should have good manners. To be deficient in manners or to be deemed vulgar is the death of a young women in Society."

"I am persuaded your niece lacks neither breeding nor manners, ma'am. Her ancestry is of the finest." Felix bowed with old-fashioned courtesy.

Priscilla could see he pleased her aunt with his comment. Actually, he rather pleased Priscilla as well.

He turned to study her. "You are ready. Shall we be off to a pleasant afternoon?" He turned to Miss Herbert. "I trust you will not be too down pin while remaining home alone?"

Miss Herbert turned a delicate pink. "Your uncle George is coming over to spend the afternoon mulling over past times. That is what old people tend to do, you know."

"You will never be old, dear aunt. You wouldn't know how." Priscilla gently hugged her aunt, then left the house with Felix quite in charity with the world.

"You know," she confided, "your uncle has been over to see my aunt a number of times. Do you think there could be an interest there?"

"I doubt it. After his wife died, he has seemed happy to lead a bachelor life. They likely enjoy a good chat."

No more was said on that subject as he directed the conversation to the panorama, wanting to know if she desired to see both tiers or merely one.

"Both, if we have time. I read in the newspaper that they are showing the Siege of Flushing."

"Indeed. It is in the greater circle. I believe the Bay of Messina is in the smaller upper circle. I think you will enjoy it."

"I confess that life in London, all I have seen while here, is considerably different from life in our village."

"You are happy you came?"

She afforded him an amused look. If she said yes—which she ought to—would he take it as praise? Fortunately she was spared a reply. Traffic had increased to the point where it took all his attention to guide his horse through the throng of carriages, drays, and the people who persisted in wanting to cross from one side of the street to the other. She had no desire to distract him.

When they reached Leicester Square, he handed the reins to his groom before assisting Priscilla from the curricle.

She thought the matter of her pleasure in London was forgotten until he said, "And how long must I wait for a reply to my query?"

"Of course I must say I am happy that my aunt brought me to London. I would have never met you had I not come. Is that not what you wished to hear?" She gave him an impatient glance, then turned her gaze to the exterior of the panorama. Viewed from the pavement, it was not a very prepossessing building. The entrance was modest—a narrow door hard by a shop selling coffee, tea, tobacco and cigars that she thought a strange combination for a shop to offer.

Cranbourne Street ran off from Leicester Square at this point. She could see the curricle, driven by the groom, disappearing down its length.

Felix paid the entrance fee of two shillings each, and they went inside to walk up the stairs.

She wasn't sure what she had expected, but the scene was overwhelming. It was as though you had been placed in the middle of the town on the top of some tall building. Around you bombs and rockets pierced the roofs of houses from which terrified inhabitants fled. They carried whatever they could manage from their burning homes, some dragging children with them. Others helped the sick and wounded escape as best they could. It was pure horror.

"I have never thought war a pleasant matter. I see I grossly underestimated its mayhem. What a terrifying spectacle." Priscilla longed to bury her head against his shoulder, to shut out the impact of the painting.

"It isn't too much? I had not thought you to be so sensitive." Felix seemed alarmed at her reaction, and she sought to reassure him that she was not such a wilting pansy as all that.

"Who would not have pity for such people in such circumstances? We are blessed to have been spared."

He guided her from the room to ascend to the upper floor to see the smaller view of the Bay of Messina.

"My heavens," Priscilla cried as she stared about her, still clinging to Felix's comforting arm, "it is quite as though you are there. The effect is astonishing and not a little deceptive. Look—over there you would swear you are thirty miles away, and over here it seems as though you are but a few feet from the scene. I do not wish to demean the Flushing painting, but I think I prefer this one. Why, I would swear I can feel a breeze from the bay against my face, it is so real. It is illusion at its best, I would think."

Felix was not studying the painting; he was instead watching Priscilla. "Yes, the very best, I should say."

She flashed him an intimate smile of great warmth at his understanding.

"Well, I am surprised to find you here."

Priscilla knew that voice. She had heard it only some hours ago in the park. Could that dratted girl have trailed them here? It was the last place Priscilla expected to see Miss Bolsolver. Yet, hadn't Priscilla said something about seeing this place? Had she mentioned this afternoon, though? She couldn't recall. It had been one of those polite passing remarks one makes when conversing with a stranger about seeing the city.

"Miss Herbert desired to view a few of the sights in London. Naturally I wish to do all to please my dear Priscilla." Felix gazed at Priscilla with a fond expression that she would swear was genuine. All around them was a painting that depicted an illusion. Was his seeming affection an illusion as well?

"This is an astonishing exhibit, is it not, Miss Bolsolver?" Priscilla gave her a smile as false as the one that the girl flashed at her.

"Well, I did not care for the Siege of Flushing view, but this is agreeable. My nerves simply will not tolerate such violence as expressed in the other. I prefer the calm tranquility of Messina." She simpered at Felix.

Priscilla hoped Miss Bolsolver annoyed him as much as she did her.

"Lovely," Priscilla murmured, shifting closer to Felix. If the chit wanted to tag after them, Priscilla would make it clear that the girl was wasting her time.

Felix cleared his throat. "I believe we have seen what we cared to view. Would you like to depart, my dear?"

Priscilla gave him a blinding smile of devotion. "Yes. I believe that would be utterly lovely."

He blinked, but recovered quickly. "We shall perhaps see you another time, Miss, er, Bolsolver." His manner was civil, his voice downright frigid.

Priscilla sensed he stretched his courtesy to the limits in being polite to the girl. Pity she wasn't truly sensitive. Priscilla would wager she had the hide of an elephant.

Miss Bolsolver was obviously stumped. There was no way she might intrude on their outing. They hadn't asked her to join them, nor acknowledged the young chap who trundled along behind her. She was a perfect example of frustration, and Priscilla thought it most delightful.

She gave the girl, who was possibly approaching twenty and thus ought to know better, a cool stare before turning away. Felix smartly marched Priscilla to the exit, down the stairs, and out the door in a trice.

"You do move quickly when you are determined." Priscilla withdrew her arm from the protection of his, walking at his side with caution.

"You know what I think of that girl. How in the world did she manage to turn up here to spoil our afternoon?"

"I may have mentioned that I intended to view the panorama, but I doubt I indicated I would do so today."

Felix looked thoughtful, but said nothing in reply.

They sauntered along Cranbourne Street until they found the curricle and his groom. The horses had been walked and appeared ready to go whenever asked.

"Now . . . Gunter's is the next item for the day, if I recall correctly."

"I must say, I do hope Miss Bolsolver doesn't follow us there. I fear she would quite spoil my ice."

He laughed at that. "Perhaps her frosty looks would be enough to keep your ice from melting. She was not exactly warm to you."

Priscilla chuckled, as she supposed he'd intended. "I agree. I fancy she saved her warmth for you."

It did not take long to reach the tea shop. It took even less time to order two pineapple ices. They relaxed in the comfort of the curricle, allowing the waiters to dash from the carriage to the shop and back again with their ices.

"Um, this is one thing I should miss away from London. I doubt if such as this can be had anywhere else." Priscilla savored a spoonful of her ice, permitting the flavor to be fully enjoyed.

"Actually we have an ice storage on our estate—I should say, my family estate. When I was a lad the cook made ices for us a number of times." Felix spoke in an offhand manner, idly, as though not really considering what he was saying.

"You do not spend any time there at present?" She hoped he would continue with his reminiscences. Everything she learned about him was of interest to her.

"No." He set aside his empty dish, then took hers, handing the little tray upon which they had been brought to the carriage back to the waiter. "No more than necessary."

Knowing he had ended all closeness, at least for the time being, Priscilla leaned back against the cushions. Waiting.

"It is a pity to end the day, but I imagine you must dress for the evening." Felix lounged across from her. He did not inquire what her plans were and she decided to say nothing to him. Apparently it mattered not to him whether she was at home or out.

She thanked him prettily for the afternoon's pleasures

once they reached Miss Herbert's residence. "Would you care to come in for a bit?"

"No, not at this time. But thank you just the same." He wore an odd expression. She couldn't guess what it concealed.

She didn't stand there, but hurried into the house. After handing her pelisse and bonnet to Lily she joined her aunt, alone in the drawing room.

"A message came for you while you were gone." At Priscilla's look of inquiry, Miss Herbert added, "Lady Beatrice requests you come over in the morning to meet Lord Silverstone."

"Oh, my."

Chapter Fifteen

They spent a quiet evening at home. Priscilla had been thankful for that; she wished to mull over what she would do—or say—when confronted with Felix's father. Her aunt had been terribly reassuring, something Priscilla needed.

While she had met a marquess at home, he had been a distant figure. His son, the earl, had married Lady Harriet Dane, a young woman Priscilla admired greatly. But Priscilla had never imagined *she* would wed an earl.

Of Felix she had not seen a thing, nor had any message. He had said nothing about setting a date for their wedding. To her, the entire affair had assumed an unreal quality. She thought she understood his position, but did he give any thought to hers? The more she considered it, the more incensed she became. Was it because of his elevated position that he assumed she would fall in with his every wish? Oh, she loved him. She admitted that readily to the face she saw in her looking glass.

But it seemed to her that while he liked her well enough, seemed pleased to escort her about town, appreciated her dealing with Miss Bolsolver, he didn't love Priscilla as she would like to be loved. Even a little. On that unhappy thought she drifted off to sleep.

Morning did not bring any reassurance. She had no idea how Felix had spent the previous evening. But then, gentlemen—especially unmarried ones—were not given to spending their time in a woman's pocket. This would be even truer in his case. He had no obligation to dance to her tune. Yet she had missed his presence dreadfully. The evening had crawled by on leaden fingers.

Even though he did not owe her an explanation she would have welcomed a word from him. It certainly would have bolstered her spirits as she went to this fateful meeting with his parent. But of course, he didn't know she was to meet his father. He'd likely have objected strongly to such a talk had he known. Since he hadn't come around to see her, or invite her anywhere, or even communicate in any way, she couldn't see that she owed him an explanation.

It was around one of the clock when she presented herself at the fashionable Aston residence. For people who had been out of Society, they lived in the midst of it, and very nicely too if the house was anything to go by. Lily had gone with her and now settled on a chair in the entry. Priscilla did not expect to stay long.

Shown to the tasteful drawing room by a reserved butler, Priscilla entered to find the room empty. Looking about, she admired the quiet charm of the room, furnished in a classical manner with pale gray and rose predominant. The Savonnerie rug in the center of the room was a marvel of delicate flowers and scrolls incorporating these colors along with cream and subtle greens. She liked the simple design of the furniture she suspected came from the Hepplewhite workshop, with neat chairs upholstered in either rose or gray-striped satin. Draperies of the same gray-striped satin hung at the windows, allowing the sun to brighten the interior of the room.

Her first thoughts of being alone were shattered when a tall gentleman rose from the concealment of a vast rose damask wing chair. "You are Miss Herbert, I expect."

She knew he had to be Felix's father, the similarity was too great for him to be anyone else. He crossed to take her hand, placing a light kiss upon it. Priscilla was shocked at her reaction to his touch. His son could take lessons from his father. She withstood his scrutiny with equanimity. The same green eyes that Felix had searched hers with an intensity she found unsettling.

"I am delighted to meet the young lady my son is to

marry." He released her hand with what appeared to be reluctance.

When it seemed his lordship was about to study her at some length, he gestured to the sofa. He returned to the wing chair, where he could continue his chat with her.

She, in turn, studied him openly wondering how this interview, or whatever it might be called, would go. Subsiding uneasily onto the sofa, she waited and watched.

She began to see what it was that made him such a success with women. He possessed a magnetic allure that Felix already had to some degree. Lord Silverstone's voice had the same rich vibrancy that Felix had in abundance. They were more alike than she expected. Gray threads were streaked throughout Lord Silverstone's dark hair, giving him a distinguished appearance. Felix would likely have that same look as he grew older. She liked it.

"My sister will join us shortly," he said at last, breaking the silence. "Tell me how you met my son," he invited with suave courtliness. He was a knowledgeable gentleman, skilled in conversation, and well versed in the art of putting a young lady at ease. This he proceeded to do with autocratic grace.

Once Priscilla had explained the meeting, he smiled and reminisced how he had met his wife, then drifted on to other impersonal topics so that she lost her stiffness, became less wary of him. It was difficult to imagine that this pleasant gentleman with such beautiful manners could be that same man who had caused such scandal and alienated his son to such a point.

But he was handsome still to a degree that she could understand how he might have women begging for his notice. There was a compelling charm about him that drew one. It would be difficult to pay attention to another man when he was in the room, she mused. This was a dangerous appeal and he was likely a dangerous gentleman. What a pity her eldest sister, Claudia, was married, this man would have suited her to a tee.

A rustle of silk drew her gaze to the door.

"Oh, good, you have had a comfortable coze while I finished dealing with the arrangements for flowers. This ball is beginning to assume a life of its own, I vow."

Lady Beatrice sailed across the room to sit next to Priscilla.

Her brother smiled at her, one of those humoring sorts of smiles brothers tend to give tiresome sisters. Priscilla recognized it at once—she had been the recipient of far too many from her own brother.

"I trust you two are becoming acquainted?" Lady Beatrice patted Priscilla's hand. "I warn you, dear brother, I am very fond of this young lady. Whatever you may do, I beg you not to frighten her away from your Felix. She will be the best wife for him. See if I am not right."

Priscilla could feel the heat rising in her cheeks. Blushing was something she could not control. "I shall do my best to be a good wife for him."

"I feel that you will be precisely what he needs," the marquess said. "How fortunate Felix is to find a woman who not only is beautiful but possesses breeding as well. I should imagine that would be important to him." His lordship rubbed his chin while watching Priscilla from beneath silvered brows.

She would have liked to inform his lordship that he had assessed his son quite well. However, there was no way she would reveal Felix's wish to find a proper, decorous wife as blurted forth by Mr. Chauncy Renshaw. She rather thought that young man now avoided her, rueful at having spilled something that ought to have been kept secret.

A glance at the clock gracing the mantelpiece reminded her that she really ought to leave. Much as the marquess intrigued her, she knew it would be improper to remain too long. Perhaps once she was married to Felix she might persuade him to renew his relationship with his father. It would be a pity for any children they had never to know such a remarkable grandfather.

"Lady Beatrice, I had best go. My aunt will be waiting for me." Priscilla paused, then added, "Are you aware Lord George has been calling on her often? They play cards and reminisce about days gone by. I believe they enjoy their tranquil afternoons."

Lady Beatrice exchanged an enigmatic look with the marquess. "How interesting. I am glad that he finds favor in Miss Herbert's eyes."

Deciding she had said more than enough, Priscilla rose and curtsied to Lord Silverstone, then said her farewells to him, adding that she hoped she would see him at the ball. With Lady Beatrice's arm linked in hers, they slipped from the room to head down the stairs. In the entry hall, she paused. "I like Felix's father. It's difficult to see how their breech can be healed, but healed it must be.".

"I agree. Much as I love my nephew, he can be remarkably pigheaded at times."

Priscilla chuckled at that, as likely intended. She shook Lady Beatrice's hand, then left the house. It was but a short distance to Hanover Square from the stylish Aston residence. Rather than call for a carriage, she simply walked home, Lily trailing silently behind her.

Upon arrival at the Herbert house, Priscilla found her aunt in a dither.

"What is going on, pray tell?" Priscilla removed her gloves and bonnet, handing them to Lily. After shrugging out of the pelisse and giving that to the girl as well, she shooed the maid away. "Now, explain, please."

"Lord Latimer was just here, and I was hard-pressed not to tell him where you were. He said he would call back in a short time, perhaps calculating you had merely gone for a brief walk. Oh, do say you have been walking." Miss Herbert wrung her hands until Priscilla gently wrapped hers about them.

"Calm yourself, dearest aunt. I did chance to walk home from Aston house. If I say I have been walking, I shall be telling the truth."

"Oh, I hope he comes while you still have that fresh rose color in your cheeks. Now, you must tell me all about your meeting with the marquess."

"I do not understand why you were not invited as well. However, I had a pleasant conversation with him before Lady Beatrice joined us. He has beautiful manners and more charm that any man has the right to possess. I do not see how the rift between Felix and his father can be mended, but we ought to try. Perhaps it will come to me later."

She had taken a turn about the room when Simpkins entered with Lord Latimer behind him.

Priscilla had the opportunity to compare the two men, having so recently seen his father. Of the two, she thought the marquess a trifle overrated. Felix might not have the suave allure his father had cultivated but he had more: a well-bred and understated elegance. And there was a sincerity within him that shone forth from the green depths of his eyes.

"I am happy to find you at home. You had an enjoyable walk? I can see the roses are blooming in your cheeks as evidence."

"My walk was most pleasant, my lord." She dipped a polite curtsy, then gestured he be seated.

"I meant to see you last evening." He gave her a sheepish look before continuing. "I was working on my stereopticon and totally lost track of time. Perhaps you will come with me next time I go to the charity school. I have a new set of slides—*The Remarkable Adventures of the Old Woman and Her Pig*."

"How nice," Miss Herbert cried. "Is it not nice, Priscilla?"

"Indeed. It is most admirable. I shall admit I hoped to see you last evening. I confess I enjoy your company, my lord. How lovely you are putting together another showing for the little children. Won't they be happy!"

"Come with me tomorrow?" Green eyes so like his father's beseeched her.

"I would never refuse you." And this was true enough. She had fallen so completely under his spell that she would foolishly go wherever he wanted, whenever he wanted.

"Perhaps you would care to join me for a drive in the park? Or would you rather ride? Beauty would likely welcome a chance to stretch her legs."

"I daresay she would. I took her out yesterday, though." Priscilla gave him a dubious perusal. She accepted his absorption in his stereopticon; it was a fascinating thing. Why was she doubtful about his present attention to her? Or was she hunting for things that didn't exist?

"When you return, you must try on the gown that came from Madame Clotilde today. I think you will be very pleased," Aunt Mercy said, smiling with her delight.

"Ah, yes, the ball. What color do you wear?" Felix glanced from her aunt to Priscilla.

"It is pale aqua crepe with pretty embroidery."

"Why do you not go up to change into your habit while I wait here with your aunt. You can at the same time snatch a look at the ball gown. I understand most women set great store by a new gown. I shall send my groom for our horses—if that is agreeable with you?"

She made a face at him. "How well you guess my mind, sir. I shall do precisely that." She curtsied to him, gave her aunt an affectionate smile, leaving the room in a flurry of periwinkle blue.

In her room she first examined the pretty gown laid out on her bed.

"Oh, Lily, it is fine, is it not? I vow that Lord Latimer will like it excessively."

"How could he not, miss?" The maid helped her from the dress and into her blue habit, then to change footwear.

Priscilla trailed a hand over the exquisite aqua silk, touched the tulle trim. Next, with hat and gloves in hand, she hastened to the drawing room. She plopped her hat on, catching sight of it in the looking glass to make certain she had it right. Lily had followed with her crop that Priscilla took after donning her gloves.

"You are a marvel of speed, my dear." Felix looked pleased, as well he should given how she had hurried.

"I wanted to see if I could change before the horses get here. Shall we see if I managed it?" Before leaving the room, she paused to direct a warm look at her aunt. "And I do like the gown. Very much."

"That's nice, dear." Her aunt reposed in her chair by the sofa table. The Argand lamp had been lit to offer better illumination for her needlework. Settled happily with that, she waved off her niece.

Felix rattled down the stairs with Priscilla at his side. Upon opening the front door, they found the horses saddled and awaiting them.

"Oh, dear, I was so sure I would win."

Felix boosted her up to her saddle on Beauty, then mounted Beau. "It is a nice day, far too nice to sit inside."

"I expect we shall see many others of the same opinion when we reach the park." Priscilla urged Beauty forward and Felix had Beau match her pace. In short order they were in the park and trotting along Rotten Row among far too many others.

Felix found he had missed her when she wasn't around. Even if she said not a word, he liked her company. She soothed him, yet she always excited him. What a contradiction she was. Would he ever understand her? He appreciated that she was always ready to listen to anything he had to say on a subject. Too many women either paid no attention or interrupted with their own thoughts. Priscilla listened to him. He liked that.

They saw Chauncy before long, riding with several other chaps he knew. Darting a sidelong glance at Priscilla, he was extremely glad he had nailed down the betrothal. She looked good enough to eat, and those chaps were not blind. They came prancing over on their high-bred mounts to join Felix and to meet Priscilla. He politely introduced them, giving thanks he had been able to keep Priscilla to himself as much as he had.

She was civil to the gentlemen, proper to the core, and how Felix appreciated that. She didn't flirt as so many girls felt necessary when around men. Nor did she think it essential to show off on her horse. She gave Felix a look, then cast her gaze on the lane ahead of them.

"We are not wasting our time with you fellows," Felix quipped. "Be gone." He grinned to take away any sting from his words.

They understood. They edged away and went on to see others. One good look at Priscilla Herbert made it clear to one and all why Felix had no desire to share her company.

"You have interesting friends, my lord," she remarked when they had distanced themselves from the cluster of Dandies and Corinthians.

"I suppose they are. Not a bad lot, though."

At that precise moment Priscilla caught sight of Lady Beatrice and Lord Silverstone tooling along in a graceful curricle not far from Rotten Row. What on earth could she do? Somehow she didn't think it the best thing to have the pair of men confront each other in the middle of Hyde Park at the height of the afternoon parade. In among the other phaetons, chaises, and barouches, the curricle was scarcely to be seen. But if Priscilla caught sight of it, couldn't Felix as well?

There were some trees up ahead. She was suddenly inspired. "I shall race you to those trees, Felix."

"Race? Are you mad? This is Rotten Row at the fashionable hour."

"Very well—a discreet canter. But I will wager Beauty can best your Beau." She gave him a mischievous grin and was off.

Felix followed, as she hoped he would.

When they reached the cluster of trees, Priscilla casually looked back and no longer could see the curricle. They had vanished. "I won!"

She conducted herself with utmost decorum the rest of the ride to compensate for her cantering race to the trees. Felix seemed pleased and that was what mattered.

Her ordeal was not over, however. Upon the return down Rotten Row whom should they encounter but Miss Bolsolver. Priscilla considered the girl with disfavor. She was garbed in a showy scarlet habit in a military style. Her mount was equally showy—and skittish as well.

"Fancy meeting you in the park, my lord," the chit said in her breathless, wistful manner. She totally ignored Priscilla, which didn't bother her in the least.

"It seems that anyone who is anyone is here this afternoon." His expression was as bland as his words.

Priscilla suppressed a grin. That ought to put the forward young miss in her place. Of course it didn't.

"Everyone is talking about your aunt's ball." She finally took notice of Priscilla politely waiting to one side of the trio. "Have you ordered your gown yet? I fancy you will be disappointed. All the *best* mantua makers in Town are utterly deluged with orders."

"My gown from Madame Clotilde has been delivered just this morning. As soon as the invitation came, we requested Madam to attend us with swatches and sketches. She already has our measurements, you see." Priscilla took a little satisfaction in the annoyance that settled on Miss Bolsolver's discontented face. It appeared to be an oft-recurring manner.

"Oh. Mama has ordered me a gown from Mrs. Ash. We look forward to seeing you in any event. It will be the highlight of the Season." She flirted with Felix, batting her lashes in an absolutely nauseating manner. How he kept a straight face was beyond Priscilla.

Mrs. Ash was not a premier mantua maker. Her shop produced insipid gowns of inferior workmanship and designs. Marshaling her countenance into one of prosaic interest, Priscilla waited silently until they could politely excuse themselves.

Seeing Felix growing impatient, Priscilla spoke up. "It is a pity we must hurry off. I promised my aunt I'd not be overlong. Lord Latimer and I have much to discuss." She gave a languishing look at Felix, hoping to offer Miss Bolsolver the impression that in truth they could not wait to be alone. Actually, she thought they *did* have a good deal to discuss, but did he see that? Priscilla slowly edged her horse forward.

"Oh." Since there was nothing the girl might do about this, she said nothing more. She struck her mount with her crop, a nasty hit that certainly set him off down Rotten Row at a fast clip.

"Remind me in the future to avoid her at all costs." He glanced after the departing miss with a stern expression before turning to study Priscilla. "But, my dear, you gave a performance worthy of Drury Lane just now. You really are talented in that line." He nudged Beau to join Beauty in a proper walk toward the Stanhope Gate.

"I surprise myself at times. I thought perhaps if I gave her the impression that we were madly in love she might abandon her pursuit of you." Priscilla suspected he was trying not to laugh, yet it didn't amuse her.

"One pursuit is quite enough for me," he said obscurely. "Have you seen my aunt of late?"

Priscilla drew in her breath, letting it out slowly. She could not reveal her earlier call. It would surely upset Lady Beatrice's plans if Felix knew his father was in London. If he must find it out, he'd not learn it from Priscilla. "She is up to her ears with preparations for the ball. I believe she thinks the ball has assumed a life of its own," Priscilla concluded with a chuckle, hoping that would be the end of that topic.

It seemed it was. He began a rambling discussion of his intentions with the stereopticon as well as another article he had read on experiments with capturing images on paper with a device that directs sunlight onto sensitized paper.

"I doubt the sunlight is powerful enough to set the image," he concluded thoughtfully.

"I cannot imagine how anything could be better than the lovely engravings we have now, not to mention the beautiful paintings on view in various museums." Priscilla had listened with care, thankful she had also read something on the subject after he had first mentioned his interest.

"I promised to obtain permission for you to see some of the private collections, didn't I?" He gave her a contrite frown.

"I imagine they are not going to disappear very soon," she replied with composure. "I admit it would be satisfying to see several. I have read something of a few of them. Grosvenor House is said to be very fine, as is the collection at Devonshire House. Since the Marquess of Stafford's collection is only on view in May and June, I may as well forget about seeing it—at least for the time being. But it seems well worth the effort. The *Picture of London* says it is the finest collection of old masters in England."

"You lean toward the Italian masters, I see."

"Well, I did look up the list of the private collection of pictures in my copy. You never know when a guidebook like that will be useful. It seemed to me that those paintings would be most pleasing."

They had reached Miss Herbert's house at that point. Felix dismounted, handing his reins to his waiting groom, then assisted Priscilla from Beauty.

Felix held her a few moments longer than necessary. She was such a delicious armful. He would give her a little more time before rushing her to the altar. He understood that every young lady enjoys her first Season. A few sessions at Almack's, perhaps some private balls and routs, and she ought to be willing to settle down as a proper married woman. He also wanted to be certain that she had not the slightest interest in any other man. That, he would not tolerate!

At last he set her on the bottom step of the shallow stairs to the front door. Simpkins had the door open and stood waiting.

"Shall you come in?" Her warm smile invited him.

"I think not. Do you attend the Dixon ball this evening?"

She nodded. "Will I see you there?"

"I will come for you. We may as well share a carriage." It would give him an opportunity to claim her company before they ever entered the Dixon house.

"Of course. So practical." She wore a wistful expression briefly, and he wondered what prompted it.

He released her, then waited until she entered the house before instructing his groom to take both horses to the mews. Felix walked to his house in deep reflection.

He ought to do something about the annoying Miss Bolsolver. Was it as Priscilla said—that the girl had decided that since his family was close to becoming respectable in Society's eyes that he was now acceptable? He cynically wondered how her estimable father felt in regard to that opinion.

What a dilemma! A year ago he would have embraced this supposition. Now he discovered he couldn't become all that excited about it. When had he changed? He no longer viewed his uncle George with the same disfavor, and he thought his aunt Beatrice amazingly charming. Could he actually *like* his family! The very idea shook him.

He went into his house still in thought. His aunt's ball loomed on the horizon, the date moving closer and closer. She had indicated all the family was to attend. Would his father show up in London to be there?

And if he did, how would Felix handle what was bound to be an uncomfortable encounter? No easy answer was forthcoming. But the thought crossed his mind that he would not wish Priscilla to meet his father just yet. After the marriage would be soon enough. That he felt a little intimidated by his father's success with women lurked in the back of his brain only to be dismissed as nonsense. Surely Priscilla of all women would be immune to someone like his father, with his practiced charm.

"Did you have a nice ride, dear?" Aunt Mercy inquired, peering at Priscilla while steadying her embroidery on her lap.

Nice. She wanted to know if it was nice. "Well enough, I suppose. The days grow warmer. I spotted Lord Silverstone and Lady Beatrice dashing along in a curricle. I don't believe Felix saw them—at least he gave no sign he had."

"Be thankful for small mercies," her aunt intoned.

"We also encountered Miss Bolsolver. Dear heaven, she obviously has decided that Felix is about to become respectable once again, for she plagues him to death. One would think she hired a Bow Street man to tag behind him, and report his activities to her. She follows him everywhere."

"I doubt she will be at the Dixon ball this evening. They are terribly discriminating—like Lady Beatrice. Only I doubt they will alter their guest list to include those mushroom Bolsolvers."

"That reminds me, Felix said we are to drive with him this evening, as we are all going. It will be practical, save trouble as it were."

Priscilla spun away, going to the window to stare down at the tiny garden in the back of the house. "I wonder why he is content to wed me. I suppose it is sensible." The irony of the situation assailed her. She was deeply in love with him. He was practical in wedding her. She would assist him in reestablishing his family with Society.

She truly cared not about Society. She only cared about Felix.

"We had best change before long." Aunt Mercy reminded. "Dinner will be slightly early. Do you wear your lavender silk? Do not forget the amethyst ear bobs. Very nice, my dear."

"Indeed, Aunt. I am very fond of that gown." It was early on, shortly after she had met Felix, before he had made his intentions known, that she'd worn it. Now she wondered if he was still firm in his intentions. He was a rather cavalier gentleman!

Chapter Sixteen

$\mathcal{A}$ whirlwind of activity marked the week following the Dixon ball at which she had danced three wonderful waltzes with Felix. He had been intense in his regard, pleasingly so. He had claimed her as his and kept a suspicious gaze on any gentleman who dared to ask her to dance. Surely that was a good sign?

The next morning Priscilla had gone with Felix to the charity school where the children had been entranced with the stereopticon showing. She enjoyed it as well.

Then Felix had patiently sauntered through the two exhibits of paintings that she had mentioned wishing to see—the one at Devonshire House and the other at Grosvenor House. Works by Titian, Tintoretto, Rembrandt, Claude, Correggio, and Rubens dazzled her eyes. That he had entree to such great houses told her a great deal about his place in Society. While Miss Bolsolver and her father might not value Lord Latimer, it was clear many others found him more than acceptable.

In between these outings she found time to obtain the perfect slippers, gloves, and evening hat for the Aston ball that loomed on the horizon.

She was thankful that they didn't see Lord Silverstone out and about, nor were they accosted by Miss Bolsolver. Priscilla hoped the girl had given up her silly quest for marriage to Lord Latimer. It was unsettling, to say the least, to have that dratted girl popping up unexpectedly.

At long last the day for the Aston ball arrived.

Priscilla took great pains with her appearance, delighting in the feel of the beautiful pale aqua silk as it skimmed over her body. The embroidered tulle border was exquisite and very fashionable. She tugged at the low neckline, thinking it was a trifle more daring than she had worn before. The tulle trim accentuated the bodice and nicely edged the puffed sleeves.

Lily placed the tiny scrap of aqua silk and tulle that passed for an evening hat atop Priscilla's blond curls. "You look exceedingly fine, miss."

Priscilla murmured her thanks, rose to draw on her gloves, then gather her reticule. Taking her evening cloak from Lily, she left to meet her aunt in the drawing room.

Felix was waiting. That is to say, he was in the room, pacing back and forth before the fireplace in obvious agitation. His floral offering of a cluster of white gillyflowers would set off the delicacy of her gown. What excellent taste he possessed.

"Good evening, my lord," she said primly. She immediately picked up the flowers, inhaling their spicy scent while studying her escort.

"You will doubtlessly outshine every woman attending the evening." He swiftly walked to her side, taking her cloak from her so to better admire her new gown. He placed the cloak on a chair, then stood back to study her.

She knew he would surpass any male in attendance—including his father. Over dark gray breeches he wore a deep blue Bath wool tailcoat. A complicated cravat was tucked into a waistcoat of subdued splendor—white Marcella woven with faint gold lines. His black patent dancing slippers gleamed brilliantly, and those sheer black hose revealed a fine masculine leg. Very nice, indeed.

"Thank you." She pounced on his disquiet. "It would seem that something is bothering you on this auspicious occasion. May I know what it is?"

"I had word that my father has been seen in Town." He stood before her, hands behind his back and resembling a belligerent schoolboy about to be called on the carpet.

"And that is so bad?" Priscilla spoke with care, thinking that perhaps it would be a good thing if Felix knew the truth in advance.

"I do not wish to see him." He dropped his hands to resume his pacing. "He has caused me quite enough grief. It is insupportable that I must deal with him this evening."

"This is his sister's ball. I should imagine she may invite anyone she pleases. If she wishes to ask her brother, what can you, a mere nephew, have to say to the matter?" Priscilla toyed with the tapes of her cloak where it draped over the chair. The more she considered it, the more she thought that it would be wise for Felix to be prepared.

"Have you heard the same rumor?" Felix halted in his steps to stare at Priscilla.

"I have heard he is here, yes." She had not lied. She had not, however, told him the complete truth—that she had actually met his father, chatted with him briefly.

"You said nothing of it to me?" His gaze was as cold as ever she had seen green eyes become—pure emerald ice.

"Was I supposed to say anything, my lord? Whenever your father is mentioned, you do not respond well." She turned her head to check the time on the mantel clock. "As soon as Aunt comes, I expect we must leave. I'd not be responsible for holding back dinner."

"Ah, yes, the family dinner, just for the close relatives. Why are you there?" He snarled like some wounded animal. Priscilla believed that he was feeling something like a wild thing, cornered, trapped.

"I was invited." Priscilla spoke in a voice as calm and soothing as she could, given her shaken emotions. She hadn't seen Felix like this before, in a tightly controlled rage.

Before he could continue his angry words, Aunt Mercy whisked into the room. In her gown of plum-colored India mull with a bit of the lace sent to Priscilla as trim, she looked very charming.

She paused not far from them, sensing the tension in the room. Giving Priscilla an assessing look, then fixing her gaze on Lord Latimer, she said. "I expect it is time we departed for your aunt's house, my lord. Time has a way of ticking by whether we like it or not."

"As you say, Aunt Mercy." Priscilla gathered her cloak from the chair, but Felix was immediately at her side to drape the soft wool garment over her shoulders. He helped Aunt don her mantle before escorting the two women to the top of the stairs. Amazingly they met a fine gentleman coming silently up the steps.

"Well, Uncle George! I did not expect you here." Felix looked taken aback, as was Priscilla.

They all waited for the fashionably groomed gentleman to gain the landing.

Aunt Mercy looked somewhat bemused at the sight of the aristocratic gentleman dressed in deep violet and gray.

Priscilla wondered if every man in the Sutton family, no matter what his age, possessed this degree of handsome elegance. Even Alfred might attain it one day.

"I was passing and thought I would join you."

They all smiled, as likely intended. Lord George offered his arm to Miss Herbert. Priscilla walked close to Felix while they all descended the stairs.

Since Lord George had taken a hackney to the Herbert house, they went in Felix's town carriage. Priscilla enjoyed sitting next to Felix, but was surprised that her aunt didn't wish her to sit by her. On the other hand, perhaps Aunt wished to be alongside Lord George.

It did not take long to reach Aston house. Because they attended the dinner, there was not the surfeit of carriages that would crowd before the house later.

Priscilla took note of the shuttered expression on Felix's face. "Courage, my lord," she whispered. He assisted her from the carriage, standing silent as his uncle and her aunt got out of the carriage.

Felix took a deep breath, drew her arm close to him, thereupon mounted the shallow steps to where the shiny black door opened before them. The austere butler bowed, escorting them inside. They left the outer attire with him.

Priscilla decided she needed a breath as well, and inhaled deeply.

"I think you are as apprehensive as I am," Felix murmured while they made their way up the stairs to where the beautiful gray and rose drawing room awaited. That the other relatives, particularly Lord Silverstone, would be watching the doorway, she had no doubt.

"Ought I not be uneasy? This is an auspicious occasion for many reasons, my lord."

"Tell me, you rarely use my name, although we are betrothed and I have asked you to make free with it. Why?" He paused at the top of the stairs, studying her face. He stood so close she could speak confidentially to him.

"It is not proper, even though you ask it. I do think of you as Felix, though. I will overcome the tendency in time." Her gentle smile seemed to reassure him. Once they were wed, her life, her very thoughts, would alter.

Yet she still had this wariness about her future. Last night she had dreamed that she was lost in a wilderness, alone, forsaken. Darkness closed in on her, oppressed her. Was it merely her worries intruding on her sleep? Or was it an omen of what was to come? She wished she knew.

Felix drew her forward, following her aunt and his uncle into the drawing room.

Priscilla could immediately tell when he spotted his father on the far side of the room. He clamped her arm tightly against his side. He turned stiff, almost frozen in place for several seconds. There were several chairs and small tables between them. Glorious arrangements of flowers scented the air. Several gorgeous Argand lamps as well as candles illuminated the room.

Lady Beatrice welcomed them all with cries of pleasure. When she reached Priscilla, tightly clasped to Felix's side, she gave him an amused look. "There is no one here who will steal your beautiful betrothed from you. We are all family. Although I do know that Alfred admires Priscilla." She glanced to where her son stood chatting with her brother Augustus, the Marquess of Silverstone.

Priscilla looked as well. The marquess dazzled in his understated elegance. He affected the style of years past in a deep rose velvet frock coat over cream satin breeches. Lace foamed from under his cuffs and at his neck, and diamonds sparkled in the buckles on his shoes.

It would be interesting to see how many women fawned over him.

Lady Beatrice continued. "I do not know what you said to Alfred, but he has become a changed person. He vows to abandon betting on horse races and rather start his own stud. It is a good thing my husband knows something about managing it. But how much better to have the dear boy occupied in something sensible!"

Priscilla cast her thoughts back to the dreadful day when she was caught at Epsom. "I should think that might prove to be an excellent thing for him." Perhaps he might at least make some money instead of being a constant drain on his mother. Naturally, it would take capital to start the venture, but that was available in seeming abundance.

The group ignored any strict precedence as to seating, with Lady Beatrice at the head of the table while her husband sat opposite her. Felix and Lord George flanked Lady Beatrice while Alfred and Lord Silverstone sat to either side of Mr. Aston.

Priscilla looked across to where her aunt murmured something to Lord George. Then she cast a sidelong glance at Lord Silverstone before turning to Felix. This was not going to be the easiest of meals. She was extremely aware of the congenial marquess at her one side with Felix frowning on the other.

The crystal glittered, becoming a beautiful red as claret was poured into it. There were two branched candelabra on the table, thus affording a pleasant light. Priscilla picked up her silver fork, taking note of the plain shape with a pretty letter A engraved on the handle. Rather than the elaborate centerpieces Priscilla had read about for the prince's dinners, there was a simple epergne with fruit.

Since she had dined once or twice at the home of the Marquess of Lanstone and was thus familiar with the array of fine silver, the finger glasses, and napkins of heavy linen, Priscilla did not feel inadequate on that account. It was this particular marquess and the knowledge that his son—who happened to sit on her other side— was at odds with him.

Somehow they managed to get through the meal without incident. Priscilla gave mental thanks when the tablecloth was removed for dessert—a delicious assortment with baskets of tiny pastries, dishes of nuts and dried fruit, and in particular a splendid syllabub.

Since syllabub was a favorite, she nodded when it was offered, savoring every bite.

"I won't remain when the women leave," Felix murmured just loud enough for her to hear. "I do not wish to speak with my father at this time."

She nodded in reply, unwilling to say anything that his father might overhear.

And so when Lady Beatrice got up, it was a relief that her husband did as well. The remaining gentlemen also rose with Priscilla and Miss Herbert.

"The others will be along shortly, so we will forgo the usual port and tea after dinner. Why do we not all go up to the ballroom?" Lady Beatrice linked her arms with her older brother and husband, allowing her younger brother to escort Miss Mercy Herbert. Alfred strolled along after them, ignoring his cousin completely.

Felix hung back, holding Priscilla by his side. She raised her brows in question.

"So far all has gone well, Felix. I see no need for any conversation with your father unless you wish it."

"Just keep *your* distance from him."

"Will that not seem odd to the others who come this evening? Your aunt desires this to be a reconciliation of sorts. As well, she wishes to reward those who have been her friends these past years. Would it not seem strange if you and I remain aloof from the family you seek to restore to their rightful position in Society?"

He mulled over her words for a minute, then nodded. "Very well. Outwardly I will be as agreeable as you might wish. Just do not expect me to have any meaningful discussion with him."

"What is there to say?" she wondered aloud. "You do not like the style of life he enjoys. He disagrees. I cannot see that you can find a compromise."

Felix said nothing in reply. From his disgruntled expression Priscilla suspected he did not care to have his views revealed so bluntly.

In short order the ballroom, decorated simply with

arrangements of flowers and greenery, began to fill with guests. No one had sent a rejection. Priscilla soon spotted the Bolsolver trio, looking about them with unfeigned amazement. If there were a single member of polite Society absent, it would have been difficult to say who it was. Even the haughty patronesses from Almack's attended, surveying the assembled throng with varying decrees of interest.

Felix partnered Priscilla, Lord George persuaded Miss Herbert to dance, while Lady Beatrice—smiling with pride and delight—took her husband's hand. She had chosen to open the ball with a stately minuet, appropriate since many of the couples were of the age that favored that particular dance. It was all bows and curtsies with elegant footwork.

Priscilla acquitted herself without too much difficulty, her father having preferred minuets as well. Following that came a collection of lighthearted country longways dances, where she faced her partner, and a quadrille, a favorite of hers. She could see her dear aunt taking note that Priscilla and Felix remained at arm's length as was proper.

Propriety. That was what had prompted this evening's event. How strange it was that this group of people held propriety so high when so often in private life they behaved in an utterly scandalous manner. It was all for outward show. How ironic.

Felix's father approached her when she stood close to one of the several Almack's patronesses, the Lady Sefton. There was no way she might reject his request for her hand in the next dance. It could undo much of the good work the evening had accomplished to this point. She took his hand with apparent goodwill.

"Lord Silverstone, what a pleasure."

"I have been wanting a dance with you this age, my dear." He led her away to join in a lively reel.

When they had a few moments of quiet during the dance, he spoke. "I should like to give you something that belonged to Felix's mother. Will you come down to the library with me? I left it in my sister's safe."

"I would deem it a great honor, sir. I believe your son missed his mother very much."

"So he did—as did I. Life is not always kind, my dear. But then, as a daughter of a rector, I imagine you already know that."

She murmured an agreement, then went on to conclude the dance. She looked about the ballroom, hoping to find her aunt or Felix so they would know where she was. Most vexingly she couldn't catch the eye of anyone she would trust to relay a message.

She joined him to slip from the ballroom. They made their way down the stairs and around to the side of the house where a fine, if small, library was situated.

"This is a pleasant room—warm paneling and an equally warm fire." Priscilla slowly pivoted to note the details of the wood carvings around the fireplace and fine paintings hanging here and there. "I marvel at all those books, and they look as though someone had read them, too.

"Both Guy and Beatrice are famous readers. Come," he beckoned her.

Priscilla followed him to the far side of the room, where he swung a painting aside to reveal a small safe set into the wall. She averted her gaze while he opened the door to remove a small velvet-covered box. He restored all as it was before leading Priscilla to stand by the fire.

Upon opening the box, Priscilla caught her breath at the dainty trifle within. Intricate threads of gold had beautiful rubies and diamonds tucked here and there to create a brooch of remarkable design and splendor. She had certainly never seen anything to approach it in brilliance.

"I don't think I should accept this. Felix and I are not wed as yet, you know. I should feel far better if I waited until after our marriage."

"Rubbish. He is besotted with you, just as I was with his mother. There is no way he will ever let you go. Here."

Priscilla froze as he removed the brooch from the box and began to pin it to her bodice. His hand slipped inside just a wee bit. His gloves prevented him from actually touching her skin, yet it was an intimate gesture.

"Well, well, isn't this a touching scene." Felix pushed the door open to stroll into the room, fixing his stare on Priscilla, then his father. "Isn't she a trifle young for you, Papa? Or have you exhausted your current crop of beauties to take aim at younger women."

"This isn't what you think, son," the marquess protested, backing away from Priscilla.

"Felix, listen," Priscilla begged.

"You may consider our betrothal at an end, my dear. I refuse to share you with anyone." He turned on his heel and left the room. He could be heard dashing up the stairs.

Priscilla slowly removed the brooch, then withdrew her left glove to take off her engagement ring as well. It was a bit difficult to see, what with tears pooling in her eyes.

"Perhaps you can see these are properly taken care of, my lord. I no longer wish to be responsible for them." She spun about and left the room to fetch her cloak.

When she returned to the entry she found the marquess awaiting her. "Allow me to see that you get home safely."

"I can walk—it is a very short distance from here."

"All the more reason you should have company." He refused to permit her the solace of a solitary walk or the tears she could shed on the way.

At her aunt's door she bid him good-bye with barely held-back tears. "I shall not see you again, sir. I beg you to talk some sense into your son, but knowing Felix as I do, I doubt it possible."

He bowed over her hand, murmured soothing words, then left once she had stepped inside.

Priscilla did not cry, at least not then. She ran up the stairs to her room to demand that Lily fetch her trunks and cases. "I am going home."

"At this hour of the night?" Lily rubbed sleepy eyes.

"Well, no, of course not," Priscilla admitted upon reflection. "But I intend to leave at first light. Perhaps a few cases? The rest can follow me later if needs be."

"As you will, miss." The maid was too well trained to

question why Priscilla had made such a drastic decision. But it was plain that her mistress was feeling hurt and angry.

With Lily's help drawers were emptied and cases filled. Priscilla would have tossed items in any old way. Lily neatly folded gowns and finally suggested Priscilla write a letter to her betrothed if necessary, since she was bent on leaving London.

Aware she was behaving just as badly as Felix, yet upset with him, Priscilla agreed. It was probably best that Lily do the packing. Priscilla would only make a muddle of things. All those lovely gowns would do her little good at the rectory. Maybe her younger sisters might make better use of them? The letter was a jumble of words, soon tossed out. What could she say that would express her feelings?

She had fallen into a restless sleep by the time her aunt returned to the house, concerned about her niece's strange behavior. The Marquess of Silverstone had made a vague explanation, but Miss Herbert sensed there was something else afoot. Felix behaved like a bear with a sore paw, leaving early, to Lady Beatrice's dismay.

It was morning before Miss Herbert received her account of the event. "He said what?" she cried, shocked to her core when Priscilla concluded her tale of woe.

"He announced in no uncertain terms that our engagement is at an end. I left my ring with his father. I have no wish to see Felix again. If he could possibly believe such a dreadful thing of his father and of me, he is not the man I thought he was."

There was nothing to do but agree with Priscilla on that score. Miss Herbert, distressed to see her dearest niece depart on such a grim note, begged her to stay just another day.

"I hoped he might rush over here this morning to plead forgiveness. As you can see, he has not come. No, I shall not impose on you another day, dearest of aunts. I intend to leave at once. Lily has everything packed. All I need is a hackney to convey me to the nearest posting inn."

Reluctantly, Aunt Mercy—tears in her eyes—agreed. One thing she insisted upon, that her footman obtain a post chaise for Priscilla. By ten o'clock the house was empty of everything that had to do with her niece. It was comforting when Lord George came to call. He allowed that his nephew was an utter nodcock and must have picked up that trait from his mother's side of the family.

"For Augustus and I would never do anything so rag-mannered."

She permitted him to hold her hand, then offered tea and those little biscuits he liked so well.

Priscilla was miserable. Fortunately, the post chaise had proven better than a stage would have been. She was in no state to sit with a clutch of other people. Lily and she jounced out of London, headed for the village and her home. She would become an old maid. She never wanted anything to do with another man as long as she lived. They simply were not to be trusted—even if loved.

Lily offered another handkerchief from the stack she had prudently kept out.

Priscilla blew her nose, then patted her eyes dry. "I shall cease this foolish crying. He is not worth it. Not in the least. Oh, if only I didn't love him so dearly!"

Wisely, the maid kept silent.

In London a very embarrassed Felix sat the next morning listening to his father and aunt lecture him at length on his stupidity.

"I see what it is," Aunt Beatrice declared. "You are so mad for this girl, your brain has ceased to work!"

"We are both single men, are we not?" inquired his father casually.

Felix admitted they were.

"Have I ever harmed a soul with my attentions to the fair ladies?"

"As to that, I could not say. A handsome gentleman can possibly wound a tender heart." Felix gave his father a stubborn look.

His remark was met with a chuckle. "Believe me, none of these women had a tender heart—at least to that degree. They understood that I was merely an escort. I would say that if a tender heart was wounded, it was you who did the harm. Your Priscilla was greatly hurt."

"Dear, you must go to her," Beatrice advised. "Tell her it was all a horrible misunderstanding."

"Worse than that," his father muttered. "In all my life I have never treated a woman like you treated her last evening. I can hardly believe you are my son."

"I am an idiot and a fool—anything else?" Felix spoke in a dry voice, pacing back and forth before the fireplace.

"Rather slow, if I may say so," his father pointed out. That he had kept Felix from going earlier was ignored.

Felix glanced at the clock, with the hour approaching one-thirty. "I am off." He shook hands with his father, bestowed a light kiss on his aunt's cheek, and left.

It didn't take long to go to the Herbert residence. Miss Herbert seemed to take great pleasure in informing him that Priscilla was not there, nor was she likely to return anytime soon.

"What do you mean?" Felix grew chilled.

"She left London earlier today, perhaps three hours ago. My footman arranged a post chaise for her."

Felix hurried to his home, sending his groom to the mews while stuffing a generous sum of money into his pocket. A change of clothes went into a saddlebag, although his valet was horrified that Felix would go anywhere without him.

Since he knew the route the post chaise would take, Felix headed south out of London, tearing along the road in the hope he would catch up with her before she actually got to her home again. The longer the time lapse, the more difficult it would be; his aunt had convinced him of that.

It had to be the most frustrating time of his life. Every posting inn where he changed horses, an ostler admitted that the yellow post chaise had been there perhaps two hours before. But they had to change vehicles and shift the baggage at each posting stop so that favored Felix.

But as time passed, he gained on them.

Still it was hours before he arrived in Tunbridge Wells. She would change her chaise here. With any luck at all, she would be required to wait just a little. That was all the time he needed. If only they were short a vehicle.

At the fine posting inn favored by the chaises, he leaped from his horse and strode inside, searching for her. She was there! Two forlorn young women—one wearing an apple-green pelisse—huddled by the fireplace.

Felix marched up to tap Priscilla on the shoulder.

She spun around to glare at him with vivid blue eyes. "You! I never want to see you again!" Anger gave her skin a lovely rose tint, and her eyes glittered with irate fire.

"I have come to apologize, my dearest Priscilla."

"Go away. You do not love me. I have decided that I would rather be an old maid than wed to someone who merely wants a proper wife. I am assuredly not your dearest!" She stamped her foot, turning away from him.

"But I *do* want a proper wife—you. My dearest girl, I love you with all my heart! I think I fell in love with you when first we met. It has been growing since."

"Well, if that is love, you have a peculiar manner of showing it! You have no trust in me. As if your father would seduce me! I have never been so angry or humiliated in my life! Did I ever give you cause for doubting me?"

Frustrated, Felix ran a hand through his hair. He hadn't expected this cold rejection, although after the lecture from his father and aunt, he probably should have. "Priscilla, my dear . . ." She darted him a black look that chilled his soul and scared him witless. "Please give me another chance."

"Go on." She spoke reluctantly, but it gave him hope.

"I confess that I at first sought propriety. But as I began to pursue you, I had this feeling inside—so alien I scarce knew what it was. Little did I realize you captured my heart. Now you have it, I find I do not wish it back. Please, dearest love, forgive my stupidity. Marry me, for I will love you, cherish you, treasure you for all time."

He fell to one knee, took her hand in his to pull off her glove, placing her ring back where it belonged.

"Now, what do you say?" He stood to draw her close to him, loosely embracing her. His eyes pleaded with her.

"What can I say to those precious words." She lovingly stroked his cheek. "I love you." And then she kissed him.

"I'm so glad I got that special license," he murmured. "How nice your father is a rector." And then he kissed her as well, a deliciously wonderful promise of things to come.